A Queer Kind of Love

OTHER NOVELS BY GEORGE BAXT

THE PHAROAH LOVE TRILOGY
A Queer Kind of Death
Swing Low, Sweet Harriet
Topsy and Evil

THE CELEBRITY MURDER SERIES
The Dorothy Parker Murder Case
The Alfred Hitchcock Murder Case
The Tallulah Bankhead Murder Case
The Talking Pictures Murder Case
The Greta Garbo Murder Case
The Noel Coward Murder Case
The Marlene Dietrich Murder Case
The Mae West Murder Case

THE MAX VAN LARSEN SERIES
A Parade of Cockeyed Creatures
"I!" Said the Demon
Satan Is a Woman

ALSO:
The Affair at Royalties
Process of Elimination
The Neon Graveyard
Burning Sappho

A QUEER KIND OF LOVE

A Pharoah Love Mystery

GEORGE BAXT

**OTTO
PENZLER
BOOKS**
NEW YORK

Otto Penzler Books
129 West 56th Street
New York, NY 10019
(*Editorial Offices only*)

Macmillan Publishing Company
866 Third Avenue
New York, NY 10022

Maxwell Macmillan Canada, Inc.
1200 Eglinton Avenue East, Suite 200
Don Mills, Ontario M3C 3N1

Macmillan Publishing Company is part of the Maxwell Communication Group of Companies.

LIBRARY OF CONGRESS CATALOGING-IN-PUBLICATION DATA
Baxt, George.
    A queer kind of love/by George Baxt.
        p.   cm.
    ISBN 1-883402-01-8
    1. Gay men—New York (N.Y.)—Fiction.   2. Police—New York (N.Y.)—
Fiction.   I. Title.
PS3552.A8478Q44 1994
813'.54—dc20   93-35517

Otto Penzler Books are available at special discounts for bulk purchases for sale promotions, premiums, fund-raising, or educational use. For details, contact:

Special Sales Director
Macmillan Publishing Company
866 Third Avenue
New York, NY 10022

Printed in the United States of America

10   9   8   7   6   5   4   3   2   1

For Cynthia Lindsay and her husband, Robert Patton

A Queer Kind of Love

chapter

1

Pharoah Love tightened his grip on the 9-millimeter. It had been issued to him that morning as a replacement for his old .38-caliber revolver. The semiautomatics were being phased into the department. A 9-millimeter can fire as many as sixteen rounds in one magazine and can be reloaded faster. The .38, until recently the standard police revolver, can only fire six shots before reloading. Pharoah liked the feel of the gun. What he hated was the sound of Herbie Marks's feet racing up the stairs of the derelict tenement.

"Herbie!" Pharoah shouted.

"Stop bothering me!" Herbie shouted back.

"Couldn't you have found one of these crap holes with an elevator? I'm getting winded!" Pharoah rested for a second. He saw two of his backup detectives coming up behind him.

One, Al Drexel, was droning news of their progress—or lack of same—into a portable telephone. The other, Moe Holding, was scratching his chest. Both were perspiring. Pharoah yelled, "Herbie!"

Herbie shouted back, "Will you please stop invading my privacy? I'm trying to make a getaway here!"

"You ain't getting away, Herbie. You can't off three people and expect to get away with it." Or perhaps he could. "Herbie, you got a good lawyer?"

"Yeah. A real ganef. He has a way with juries. He gets the best that money can bribe."

"Herbie, please. For old times' sake, give yourself up."

"Ain't you copped enough citations?"

"I don't want any more citations. I want you, doll. Come on, Herbie." He mimicked a twelve-year-old's voice. "Come out, come out, wherever you are!"

Herbie laughed. "Man, how I wish this was a game of hide-and-seek! Hey, Pha'!" Pronounced Fay or fey.

"What?" Pharoah and his men had resumed the climb.

"Remember we used to play red rover and ringalievio. Remember? You, me, and Marco Salino."

"We ain't kids anymore, Herbie." A sadness had suddenly overtaken Pharoah. A memory of three kids who were the Three Musketeers almost three decades ago in Brooklyn. Three Canarsie kids. One Jew, one black (oops! African-American), and one Italian. Three buddies. Three pals. The two whites the only ones in the neighborhood to invite the friendship of a black kid. Not all that black. A light coffee color. A smart kid. The three of them were smart.

"You seen Marco lately?" Herbie's voice betrayed its weariness. He had offed three drug dealers who had double-crossed him. They weren't the first he had iced, but it was the rare time that there were witnesses. Herbie's roll was over.

"Yeah. I been seeing a lot of Marco lately. He's been buying me expensive dinners."

"Oh, yeah? Hey, Pha'. You ain't turned sneak, have you?"

"Fat chance of that. Come on, Herbie! Stop horsing around. Throw your gun down and come down the stairs."

"No way. I'm going out on the roof and behind the chimney stack, and we're going to have a good old-fashioned shoot-out."

"Herbie. We won't be pointing fingers at each other and yelling, 'Bang, bang, you're dead.' These are real guns. These are real bullets. Hey, Herbie! We've got them new nine-millimeter handguns!"

"Hey! Hey! I read about them the other day. You iced anybody with it yet?"

"No, Herbie." Sadly. "I'm holding a virgin." Please don't make me use it on you, Herbie. *Please.* We used to go halfies on a two-cent slice of halvah. We shared our Devil Dogs. We sneaked into the movies together every Saturday. Gene Autry. Roy Rogers. They ran the old westerns on Saturdays. Bad prints but great action.

"Pharoah?"

"What?"

"I didn't know there were any virgins left." He raced across the roof and positioned himself behind the chimney stack. His gun was a .45. He hadn't fired it in hours. It was loaded. He always kept it loaded. A handsome man with a two-day growth of beard, he was a few years short of forty, the same age

3

as Pharoah and Marco Salino. He and Marco were Libras; Pharoah was a Gemini. The signs were compatible. Herbie liked Geminis. He didn't want to kill one.

Pharoah said from the doorway leading to the roof, "Herbie, please throw your gun out. It's beginning to drizzle. You'll catch cold. You know how your mother's always yelling at you."

"She hasn't yelled in a real long time, Pha'. Now it's Gracie who yells." Gracie and the two boys living the good life in Carroll Gardens in a brownstone all paid for with blood money. He wondered if Gracie ever gave that a thought. Nah. To Gracie, money was money, and the more the merrier. And all that insurance. Well, what the hell. She deserves it, with what she's been putting up with the past fifteen years or so.

Al Drexel looked at Pharoah. "Maybe I should ask for more backup?"

"Why? You lonely?"

Moe Holding had another idea. "Do you think we should try to circle him?"

"You got a helicopter?"

Al Drexel brightened. "Should I ask for one?"

Pharoah spoke to the sky. "Dear God, spare me." Then he shouted, "Herbie! Come on, babe! Be a good guy! Drop the gun!"

"Pha', you know who I'm thinking of right now? You'll never guess."

"So tell me."

"Miss Morgan"

"Miss Morgan? You mean from P.S. 115?"

"Remember her knockers?" It sounded as if he were asking Pharoah to remember the *Maine*.

"Herbie," said Pharoah, his voice tired, "you know I was never into knockers."

"I like your ponytail, Pharoah. You're one of the few black guys who looks good with a ponytail."

"Racist."

"You know what I mean, Pharoah. Most black guys ain't got the hair for ponytails. Dreadlocks, yeah, ponytails, nah. You still wearing that crazy earring you had designed for yourself. Jesus with his arm around Moses."

"Yeah, Herbie. It's still in my left ear. It gives me comfort to have the guys so close to me."

"Hey, Pha'?"

"What?"

"Did you know at the Last Supper Jesus asked for separate checks?"

"Stop horsing around! Come on out, damn it. You got no choice!"

"I'm not ready yet, Pha'." He went silent.

"Herbie, don't do anything dumb!" Christ, thought Pharoah, I feel like bawling. That's all I need in front of Al and Moe. I'll never live it down.

"I already done what's dumb, Pha'. Killing those three bastards was dumb."

"They were bandits."

"Sure. Sure. But I should have played it smart. Smart the way Marco plays it. I should have hired a hit to do it for me. Marco was always smart, wasn't he, Pha'."

"Not as smart as you were, Herbie. You were the boy they voted most likely to succeed."

Pharoah couldn't see Herbie preening. "Damn right! I was

the first kid on the block to buy four insurance policies. Boy is Gracie gonna be one hell of a catch. Hey, Pharoah, Marco still married to Fat Selma?"

"I suppose he is. He never mentions her."

"I'll bet she's still fat."

"The last time I saw her, she was so fat, the post office was thinking of giving her her own zip code."

"Ha-ha-ha-ha-ha."

"It's nice to hear you laughing, Herbie. I ain't heard you laugh in a long time. You were always a great laugher."

"Marco's in bad trouble, ain't he. I saw the papers. Who's knocking off his soldiers?"

"That's what I'm supposed to be finding out, Herbie."

"So what are you doing up here bugging me?"

"I asked for the assignment, Herbie. For old times' sake."

Herbie stared at his weapon. "Pha'. Remember that time my father brought the TV home. How excited we got. You, me, and Marco. We watched Jimmy Cagney in *Yankee Doodle Dandy*."

Pharoah smiled. "How can I forget." He mimicked Cagney as George M. Cohan. "'My mother thanks you, my father thanks you, my sister thanks you, and I thank you.'"

Al Drexel held tight to the portable phone. He had asked for an ambulance. He knew there was only one ending to the drama in which he was participating.

"That's pretty good, Pha'. You're still pretty good! Now do Katharine Hepburn!"

"Cut it out, you nut. Don't make me come after you. You know what happens when I get mad!"

"How could I forget? You stamp your foot and spit."

"Herbie, you're a bitch."

Softly, Herbie said, "I love you, Pharoah. I always loved you. When you were a kid, you didn't have a mean bone in your body."

"I do now!" Pharoah shouted.

"No, you don't. It's the cop in you that's mean, but not you yourself. Marco had the mean streak. Tell me what's going on with him."

"Herbie." The voice was agonized.

"Tell me and then I'll come quietly."

Drexel said, "Go on, Pharoah, until the meat wagon gets here." He didn't dare confess he was getting to like Herbie. He sounded so sweet-natured.

Pharoah asked Drexel, "You falling in love with him?" Moe Holding guffawed. "Herbie," said Pharoah, "like you read in the papers, four of Marco's lieutenants have been murdered. Two at a time. Gunned down."

"Is there a war on?"

"There isn't, not according to Marco. That's what's puzzling him. What with Gotti stashed away for life and a few others that were troublesome taking singing lessons from the feds, until these killings, it's all been quiet on the eastern front. Rival capos have been seen in restaurants exchanging cigars. The Mafia's been having a rough time, what with the shaking up going on now in the mother country. No, this ain't no ordinary killer. Whoever he is, he's angry. In fact, he's mad as hell. I also think he's crazy."

"You sure it ain't an eye-for-an-eye thing?"

"Marco doesn't think so. He hasn't had four rivals offed in months. This is from out of the clear blue. Sounds to me like some kind of revenge motive, but Marco can't think of who might want revenge and for what? No, this is someone who's just plain angry."

"You got any ideas, Pha'?"

"I got one great idea. You throw your gun down and come on out with your hands up, and we'll go to the precinct and book you. I'll make sure you get the best cell in the house."

"And after that?"

"Depends on your lawyer. We got no death penalty in the state, so you'll probably end up in Attica or some other university like it."

"In an eight-by-ten cell? For the rest of my life? Don't you remember? Don't you remember I couldn't stand going to the Prospect Park Zoo. I couldn't stand them animals pacing back and forth, back and forth. I couldn't stand it. I just couldn't stand it. Not for them. And not for me." He heard the siren of the approaching ambulance. "Hey, hey, Pha'! They're playing my song!"

He came out shooting. Shooting wildly. Shooting in all directions. Pharoah caught him with one slug. Herbie clutched his stomach, dropping the gun, and sank to his knees. Pharoah rushed to him and knelt by his side, holding his dying friend in his arms.

"Herbie, you dumb, rotten, mean son of a bitch! You weren't aiming at anything! You wanted me to kill you!"

Herbie opened his eyes. He reached up and with an effort tried to pat Pharoah's cheek. "I love that earring, Pha'." It was a whisper. The whisper continued. "'My mother thanks you, my father thanks you, my—'" The death rattle was ugly.

Guided by the sound of the shooting, the ambulance attendants made their way to the roof, carrying a rolled-up stretcher.

"What a stench," said one attendant to the other.

"Very inexpensive co-ops here" was the other's reply.

Pharoah still held Herbie in his arms. Al Drexel said, "Pharoah, the meat-wagon boys are here."

"In a minute," Pharoah said hoarsely. Drexel and Holding looked embarrassed. The ambulance attendants were anxious to get on with it. They were having a very busy day. A pregnant woman shot in a drive-by on East Fourteenth Street. Three high school kids knifed when a drug buy went sour. An elderly couple hit by a speeding motorcycle on Central Park West. A jumper who'd leaped from the balcony of a high rise on East Fifty-seventh Street and landed on a young actor who would never know he had a callback. So far, it was proving to be a very interesting day.

On the street, a small crowd had gathered. There were reporters, cameramen, and TV-station trucks, all anxiously waiting to get the story. It wasn't as though Herbie Marks had some kind of notoriety or celebrity of the sort that had embraced Marco Salino. Marco was colorful. He had charisma. He was flamboyant and stylish. He was also handsome in an old-fashioned, gigolo-like way. And like old-fashioned gigolos, he had a smooth line for the ladies and was a graceful dancer. In the boudoir, as one celebrated Hollywood actress said of him, "he has a master's degree in engineering." His fat wife had been a slim bride, but years of verbal and physical abuse and further years of neglect had added unnecessary and unwanted weight to her frame. She was too shy at first to take a lover. Now she was too fat.

Marco had never dreamed of being a mafioso. He wanted to be a dancer. Until an uncle arrived from Sicily who took a shine to the handsome youngster and seduced him away from his dream. The dream stolen, Marco made do with becoming his uncle's lieutenant. His uncle became a capo, a powerful leader who had no tact or finesse. After his funeral, Marco was awarded the position as replacement. And he never abused it. He was always a smart kid from Canarsie. Always a charmer. He charmed the Russian Mafia in Brighton Beach and the deadly Oriental gangs of Chinatown. He charmed everyone. He continued to charm Pharoah, little realizing that Pharoah, after making detective, well understood Marco would come in handy one day. Pharoah had always known how to manipulate his old friend. And Pharoah knew Marco enjoyed being manipulated by him. Once, soon after they first met, Marco kissed him on the lips. It had never happened again, but Pharoah didn't misread the offering. This was Marco's way of telling him they were pals: all very hot-blooded, very Latin. Later, when Pharoah found out Mafia hit men often kissed their intended victims on the lips before lowering the final curtain, then and only then did Pharoah shudder.

Herbie was no Marco Salino. He had been a nice, smart Jewish kid of ordinary origins. His father and mother barely eked out a living from their dry-goods store. There was enough to pay Pharoah's mother to clean the four rooms behind the store. (She also did the Salino place, a small six-room cottage that boasted a thriving fig tree in the backyard, planted by Marco's mother shortly after their move to Canarsie from the Brownsville ghetto, just five BMT stops away.) Herbie was the nice kid with the perenially runny nose. And very,

very smart. A voracious reader. He introduced Pharoah to the local public library, to which they made frequent visits, hunting for the books recommended by their teachers.

Herbie's mother and father died tragically of serious illnesses within months of each other, and he and his siblings, a brother and a sister, were farmed out to relatives who weren't into farming. The aunt and uncle Herbie lived with were small-timers in the numbers racket. They taught Herbie, who was a quick study. He graduated from numbers to horse races and dog races and became adept at fixing wrestling matches and hockey games. Then Herbie really scored big when he got into dealing drugs. He became rich and then richer, and there was Gracie, who loved money and never asked Herbie where it came from as long as it arrived.

As he descended the tenement stairs, Pharoah pondered Herbie. Ahead of him, Herbie's body, wrapped in a white sheet and strapped to the stretcher, was being carried out of Pharoah's life, out of Gracie's life. Pharoah chuckled, and it surprised him, because he was thinking, Herbie, at last you're really out of this world. Herbie had been a real swell pal. Herbie wanted Pharoah to be his executioner. Pharoah had complied, as if the scene had been choreographed. Al Drexel was wondering why Pharoah was talking to himself. Moe Holding was wondering if anyone would ever cry for him the way Pharoah had cried for the dead perp on the roof.

On the street, the photographers went into action. The reporters strafed Pharoah with questions while scribbling his replies in their notebooks. Microphones that were the property of the major television networks were poised at Pharoah's mouth. Television cameras moved from Pharoah to the body being loaded into the ambulance and then back to Pharoah. He'd been assured this was not live coverage. Herbie's wife stayed glued to the TV set all day, a soap-opera junkie. He didn't want her to find out Herbie was dead until he told her. There had to be a phone nearby. As he continued fielding questions, he spotted the Grey Ghost.

chapter

The Grey Ghost had materialized only a few weeks before and immediately become Pharoah's favorite homeless person. Pharoah first noticed him hanging around one of the two alleys adjoining the town house of Manhattan's favorite and most heavily patronized madam, Rita Genari. Rita's housekeeper, a jolly Mexican named Juana Gomez, was also partial to the Ghost. She seemed oblivious to his nervous twitch and the stream of obscenities that emerged from his mouth, meant for no one in particular and spoken so softly that they had a certain perverse charm. Pharoah recognized that the obscenities were uncontrollable, some sort of affliction that medical science could probably identify. Juana ignored them. The Ghost was charming and courtly and effusively grateful for her generous handouts of food, cans of soda, and the occasional dollar bill.

It was Pharoah who had dubbed him the Grey Ghost. The man wore a gray jacket and gray trousers, and on his head a knitted gray ski hood pulled down to his ears. A scraggly Vandyke beard and bushy mustache camouflaged most of his face. At times, he covered his piercing blue eyes with dark glasses. Pharoah, who sometimes wondered if it was more appropriate to feed the hairy face peanuts, figured him to be somewhere in his mid- to late twenties, possibly freshly released from a mental institution. There were too many of these unfortunate creatures aimlessly prowling the streets. Though he couldn't have explained exactly why, Pharoah considered him someone special, and it pleased him that Juana concurred. She was one shrewd cookie with a unique gift for sizing up character. You needed that gift working in a whorehouse.

Pharoah moved away from the reporters and photographers; he sensed they had no further use for him. The ambulance pulled away, siren shrieking mercilessly, a mechanical banshee. Pharoah had a few words with Drexel and Holding, who had already dismissed the four other detectives who'd been part of the team pursuing Herbie Marks.

"I'm going over to Rita Genari's." Drexel and Holding exchanged glances. "That bothers you? Rita's my friend."

"Rita has lots of friends," said Drexel snidely.

"Al," said Pharoah, "you're so mean, I think if you could, you'd cancel Christmas."

Drexel was now uncomfortable. "I didn't mean anything, Pharoah."

"Sure. I'll see you guys later at the precinct." He went in search of a telephone. The Grey Ghost seemed riveted to the pavement.

"Hi, Ghost, how goes it?"

He caught the man in mid-obscenity. The Grey Ghost adjusted his gray gloves and said in a whisper, "I am busy mastering the external."

"The external what?"

Twitch, twitch, twitch. "The ozone. The hole in the ozone."

The foul words and phrases fascinated Pharoah, the Grey Ghost having mastered and memorized such a serendipitous variety of them not only in English but in an impressive array of foreign languages.

Pharoah knew the stream would diminish when he started questioning the Grey Ghost. "You getting enough to eat, babe?"

"I have been enjoying Lucullan feasts." His steel-blue eyes betrayed nothing. His voice was soft, almost faint, and Pharoah had to strain to catch the words.

"You got someplace to sleep tonight?"

He stretched out his gloved hands. "The city is my hotel. The doorways and the crawl spaces are my boudoirs." Boudoirs, thought Pharoah. Rather pretentious.

"I suppose you're warm enough."

The Grey Ghost nodded and twitched. This guy is a mess, thought Pharoah, albeit a very appealing one. "Who was the man you killed?"

"How do you know I killed him?"

"He was someone you liked. Your eyes tell me you mourn him."

"One of the other guys could have done him."

"No. You're the man in charge. The man in charge pulls the trigger. We all know that."

"You're pretty smart, babe. You go to college?"

"One doesn't have to be educated to be smart."

Pharaoh asked the question the Grey Ghost would never answer, though this didn't discourage Pharaoh from continuing to ask it. "Where's your family, Ghost? Where do you come from?"

The Ghost smiled, revealing remarkably even and white teeth. "That's for me to know and you to find out."

"That's what I'm trying to do." He gave the vagrant a dollar bill. "I'd give you more, but I don't want to spoil you."

"We are grateful for all contributions." The royal "we" seemed appropriate to the mysterious wanderer.

"Ghost, why do I have a hunch you've got royal blood in you."

Pharaoh was rewarded with a fresh batch of obscenities, hot from the oven that was the Grey Ghost's mouth.

"I've got to find a phone." The Ghost pointed to a sleazy bar across the street. Pharaoh studied the gloved hand. He recognized that when the gloves were new, they had been expensive. "I like your gloves." The Ghost raised his hand higher and studied the glove as though he'd been unaware he was wearing it.

"This is a gauntlet. I challenge life with it. *Ciao.*" He turned abruptly and hurried away, twitching and cursing, reminding Pharaoh of some grotesque imitation of the White Rabbit. Pharaoh crossed the street in search of the phone. The Lower East Side had once been a bustling ethnic neigh-

borhood of European immigrants, the streets once teeming
with pushcarts and outdoor stands. Now the buildings were
mostly derelict. Those that weren't reeked of miserable pover-
ty; they were hotbeds of criminals and crime, teenage criminals and teenage crime. There but for the grace of God,
thought Pharoah.

There was nothing prosperous about Canarsie when he and
his pals grew up there. It was in the past ten years that it had
suddenly become a Mafia outpost, uneasily still sharing the
territory with middle-class Jews and Irish. It was a gentrified
section of Brooklyn that succeeded and prospered, much like
Carroll Gardens and Brooklyn Heights on the opposite side of
the borough. Brighton Beach, adjoining sleazy Coney Island,
was now a haven for Russiam émigrés, and from them had
sprung a Russian Mafia as ruthless and as dangerous as the
Italian. Pharoah wondered if New York City would ever recov-
er from its illness, if it ever again would show a bright, shiny,
healthy face. Probably not in his time, probably not in anybody's time.

When Pharoah entered the bar, the bartender's practiced
intuition told him it was the fuzz. He could also have seen
him through the plate-glass window participating in the drama that had starred, tragically, briefly, Herbie Marks. "You got
a phone?" The bartender invited him to use the one on the
bar. Pharoah searched in his address book for Herbie's home
number and then pushed buttons. He gave it six rings and was
about to hang up when he heard Gracie's shrill "Hello?"

"Gracie, it's Pharoah Love."

"Wait a minute, Pharoah. Let me turn off the set." On the
table next to the Marks's television was a framed photograph

of herself and Herbie taken a decade earlier in Las Vegas, when they kidded themselves into believing they were still in love. She touched her wedding ring and her engagement ring for reassurance. Instinct told her Herbie was dead. Pharoah phoned the house infrequently, certainly never in the day-time, not if he was looking for Herbie. Today, now, Pharoah obviously knew where Herbie was. She picked up the phone. "Pharoah, you got bad news for me?"

Not really all that bad, thought Pharoah. There's all the money and four—count 'em—four insurance policies. Like Herbie said, you're a great catch now, Gracie. "Right on the nose, babe. You're always right on the nose. I shot him."

"Well, that keeps it nice and friendly. Is he dead?"

"He's resting at the morgue, or should be in another couple of minutes. He iced three dealers."

"They deserved it," said Gracie, in death Herbie's surprise ally.

"Well, if he hadn't come out shooting and survived, it'd be life."

"He couldn't take that. Herbie hated cages, you remember. Zoos. Prisons." Our marriage. "When can I have him sent to a funeral parlor? We've got a real nice one just a couple of blocks away. He'll feel at home there." She was babbling, go-ing on and on about who else had been buried from the place. Her mother, her father, an aunt, a neighbor who had been al-coholic; for a laugh Herbie had slipped a pint of gin into the coffin—real good stuff.

"Gracie," Pharoah interrupted abruptly, "why don't you call a girlfriend to come over."

"You won't believe this, I'm expecting three. This is my

bridge day. Every week we play bridge at somebody else's house. I've got the nosh all prepared, and I bought fresh decks and oh, Christ!" She sobbed bitterly, slamming the phone down, sinking onto the sofa, suddenly remembering Herbie had been her boyfriend, then her lover, then her husband, then the father of her two kids, and then the two-timing chiseler with girlfriends all over the place, sometimes even in this house, when she and the kids were away for the summer.

She cried Herbie's name over and over again until, exhausted, she leaned back onto the couch. Her sobs subsided into heavy breathing, and then a cooler head prevailed. Bank accounts. Life insurance. She's wealthy. She's not yet forty. She's still a good-looking broad. Now composed, she found the phone number of Herbie's dishonest lawyer (and he better not try any tricks with me), dialed, told the receptionist she wished to speak to Mr. Lapidus, and when the receptionist asked, "Who shall I say is calling?," Gracie said with immaculate enunciation, "This is Herbert Marks's widow."

Pharoah had winced when Gracie slammed the phone down. He shut his eyes for a moment, and when he opened them, they were moist. He rubbed them with his fists and reached into a pocket for a bill with which to pay for the diet Coke he'd requested.

The bartender reminded him, "You want a shot of something stronger?"

"Do I look like I need it?"

"Can't hurt."

"Vodka." Pharoah contemplated the unpleasantness of attending Herbie's funeral. The executioner paying his respects to the victim's family. Very hypocritical. But Herbie had been a pal, a buddy, a musketeer. The two of them and Marco had lost their virginity together. What was her name? Muriel. They thought they were her first. She was only about twelve or so. They didn't know that when Muriel got home, she wrote their names in her secret diary, like a gunman of the Old West carving notches into his gun handle. The boys had been preceded by several dozen other names, the first three of which belonged to Muriel's father and her two brothers.

Muriel, thought Pharoah, fair of face and filthy of body. Could it have been she that made him opt for same-sex partners, or was it a genetic malfunction, one that he'd read about during that painful period when he thought, disturbingly, of marriage and kids and mortgages and the life-threatening boredom of the same partner for the duration. Pharoah suppressed a shudder, downed a second shot of vodka, voiced to the bartender a sincerely meant "Hang in there, pal," and then went in search of the solace he knew his good friend Rita Genari would offer him.

Rita Genari's town house on West Forty-fourth Street between Ninth and Tenth avenues had been her base of operations for over a decade. She occasionally wondered what some of her neighbors, such as Actors Studio and New Dramatists, would think if they knew what other kind of entertainment was being practiced behind the facade of her well-maintained building. Her call-girl service was conducted discreetly, with taste and grace, friendly good humor, and warmth on Rita's part. Rita's operation was coed. Her women and men were carefully screened before winning callbacks that could lead to a lucky draw. Rita's was the very best service in town. She charged the highest prices and drew the best clientele. The elite of the world made specially planned pilgrimages to her house. They came from Japan and China and India and Sri Lanka. They came in droves from South and Central America and from Mexico. She was a legend in Europe and in Africa. A fax to Rita from anywhere in the world sent one of her women or one of her men flying first-class to all points of the globe.

Four times a year she published a glossy catalog and sent copies by express mail around the world. She took pride in the fact that quite a few of her girls married into great wealth and nobility. Several of her young men were now the permanent possessions of various wealthy clients at home and abroad. Five of her boys had starred in movie box-office sensations and every Christmas sent Rita lavish gifts. Two had even gotten married and sired children. One of them was now an infamous homophobe. Rita referred to him as "that turncoat rat!" She was simply the tops, and so young wannabes of either sex bombarded her with photographs and résumés pleading for a chance to prove they were worthy of her patronage. Publishers offered generous advances for her memoirs, but Rita rejected them, always graciously. In the back of her mind she recognized that she would need a publisher in the future, when she was no longer the beautiful forty-year old goddess who reigned over her Forty-fourth Street mansion.

Rita's house, like Rita, was detached, surrounded on both sides by alleys that led to a garden in the rear. It had once been the home of a famous stage and screen star of the thirties and forties who had been the mistress of a Greek billionaire. The billionaire was long since dead, but the actress, now well over ninety, resided at the Actors' Fund Home in New Jersey, lost in the fog of Alzheimer's. In addition to mechanical devices,

Rita had the protection of the Mob and of the police. Both needed her uniquely brilliant grapevine. Pharoah had said of Rita that had she been around at the time, there would have been no Pearl Harbor. And what further endeared her to her clientele was the knowledge that she kept several physicians on daily call. Her "kiddies," as she called them, had to retain excellent health. The plague, AIDS, played no favorites. As one of her lovely, albeit not too intelligent, young ladies told a frequent visitor, a Pulitzer Prize–winning newspaperman, "We certainly practice safe sex. Rita insists we should always use conundrums."

In a very special way, Rita and Pharoah loved each other. When they needed it, they comforted each other. As Pharoah no longer had the same sort of close male buddies he had had when a youngster, Rita had no special women friends. (She couldn't, in truth, remember ever being young, she would tell Pharoah.) Her own quarters, tucked away in the back, were where only a chosen few of her clients, such as a former president of the United States and an Olympic decathlon champion with a taste for redheaded young men were permitted to set foot. The three upper floors were supervised by Juana Gomez, a lovely, middle-aged Mexican who saw to it that the reception room where clients waited was well stocked with drinks and appetizers for those who had arrived with a different kind of appetite.

Rita and Pharoah sat across from each other in her living room. A maid had served Bloody Marys, but both drinks remained untouched on the coffee table that separated the two friends. Rita wore a fashionable housecoat made elegant with two pieces of Elsa Peretti jewelry. Pharoah sat in silence, which at the moment Rita chose not to break. There was something on his mind, she could tell, and she knew she would hear what it was when he was ready to share it. A few minutes later, he shifted in his seat and spoke.

"I killed one of my best friends this morning."

"Was it something he said?" She lit a cigarette and sent a perfectly formed smoke ring past Pharoah's left ear. "How come a best friend?"

Pharoah shrugged. "What are best friends for?" Rita smiled. This was the sassy Pharoah she enjoyed. "We grew up together. Went to the same school. He was voted most likely to succeed. He succeeded into dealing drugs. He was dealing too much with bandits. I've been warning him for years to get out. You must have read in the papers about the three dudes found murdered in a Harlem apartment. Herbie killed them."

"You're sure?"

"We trust our informers. My chief sympathized when I asked him to let me go after Herbie. I knew Herbie would appreciate that. You know, for old times' sake."

"Oh, sure. Sort of a class reunion." She reached for her Bloody Mary and sipped.

"He led me quite a chase once I caught up with him in one of his pads down on Catherine Slip. You could really hurt yourself jumping from roof to roof. Running up stairs, running down stairs."

"I'm exhausted listening to you. Try your drink."

"In a minute. Then into one of those derelict tenements where I was afraid there'd be some squatters. Thank God there weren't. Herbie knew I'd collar him. He knew it meant a cell for the rest of his life." He tried the Bloody Mary. It was good.

"Herbie was claustrophobic. Allergic to close quarters, especially cells. It was up on the roof. Him behind the chimney stack, me in the doorway, behind me my backup team. You know what Herbie and me was doing? We were reminiscing."

"That's sweet."

"Then he came out shooting like gangbusters, and that was my cue, and I took it and nailed him. He was committing suicide. I know he wanted it that way. He wanted me to be his executioner. I can't say I'll miss him, because we haven't been seeing that much of each other. He and Marco Salino and I haven't been close in a long time. I told you Marco was one of the Three Musketeers back in Canarsie."

Rita was crossing to a desk to answer the phone. She spoke softly, in a sexy voice that promised everything and guaranteed nothing. "This is Paradise." She listened, quoted prices. Pharoah's mind boggled. Rita said, "We don't give any cash-back guarantees." She winked at Pharoah. "Sorry, sweetie, we don't accept food stamps." She hung up and returned to her seat. "Can you imagine that? Food stamps!"

"Now I can concentrate on Marco's boys. You had any more bad scenes lately?"

Two of the string of mob victims, the brothers Dario and Benny Lupo, had been knifed to death in one of Rita's alleys. They had been preceded several days earlier by the double murder of two other Marco lieutenants, Renato Belli and Luchino Vido, shot to death in the front seat of a car parked in front of a restaurant, La Fontana, a Mafia hangout.

"Wasn't it bad enough having the Lupos knifed practically on my front doorstep. That could be bad for business." She tapped ash into a tray. "Doesn't Marco have any suspicions?"

"Do you?"

"What do you mean by that?"

"The boys are steady customers here. I'll bet some of them talk in their sleep."

"If they do, I don't hear it. You know that song an old-time dyke nightclub singer named Spivy used to sing? It was called 'The Madam's Lament,' and the opening line goes, 'They all go upstairs but me.'"

Pharoah laughed and then said, "But your kiddies might hear it."

"You know they feed me everything they think might be of some use. What does that look on your face mean?"

"I can't see it, but I'm sure it reflects what I'm thinking."

"So what are you thinking?"

"I'm thinking you know something you're not so sure you ought to tell me."

"You must have been real smart in school."

"Damn right. I worked real hard. I didn't want to end up doing time or windows."

"All straight A's?"

"Some of them were gay."

She smiled. "How much is one and one?"

"I'm in no mood for games."

She repeated the question. Pharoah recognized there must be a method to her madness.

"Okay. I'll play. One and one are two."

"And what does two put you in mind of?"

"Twins?"

chapter

3

"Twins," echoed Rita.

"What about twins?"

"There was something about a pair of beautiful girl twins found dead in a car submerged in a lake in the Catskills about four weeks ago."

"Oh, yeah. It was the front page of the *Post*. They had a picture of them, a professional picture. They were dancers or something."

"They sang and they danced. They were babies, they were eighteen, they were just starting out."

"What were they doing in the Catskills?"

"They'd been booked into the Hotel Capri."

"The Mafia Hilton?"

"You got it."

"I thought it was closed for the season."

"The Mob doesn't know from seasons. Once a month they have a big weekend meeting up there. You know, when they decide policy and strategy and who's double-crossing who and who needs to get back in line or who needs to be erased. There's lots of food, lots of drink, I do the major catering."

"You deliver some of your kiddies."

"They pay big money."

"You mean Marco pays big money. He owns the Capri."

"Mostly, yes." She crushed the cigarette in the tray and sipped her drink.

"You sent the twins?"

Her face hardened. "No way. They were booked by an agent, Emmanuel Robinson. Manny's an all-right guy. When he books the acts up there, it's an unwritten law that nobody tries to fool around with them. This time the law got rewritten, and it ended up very nasty. After dinner and the show, the capos retire to a meeting room on the opposite side of the hotel, behind the grand ballroom. It's far away from the basement casino where the show takes place while dinner is being served."

"Does it always get out of hand?"

"It usually doesn't get out of hand at all because the boys who aren't in on the big meeting pair off with my kiddies and make hay while the moon shines. That night, eight of Marco's baboons asked the twins to join them in the basement for a nightcap while waiting for their ride back to the city. What they didn't know was that the other acts were already leaving. Some had their own cars."

"You knew the twins?"

28

"Millie and Annie Cicci. They called themselves the Chic Twins."

"Cute."

Rita was torching a cigarette. "They were gang-raped. They were beaten up brutally. They were attacked by animals. Animals."

"You said they were waiting for a ride back to the city. What were they doing in that car in the lake?"

"Don't be stupid, Pharoah. The whole damn thing was staged." She paused. "Neither of the girls could drive."

"Why'd you wait until now to tell me this?"

"Because it's been gnawing at my brain for weeks. I didn't see them raped. I didn't see them beaten up. I asked Marco Salino if this is what might have happened to the girls, and you know him. He waves his arms and yells, 'My boys don't do nothin' like that!' 'My boys.' Ha. So what I just told you is a scenario I dreamed up, and believe me, to me it sounds good."

"Oh, yeah. Movie of the Week material. Can Drew Barrymore sing and dance?"

"Does my scenario make any sense to you?" The phone rang. Rita crossed to the desk. "This is Paradise." She listened. "Hello, Walt."

Walt MacIntyre, the chief of detectives, sat behind his desk looking with distaste at a slice of cold pizza. "Is my boy there? Put him on. I need him back here." He threw the pizza into the wastepaper basket. "Pharoah? What the hell you doing in a cathouse in broad daylight?"

"Having a talk with Rita."

"Learning anything worthwhile?"

"I'll tell you when I see you."

"Make it soon. I want your report on Herbie Marks."

"What's the matter with Al and Moe? Didn't they file?"

"They seem to have a problem. Like was the perp aiming to kill or shooting wild accidentally on purpose."

"How would they know? They were behind me on the steps in the hallway. They couldn't see shit."

"You cradled Marks in your arms and cried when he died. Was he an old lover?"

"I never have old lovers. You know I like them young, fresh, out of a Yeshiva."

"Not funny, Pharoah. So come home, but not all is forgiven."

"Say, Walt . . ."

"What?"

"What was the topping on that pizza I'll bet you just dumped?"

MacIntyre exploded. "You know, sometimes you're too effin' smart for your own good! Stop off someplace and bring me one with pepperoni and mozzarella and no anchovies!" He slammed the phone down as Pharoah turned and saw a good-looking young man in the room whom he hadn't heard entering. He was too tall to have little cat feet. He wore a T-shirt on which was lettered: In Case of Emergency Give Head. His jeans were pasted to his body, making him, in Pharoah's unforgettable phrase, a real stocking stuffer. He also wore an earring in his left ear, a miniature crucifix. Rita introduced him.

"Pharoah, this is one of my prizes, Gino Vinelli. Five hundred a pop. Has tuxedo, will travel."

"I'm not in the market."

"I didn't ask if you were. Gino has a beautiful baritone."

"What's his name?"

"His voice, asshole, his voice. He sings under the name Carl Turner. I think he could be another Vic Damone."

"Isn't one enough?"

She said to Vinelli, "If you give a damn, you try getting used to Pharoah. Pharoah Love, that is. Detective."

Vinelli stared at Pharoah. A detective wearing a yellow-and-blue-striped cowboy shirt? Wearing corduroy jeans torn at the knees? A detective wearing cowboy boots decorated with multicolored studs? A detective with a red AIDS pin fastened to his shirt and on his head a cap with a blue pom-pom? The ponytail, he decided, was just right. He wondered if he moonlighted for Rita.

Pharoah heard Rita say, "Gino was one of the acts the night the twins were killed."

"That's so?"

"Yeah," said Vinelli. "I was there." He might have a great baritone, but Pharoah noted he needed diction lessons.

"Did you suspect the evening might end up in an orgy starring the twins?"

"No. I've played the Capri before. It was always hands off where the acts were concerned—unless something was prearranged."

Rita said, "I did the prearranging. I have a monopoly." She smiled.

"You sure the twins weren't prearranged?"

"I won't take offense at that one. We're good friends."

"No offense intended. How long have you known the twins?"

"A long time. Juana was their godmother."

"Your Juana?"

"My Juana."

"You know, I'm very, very puzzled." Pharoah sank back into his easy chair. Rita had crossed to her desk and sat there. Gino Vinelli was leaning against a wall, his arms folded. Pharoah thought he looked like a statue of Apollo but reprimanded himself with Hands off, Pharoah—unless Rita offers him for Christmas.

"You got a lot of puzzles, Pharoah," Rita commented. "Your cup runneth over."

"I'd prefer it didn't. When I get back to the precinct, I'm going to find out why there's been no investigation into the twins' murder."

"Maybe there's one going on and you don't know about it."

"Rita," Pharoah said solemnly, "they ain't nothin' that Pharoah doesn't know is going on at the precinct." He thought for a moment. "Of course, the bodies were found in the Catskills, that's Sullivan County."

Rita said, "Pleasant to hear an Irish name for a change."

"Sullivan's got their own force. Damn, I'm going to look into this. Maybe what it's all about is that someone connected to the twins is avenging them." He enumerated slowly, "Renato Belli, Luchino Vido, the Lupo brothers. Gino—were they at the Capri that night?"

"They might have been," replied Gino.

"What do you mean, they might have been? You were there. You must have seen them when you were doing your act."

"There's a spotlight on me. And there's an awful lot of mafioso out front blowing smoke in my face. And besides, they all look alike to me."

"God damn it, Marco Salino would know if they were there. The son of a bitch, my old buddy, my old musketeer, comes to me and says, Find this killer, Pharoah, find the son of a bitch who's thinning my herd. Does he tell me about the twins? Does he tell me there could be a connection between the girls and these mafioso murders? Say, Rita. Have you discussed the murders with Marco?"

"Not in any depth."

"Why not?"

"Marco doesn't come here to talk."

"You're not terribly fond of Marco."

"What makes you think that?"

"The way you say his name. I can hear the faint trace of distaste in your voice."

"He's not one of my favorite people, but I like his money. He gives me a lot of business. He helped get me connected internationally. He connected me with the Yakuza in Japan and the Triads in Hong Kong."

Pharoah, hands on hips, said, "Rita, you must have one hell of a file with the FBI."

"If I do, I wouldn't mind having a look at it. You know I have my protectors, Pharoah. If the files on me are ever laid bare—you'll pardon the expression—to the public, governments might tumble."

Pharoah shook his head from side to side as he went to Rita and kissed her forehead. "I'll get back to you later." To Gino he said, "In your spare time try jogging your memory. Maybe you'll remember seeing the four paisanos. *Ciao*, darlings!"

After leaving Rita's apartment and crossing the long hall to the front door, Pharoah hoped to run into Juana Gomez, but he was out of luck. He looked up the staircase, but he saw no one and heard nothing. He went out to the street. He descended the short flight of cement stairs that led to the sidewalk. He paused to reconnoiter the alley to the left of the house, the alley in which the Lupo brothers had been stabbed to death. How does one guy off two men at the same time? And how did he know they were to be found at Rita's? Rita, at first highly indignant that such an atrocity could have taken place right outside her front door, was reminded by Pharoah that there once had been a street lamp outside her door. At her insistence, it was moved several yards down the street so that her clientele could enter and exit discreetly.

The obscenities were coming from behind him. He turned and saw the Grey Ghost's twitching face. "You shouldn't creep up on a guy like that, Ghost. Especially a guy carrying a gun. Where'd you get the carnation?" The Grey Ghost was now sporting a red carnation in his gray jacket lapel.

"There was an AIDS rally in Times Square. Somebody put it in my buttonhole." He pulled it out and let the flower drop to the pavement." Ferocious curses. He moved past Pharoah into the alley in search of Juana Gomez and a handout.

Pharoah's radar warned him he was being watched from within the house. His eyes moved to the second floor and three heavily draped windows. The middle window betrayed a sliver of light. The drape was quickly moved back into place, and Pharoah was abandoned. Who was watching him? Certainly not Rita; she's in the back of the house. Juana? He ached to have a chat with her, positive she might know things that could be of value to him. One of Rita's kiddies? The room with the three windows facing the street was the reception room, the "salon," as Rita styled it, Juana's domain.

Juana moved away from the window to see if one of the establishment's steady clients needed his diet ginger ale refreshed. The man was a nattily dressed septuagenarian whose sisters started a house account with Rita just to accommodate their widowed brother when he moved in with them. They were spinsters. They and their sibling were amusingly wealthy, the money coming from a chain of amusement parks that had proliferated across the country decades earlier. The sisters had never married, their brother explained, because they were too busy counting their assets. When Juana asked if he wanted more diet ginger ale, he impatiently waved her away and said to the beautiful Lily Davis, one of Rita's veterans, a knowledgeable Creole from New Orleans, "I can't do it on a water bed. I get seasick."

"I've got Dramamine," Lily said as she took one of his hands. "Come on, Eugene, let's go make babies."

As Lily led Eugene to a field of dreams, Juana went back to the window and slowly moved the curtain aside. Pharoah was gone. She let it fall back, wondering why Rita had decided to tune the detective in to the twins' murder. Juana had been eavesdropping at the door that separated the living room from the kitchen. She was a chronic eavesdropper. It was her second-favorite sport. Rita encouraged it when one of the kiddies, not all of whom had retentive memories, was with a client, and Rita relied on Juana to supply choice morsels of information that the kiddies didn't recognize might be of some importance. For instance, Rita highly treasured stock market tips. A good number of Wall Street denizens were her patrons, and Rita considered it bad form to cross-examine them personally. She had to rely on the kiddies and her treasured Juana, who she occasionally worried might develop some form of cauliflower ear from listening at keyholes.

But now eavesdropping had slipped in priority. Juana was thinking of Pharoah Love, of the four murdered Mafia lieutenants—who got what they richly deserved, as far as Juana was concerned. She loathed them all. She loathed all *bandidos*. She had known nothing like this in Mexico. Nothing like *them* in Mexico. She adored Pharoah. He made her laugh. He treated her with respect. He brought her comic books, one of her several vices—besides watching Barbara Walters and Geraldo Rivera.

La Señora is up to something, Juana decided as she reached into a dish of walnuts and popped one into her mouth. *La Señora* guards her treasures of knowledge zealously. Why did she share so much with Pharoah all of a sudden? All of a sudden? Rita does nothing on the spur of the moment. Rita plans everything carefully. There must be a reason behind divulging to Pharoah what she knew and suspected about the murder of the twins. The murderer must be caught. This elusive phantom must be brought to justice. He murdered the four lieutenants. Could he also have murdered the twins? Were those innocent-looking babies not all that innocent? Had they learned things that could be dangerous to a mafioso? Marco Salino? That son of a whore, which Mrs. Salino certainly wasn't. Mama Salino, who at this very moment was in the Holy Family Church in Canarsie lighting enough candles to illuminate Paris while mouthing in equal proportions Hail

Marys, novenas, and the contents of a new recipe for spaghetti vongole she'd gotten from her Jewish neighbor Mrs. Markowitz.

Rita had often warned Juana that thinking could be dangerous to her health. Juana's head throbbed. Intrigue was too much for her. It was all she could do to cope with Rita's kiddies and their clients. Why couldn't they all be as smart and clever as the Creole? Lily Davis was the only whore in captivity who owned valuable real estate in Queens (no pun intended), was a college graduate, and had read Proust's *Remembrance of Things Past* in the original French. Juana went in search of aspirin and a cold towel for her forehead.

Pharoah walked slowly to Eighth Avenue. On the corner, a familiar and well-liked figure, a street performer, was holding a small crowd mesmerized while juggling six multicolored balls. He wore a harlequin costume with a ruffled collar around his neck. His face was a colorful exaggeration. Paint exaggerated his mouth and his nose, his cheeks and chin. Not even his mother would have recognized him. At his feet was a sort of carpetbag filled with materials necessary for his performances, such as barbells, Indian clubs, fans of variegated colors, all forms of whatnot and nonesuch with which he dizzied and fascinated his audiences.

Pharoah called out to him, "Yo, Yoyo!"

Without missing a beat, Yoyo acknowledged Pharoah. "Hanging in, Pharoah!"

"So I see. Where you been? Ain't seen you around lately."

"Been doing some weddings and bar mitzvahs. The recession's worse, so I'm back on the streets. How's the murder business?"

"As usual, mostly cut-and-dried." Yoyo's audience now resembled spectators at a tennis match, heads moving back and forth between the clown and Pharoah. Yoyo tossed all six balls into the air at once and then caught them neatly in the carpetbag. He was rewarded with applause, and it was gratifying. He swiftly doffed his multicolored, cone-shaped headpiece, and his eyes pleaded for donations. He didn't do too badly considering this was one of the neighborhoods not celebrated for its affluence.

"Things are looking up," said Yoyo brightly, "at least enough to buy me a subway token."

"Glad you're back, Yoyo. I was beginning to miss you."

"I wish I could hear the same from my creditors." Returning his friend's wave, Pharoah headed on uptown to his Fifty-fourth Street precinct, reminding himself to pick up a pepperoni pizza for Walt MacIntyre.

Walt MacIntyre was a good-natured man in his mid-forties. His rise to chief of detectives had been rapid and deserved. He was responsible for racking up a respectable score of homicide solutions and had ruthlessly prosecuted a group of rogue cops who he suspected were on the take. In return, his men respected him and tried to do their best work for him. It was believed that he had political aspirations, though few could envision him as a mayor of New York or even a borough president, but stranger candidates had succeeded to the pantheon. MacIntyre had his favorites, with Pharoah at the top of the list.

In an organization notorious for its homophobia, MacIntyre admired Pharoah, enjoying the way he gave as good, if not better, than he received. Though Pharoah's garish sartorial taste had been spotlighted in the newspapers and on television on various occasions, MacIntyre found it amusing, whereas to others it was an embarrassment. Pharoah was the precinct's only gay officer, though he was one of the few policemen who admitted it. As MacIntyre had explained to his wife, who thought Pharoah a delight after having him to dinner one Sunday, "When Pharoah came out of the closet, he tore off the door and the hinges."

She said thoughtfully, "That was a long time ago, wasn't it? It took a lot of courage for him to do it then, when it was more dangerous than it is now."

"Pharoah said he was tired of dissembling. And don't kid yourself, Loretta, it's still dangerous. Pharoah suffers a lot of flak, though in Pharoah's case suffer is the wrong word. Pharoah wears invisible armor. I've got some good detectives who are bad apples where Pharoah's concerned."

One of them, Albert West, an eight-year veteran, was seated across the desk from MacIntyre. He was grousing bitterly. "Herbie Marks was my case. You shouldn't have taken him away from me and given him to Pharoah. You were playing favorites." He sounded like a teenager complaining to an indifferent father accused of preferring his other children.

"I don't play favorites, Albert. This was a special case. How often do I have to tell you Pharoah and Marks grew up together. They were buddies. Pals. They were everything together but Boy Scouts."

"I'd have brought Herbie Marks back alive!" This reminded MacIntyre of Frank Buck, an erstwhile animal hunter who boasted he "brought them back alive," though on film he was seen to slaughter more then he had captured.

"I get the impression Herbie didn't want to be brought back alive," on which statement Pharoah entered without knocking and placed the carton of pizza on MacIntyre's desk.

"No anchovies, which brought a look of disapproval to the baker's face," he announced.

Pharoah sat in the office's other chair, removed his cap, and contemplated Albert West's look of displeasure and disapproval. MacIntyre offered West a slice of pizza. Pharoah said, "Think twice before accepting, Albert. The pizza man's gay."

"Up you!" was the unique response.

"Still coining them, Albert?"

"Cut it out, you two," MacIntyre flared, and then bit into a slice, fanned his mouth to cool the heat, and after a suspenseful moment or two favored them with a look of bliss. While chewing, his mouth a fleshy facsimile of a cement mixer in slow action, he said to Pharoah, "Albert's pissed off I passed Herbie Marks to you." Pharoah shrugged. Albert was always in heat about one thing or another. If he wasn't upset by a failed attempt to corner a perpetrator, he'd blithely move on to complaining about the plumbing in the men's room. "What happened on the roof? If like you said on the phone Al and Moe were on the hallway steps behind you and couldn't see much, then their report is useless."

"They spell better than I do."

"Save your lip for your face."

Pharoah recounted the event quickly and articulately. Albert West had a look of disbelief as Pharoah told them how he and Herbie had reminisced about their childhood.

Albert West interjected snidely: "How come you didn't send out for some Big Macs?"

"We weren't hungry," Pharoah said sharply.

MacIntyre growled, "You're both giving me indigestion. Pharoah, did you deliberately murder Marks?"

"I never deliberately murder anything except the Queen's English." He explained about Herbie's determination not to spend the rest of his life caged in a cell and his chronic claustrophobia. "Herbie wanted to die."

Albert West snapped, "Why didn't he shoot himself?"

Pharoah snapped, "Go ask him."

"Enough!" shouted MacIntyre, who then helped himself to a second slice of pizza, knowing full well he'd pay the consequences of acute indigestion.

Pharoah penetrated the brief silence that had settled over the room. "Herbie came stampeding out from behind the chimney stack like a fireball. He was scatter-shooting ferociously. The look on his face—I'll never forget the look on his face. It said, I love you and if you love me, you'll kill me, so I took the shot and he fell." He said to Albert West, "He died in my arms, and I cried. Don't you ever die in my arms, Albert, because I'll never have any tears for you."

"You mother!" West growled.

"No way possible."

MacIntyre wondered aloud why Marks had led Pharoah on a futile chase. Pharoah said, "I think he thought I'd nail him while chasing after him." He was thoughtful for a moment. "I could never hit anyone in the back. Not Herbie, not my pal."

West asked sardonically, "Could you hit Marco Salino in the back if you were chasing him? Wasn't he the third of your boyhood threesome?"

"It's not worth considering. If you knew Marco as well as I

do, Marco never runs away from anything. That's why he's made it so big."

Albert West had some choice obscenities for Marco Salino, putting Pharoah in mind of the Grey Ghost and the realization that the Ghost and Albert West had something in common. Both were homeless, the Grey Ghost physically, Albert West mentally.

MacIntyre said to Pharoah, "Gracie Marks has been on the phone kvetching about when she can claim the body. Seems she's got her favorite mortuary standing by to eviscerate and wax him."

Pharoah said, "Jews don't embalm their dead. And by law they have to be buried before sundown of the day after they died. Do we need an autopsy?"

"Please, Pharoah, not while I'm eating. You sure you guys don't want a slice? I don't think I can manage it all by myself." Both refused. "I'll have the body released right away." He barked the order into an intercom. "That should make the grieving widow happy. Pharoah, you got the chutzpah to attend the funeral?"

"I adore funerals," Pharoah replied archly.

Albert West inquired with sarcasm, "You going to wear an outfit like the one you're wearing now?"

"Well, that depends," Pharoah said, crossing one leg over the other and folding his arms as he swung the crossed leg back and forth like an anxious B-girl in a waterfront saloon. "My harlequin leotards and my pailletted tutu are at the French cleaners. If they're ready by tomorrow, I'll wear one or both and a corsage of orchids pinned to my hot blouse, the see-through one. What do you think, Albert, will I make page six of the *Post*?"

"Go to hell!"

"If you lead the way."

"Enough!" yelled MacIntyre, who then erupted into a belch.

"Albert," said Pharoah, his voice slightly sweetened, "ain't you ever visited the museum on the second floor of the Police Academy? You know where the academy is, don't you? I'll remind you. It's on East Twentieth Street. It's very small and very tucked away, but it's there. It was put there by GOAL, the Gay Officers' Action League. You've heard of *us*, haven't you?" MacIntyre didn't try to mask his enjoyment of Pharoah. Too obvious. "There's not many of our artifacts there because there isn't that much to display. But it's significant. We formed GOAL back in 1982 because we got tired of being hassled by you and your brother homophobes. I'm thinking of doing a poster to hang on the wall over the display case." He was on his feet, warming up and enjoying himself immensely, Herbie Marks having been temporarily exiled to a dark recess of his mind.

"It will state the following. 'Who is a homophobe's favorite author? Straight Talese! What is a homophobe's favorite era in American history? The Straight Nineties! What is a homophobe's favorite European city? Straight Paree! And when a homophobe suffers muscular aches and pains, what does he anoint himself with? Ben Straight! And as for all of us, we prefer to walk the gay and narrow path."

Pharoah sat down while MacIntyre had a choking fit, then

was out of his seat, pounding his boss on his back. At the same time, Albert West emerged from his brief coma to fetch a glass of water. Five minutes later, after MacIntyre had recovered, the three were deep in a discussion of the mafioso murders. Several days earlier the unhappy Albert had been assigned to sit in for Pharoah while the latter went in pursuit of Herbie Marks. Now MacIntyre perversely decided to retain West's services, for despite disapproving of his bigotry, MacIntyre respected West's agile and probing mind. And, in criminal matters, the man was a true bloodhound. Though Pharoah begrudged him his abilities, he too, respected them. They had worked together before, and successfully, despite their sexual polarization. At least Pharoah would be out in the field, where he preferred to be, while West would work out of the precinct.

MacIntyre asked, "What have we got so far, Pharoah?"

"Four corpses and an anxious Marco Salino."

"That's all?"

"No, that's not all. I got a fresh development today."

"Come on, come on, spill!" MacIntyre was lighting a cigar, and Pharoah foresaw instant asphyxiation for the three of them.

Pharoah carefully repeated what Rita told him about the Cicci Twins, her suspicion that they were gang-raped and beaten and then put in the car that was submerged in the Catskills lake. MacIntyre needed time to digest these new revelations.

MacIntyre studied the ash at the end of the cigar, flicked it into a tray on his desk, and said, "It's pretty good thinking on

Rita's part. Maybe too good. Maybe she knows this for a fact. What do you think, Albert?"

"I think we should check with the boys in Sullivan County, and if the twins were autopsied, we should know the results."

"You get on that, Albert," MacIntyre ordered. "What's on your mind, Pharoah? I know that look."

"I'm not sure. Rita's a great gal. A good friend. She's always been on the square with us."

"And we've been more then generous with her," MacIntyre reminded Pharoah.

"I'm just puzzled by why she waited a couple of weeks before sharing this with me. Anyway, Rita's a very cautious lady, as we well know. I think she has deeper suspicions that one of these days are bound to surface."

MacIntyre's voice was bathed in menace. "The sooner they surface, the better. Keep working on her.

"I'm going to try and get her housekeeper, Juana, to have a little tête-à-tête with me. I have a feeling she knows a few things that could be to our advantage. I think she was watching me from a second-floor window when I left Rita's place."

"No crime in that," MacIntyre said.

"No, but if it was her, I had the feeling then she was trying to make up her mind about telling me something that might help." He got to his feet. "Well, I've got to get home and bathe and anoint myself with delightfully smelling oils. I've got a heavy date tonight."

MacIntyre killed the cigar in the tray. "Less heavy dates, please, and more weightier sleuthing."

"It's all in the line of duty. I'm having dinner with Marco

Salino at La Fontana. Maybe I'll take along a couple of roses to drop in memory of the two who were gunned down in their car outside the place. Which reminds me, Albert." He had the door open for a graceful exit. "Did I ever tell you about the time I was in Caracas, Venezuela, and was wooed and won by a straight caballero?" He shut the door gently behind him.

chapter

4

Pharoah's one-bedroom apartment was in a still-dignified-looking brownstone on West Fifty-fifth Street between Ninth and Tenth avenues, a short walk from the precinct. It was up one flight of stairs in the rear, and his bedroom window afforded a magnificent view of a garden overgrown with weeds and pockmarked with an assortment of tin cans fielded over the fence by a motley assortment of neighbors. It was a popular social club for stray cats that fought, copulated, and serenaded in a variety of ugly voices. Pharoah found it all very New York and very comforting.

Pharoah soaked in the tub up to his neck in suds created by a combination of bath salts—his favorite Jour D'amour—and his churning feet and busy hands. A naval battle was under way between several toy warships, submarines, and gunboats. Pharoah supplied the sound track, voom-vooming dropped bombs and yak-yaking falling flak, and his simulation of machine-gun fire was uncannily real. He reached for a sponge and lazily rubbed his arms and legs while sinking a proportion of the warring fleets. He began talking to himself.

"Herbie's gone. I hope Gracie broke the news to his folks gently. So now there's only Marco and me." He sighed. "Marco, the murdered mafiosos. Rita and Juana and the twins. God damn it, there's got to be a common denominator someplace. A link, there's always a link. Where's the link? Where's the meat?" He was scrubbing his chest vigorously. Are these revenge murders? He spoke to the ceiling. "Is Marco kidding me, or is he kidding himself? Did he order these hits to be rid of a bunch of expendables? Or is there a very dangerous nut at large? Boy"—he shook his head from side to side—"if this ain't a kooky form of ethnic cleansing." He was giving himself a headache, and he needed to think clearly tonight. There was a long night in store for him. Marco and then back to Rita's to try for a go at Juana. And then God only knew what surprises. He grappled with the perennial problem of scrubbing his back with a very tired and very worn brush. Suddenly, he shouted, "God damn Albert West!"

Ten minutes later, dried, powdered, and scented, he selected his wardrobe for the evening. Not too bizarre so as not to be too easy a target. His green T-shirt featured a fist with the middle finger erect. His brown slacks were perfectly tailored. The jacket was a Bloomingdale's markdown, one of his favorites. It was blue corduroy. He opened a dresser drawer and studied the variety of guns reposing there. "Now, then," he said, "which of my faithful darlings shall accompany Daddy on his rounds tonight? Now let me think, could there be any unpleasant, unexpected action tonight, such as more shootings outside La Fontana?" Something popped into his head that gave him pause to think and consider seriously. Is Marco a possible target? The notorious Paul Castellano didn't suspect he had less then two minutes to live when his town car pulled up in front of Sparks Steak House on East Forty-sixth Street. John Gotti ordered that hit. Castellano was a powerful godfather. Gotti at the time was a nothing Queens capo in Castellano's Gambino crime family. December 16, 1985.

Hmmm. You never can tell. Pharoah chose a powerful 9-millimeter Glock pistol. Austrian. It could fire up to eighteen rounds. It wasn't official issue, but that didn't worry Pharoah. Very little that was supposed to be official did. He tucked the weapon into his waistband and buttoned the jacket. He turned to the full-length mirror on the opposite wall. He studied himself with a professional eye. He turned to the left and then to the right. He loved what he saw. He crossed to the mirror and kissed his reflection. "Pharoah, you sexy devil!"

La Fontana was one of several Mafia hangouts on West Forty-fourth Street between Fifth and Sixth avenues. Marco Salino chose the location after forcing out a French restaurant that suffered from the delusion of grandeur. West Forty-fourth Street boasted the newly refurbished, newly elegant Royalton Hotel. La Fontana itself never advertised. It grew by word of mouth. Several excellent reviews cemented its popularity. An occasional celebrity dropped in, usually by command of a capo or a godfather. Now there was added panache in the assassinations of Renato Belli and Luchino Vido right in front of the restaurant. It made headlines, and the accompanying photographs of La Fontana destroyed what little anonymity it had managed to retain. It was soon featured on one of Embassy's sightseeing routes, and Nicholas Suggi, who ran La Fontana, had his hands full discouraging tourists.

Marco Salino sat at his favorite table in the rear of the restaurant, his back to the wall and a full view of the restaurant and its entrance. Capos and godfathers made it a point of sitting in restaurants with their backs to the wall. But sometimes there were too many of them gathered at a table and not enough wall to go around. Nicholas Suggi had solved that problem in his restaurant by placing mirrors strategically on the walls, affording a clear view of the interior for everyone. At Marco's left sat Natalya Orloff, a Russian émigré nightclub singer. Marco had found her a month earlier singing in a restaurant in Brighton Beach in Brooklyn. Brighton Beach was a hotbed of Russian refugees, mostly Jewish. It was the turf of the very dangerous Russian Mafia, which guarded its territory and its secrets zealously. On the surface Brighton Beach's tough guys were jollity itself. Lots of backslapping and generosity and lots of borscht and blini and vodka and balalaika music and soulful songs of the old country. Natalya specialized in their rendition. She could tear off a mean *Dark Eyes* (*"Ochee Chornyaaaaaa, Epeekrasnyaaaaaaa . . ."*) complete with dry sobs and heaving chest. When she tore into "Papirosson," a serenade, believe it or not, to cigarettes that the surgeon general would heartily disapprove of if he ever got to hear it translated, there was never a dry eye in the house; rather, lots of chest-wrenching coughing. Marco had "borrowed" Natalya from her Russian protector whose protestations fell on deaf ears mostly because they weren't terribly sincere. Natalya and Marco both knew he had a replacement warming up in the bullpen, and Natasha was eager to spread her wings and try for the big time that she knew eagerly awaited her in Manhattan.

Natalya had a magnificent body. Her breasts were in a class by themselves, large, firm, and dangerous. Her newly acquired Givenchy had a neckline that plunged short of suicide. She wore no brassiere, which is the way Marco liked it. As to her face, she made the most of her Slavic features. Thick, lush lips heavily rouged. Large brown eyes heavily outlined with kohl. Eyebrows thinned and penciled, and there was a seductively decorative mole where left cheek and chin met. Being fearless and perhaps a little too recklessly Russian, Natalya smoked unfiltered cigarettes in a long, menacing holder that she was prone to wave about wildly when speaking, like an orchestra conductor gone berserk. Marco adored her. She was a far cry from, and a vast improvement on, his wife, Fat Selma, a monument to obesity.

Nicholas Suggi sat with them, nursing a glass of Chardonnay. Marco glanced at his wristwatch. "He's five minutes late. Pha' is usually on time. I hope it's something worthwhile delaying him."

"Vot is vorthvile?" asked Natalya, eyes widened and palms up and outstretched.

"Maybe he's got a lead on the son of a bitch picking off my boys." Marco chose the heel of an Italian bread from the basket on the table and helped himself to some pats of butter.

Nicholas Suggi said, "Maybe he's in church lighting a candle for Herbie Marks."

"Don't be funny," growled Marco. "I can imagine what pain Pha' is suffering. It ain't easy killing one of your best friends. I ought to know. I've iced enough of them."

Suggi didn't challenge the statement.

"Vot is vit ice?" asked Natalya, wishing Marco wouldn't make so much noise when he chewed. It was almost as repulsive as the memory of her father slurping tea from a saucer. Suggi explained that icing meant killing, as did offing and a few other interesting expressions that had entered the American vocabulary during the past decade.

Natalya laughed while gesturing, almost severely branding Marco's cheek with her cigarette. "Icing, offing, vot nonsense! And who is this Herbie Marks?"

Marco briefed her quickly on the relationship that once existed between himself, Herbie, and Pharoah, to which Natalya commented, "Is very sveet. And this him standing by the door looking so immaculate and so handsome?"

As Marco waved to Pharoah, Suggi got to his feet and pulled a chair out from under the table for Pharoah.

"Sorry I'm late," said Pharoah. "I got caught in the theater traffic. How goes it, Nick?"

"Not bad, not bad."

Marco introduced Natalya. "Nice," said Pharoah with a charming smile. "Very, very nice."

"You approve of me?" asked Natalya coyly while Pharoah

wondered if she was capable of causing multiple injuries with that frantic cigarette holder.

"You're a big improvement on Fat Selma." He winked at Marco, whose face was impassive.

Natalya's eyes widened. "And vot is a Fat Selma?"

Pharoah said, "Marco, baby, for shame. Haven't you told her vot is a Fat Selma?"

Marco growled, "Pha', you're too old to be cute." He said to Natalya, "Fat Selma's my wife."

Natalya shrugged. "Vife? Vot is vife? All my boyfriends have vifes."

"How many boyfriends you got, Natalya?" asked Pharoah.

"Right now? Only Marco. Is very bad season right now. Recession!" She shrieked with laughter. Marco's eyes locked with Pharoah's, and they made it a laughing trio. Only Suggi was not amused. Natalya's laughter subsided, and she said in all seriousness, "In Minsk, from where I'm coming, is not much opportunity for boyfriend. So I steal rubles from my father, who is black marketeer, and I go seek my fortune in Moscow." She sighed. "Moscow is also not easy, only bigger. So in Moscow I am call girl." She didn't notice three jaws dropping. "You know, telephone operator. But Natalya very smott girl. Soon I meet vit gangster, who also"—she giggled—"offed and iced all over the place."

"Where's he now?" asked Pharoah.

"In Brighton Beach. He bring me to the good old U.S. of A. Marco steal me from him." She snuggled against Marco, who kissed her on the forehead.

Marco asked Pharoah, "Ain't she something?"

"If I were a pervert, I'd say I could eat her with a spoon." Pharoah said to Suggi. "Who do I have to fuck to get a drink around here?"

"Sorry, Pharoah. I was enjoying the floor show." A thumb jerked in Natalya's direction.

As Suggi signaled the headwaiter, Natalya asked, "Vot floor show? Vere is floor show? I do not see a floor show."

"He meant you, kid," said Marco.

"Me? I am floor show?" Perplexity gave way immediately to humor. "Ha, ha. So I am floor show. This means you enjoy me, yes? Vell, vait till you have the great joy of hearing me sing. If I had my balalaika, I vould sing entire repertoire." She chucked Marco under the chin. "I am vunderful, am I not, beloved?"

"You're one in a million, kiddo."

Pharoah asked the headwaiter for a bottle of Vichy.

"Vichy!" snorted Marco, "where's my two-fisted martini drinker?"

"I need a clear head tonight, Marco, preferably my own. I have an idea it's going to be a long one."

"You hurtin' that bad?"

"It ain't good."

"You speak to Gracie?"

"Yeah. She's having the time of her life arranging the funeral. Now she's a rich widow."

"She'll soon find someone who'll sucker it out of her. My money's on Gracie. So dumb, she thinks Somalia's an Italian dress designer."

"She's not all that dumb," countered Pharoah.

"So who is Somalia?" asked Natalya.

"Oh, God," said Pharoah under his breath.

Marco said, "Nick, go get the chef. I'm hungry." Suggi excused himself and went to the kitchen. Pharoah dreaded the scene that he knew from experience would be forthcoming. A conference between Marco and the chef, a hot-blooded Sicilian who could boast of more culinary awards than his nearest competition. He continuously threatened defection and each time won a bigger piece of the action for himself. Smart restaurateurs gave the chef a percentage of the take, and Nicholas Suggi was a very smart entrepreneur, which is why Marco selected him to run La Fontana. "So, Pharoah, what's new I should know about?"

Pharoah repeated the information he received from Rita Genari regarding the twins. Natalya's eyes never left Pharoah's face. He had her mesmerized. Gang rape. Beatings. Put in a car that was submerged in a lake. She suppressed a shudder while the bottle of Vichy was served to Pharoah. Suggi was a long time returning with the chef. Marco figured that he had walked into one of the many crises that plagued the kitchen.

"Did that happen?" Pharoah asked Marco.

"Sometimes Rita talks too much."

"Sometimes you don't talk enough."

"Meaning what?" Marco's eyes were narrowed, Pharoah recognizing the familiar expression of menace on his face.

"Meaning if you want me to do my job right, you've got to give me a lot of help. Is *that* what happened? *Were* they gangbanged, beaten up, dumped in the lake?"

"Maybe."

"What do you mean, maybe? For crying out loud, you ought to know."

"I was in a very serious meeting in another part of the hotel, damn it."

"You know *all* of what goes on. Don't shit me, Marco."

"I ain't doing nothing of the kind. Sometimes my boys get a little out of hand, let off some steam. Okay okay!" He held his hands up as though there were an invisible gun pointed at him. The way Pharoah had been reading him, he was now reading Pharoah. When Pharoah meant business, you took a hand in the deal or left the game. "What Rita told you is what happened, but I swear to God, I didn't know nothing about it until Rita faced me with it. Damn bitch. I told her to keep it to herself until I could figure out the angle."

"What angle?"

"Like were my boys being killed because of what happened that night. And who was it that was getting revenge?"

"Were the twins on the square?"

"Oh, hell, yeah. They knew from nothing. They were kids. Real nice kids. Believe me, if this killer hadn't gotten to my boys, I'd have given them something to remember myself."

"How many of your lieutenants were in on the rape?"

"Eight that I know of. Four are dead."

"Where are the other four?"

"Well hidden. And leave it at that."

"If you're not going to tell me where they are, how can I help them escape getting their behinds shot off?"

"I can protect my own, Pharoah."

"The way you protected the Lupo brothers and the other two?"

"Those four dummies were killed so fast, I had no chance to realize a pogrom was underway!"

"Where are they?"

"A couple are upstate. Two are in a safe house. The four he got were easy picking, two coming out of Rita's, the other two parked outside. But who knew a nut case was on the loose? When the Lupos were killed in Rita's alley, I figured it to be a mugging. Renato and Luchino in the parked car were clay pigeons. Believe me, Pha', I thought maybe 'Weeping Willie' DiLuca had declared war on me and was doing a number on my boys."

"And vot, please, is a Veeping Villie DiLuca?" Natalya was working on a fresh cigarette.

Pharoah explained, "He's lover boy's archenemy. They're very jealous of each other."

"He ain't no archenemy, damn it. We just don't agree on very much. He's jealous I got so many businesses under my thumb."

Pharoah said to Natalya, "Maybe you haven't noticed, but Marco has very big thumb."

She smiled slyly and said, "Marco has much that is very big."

Nicholas Suggi finally returned with the chef. "Maestro!" exclaimed Marco, arms outstretched. "Have you something special for us tonight?"

The chef stood looking down at Marco, hands rolled into fists and positioned on each side of his waist. "I want no problems with you tonight. I got a very busy kitchen." He did not speak directly to Marco. He trained a very professional eye on Natalya, who responded by rewarding him with a big smile that revealed her dazzling caps.

"Now, now, Maestro," cautioned Marco, "talk to me, not to my girlfriend. She ain't picking up the check."

"You ain't, either," Pharoah said. Natalya directed her smile at Pharoah. This is one smart peasant, thought Pharoah. She probably comes from a long line of cossacks.

The chef was saying, "I suggest you begin with the arugula and red pepper salad with goat-cheese croutons."

"What kind of dressing?" Marco asked. Pharoah looked at the ceiling.

"The kind I make the best!" the chef raged.

"Like what?" Marco said through clenched teeth.

"Like oil with an olive purée!"

"Not too sharp!"

"No, not too sharp. Agreed?"

"Agreed." Pharoah and Natalya weren't consulted. She was too smart to interfere. Pharoah didn't give a damn.

The chef was speaking. "I have a superb Malfatta in a beautiful stew of sherry, thyme, and mushrooms and cream with carrots, fennel, and very juicy pieces of duck."

"Is fattening?" asked Natalya, feigning alarm.

The chef's eyes twinkled. "Is delicious!"

Pharoah's mind wandered as the chef and Marco played out their vaudeville sketch. What preoccupied him was twins and a whorehouse madam and a Mafia capo and four murder victims and four more potentials sequestered where he couldn't get to them and question them, let alone try to offer them protection. Pharoah suspected there was a lot more at stake for Marco than was immediately apparent, which is why he was playing it so cool. Pharoah was in no rush. It would all come together sooner or later, give or take a few more corpses. Juana was the godmother of the twins, so she had to know something that would prove valuable to Pharoah.

Marco's voice broke his reverie. "The menu sound okay to you, Pha'?" He looked as though the future of civilization depended on Pharoah's approval.

"Sounds real cool." He said to the chef. "Hey, maestro, do me a medium-rare burger on a toasted bun with french fries on the side and a bottle of diet cream soda, *kapish?*"

chapter

5

The meal was now just a pleasant memory. Pharoah was enjoying an espresso. Natalya was repairing her face with the loving care one imagines Andrew Wyeth painted his Helga. Marco's cigar was gripped between two fingers of his right hand. "This is my own very special brand. Fidel ships them to me regularly. And I ship him girlie magazines and porn tapes. Stupid bastard."

"Vy stupid bastard? He owns island. You don't." Natalya couldn't bear to tear herself away from her reflection in her compact.

"Fidel's living on borrowed time and borrowed money." Suggi had rejoined the table now that the dinner crowd had dwindled and there was still more then an hour before the after-theater crowd would come trickling in. "Pha', baby, how'd you like something big? Something real big."

Pharoah marveled at how Marco still looked the way he looked as a kid suggesting they sneak into Canarsie's sole movie house. "Such as?"

"How'd you like to run Cuba for us?"

"I don't speak the language."

"You can have the best translators. I'll make you a millionaire."

"I didn't know you knew how to sew."

Marco said to Suggi, "Will you listen to the putz? He makes dumb funnies while I'm offering him the jackpot. How's about you, Nick? You want Cuba? You're doing a great job running this joint for us, you don't even skim as much off the top as we figured we'd allow you. You could do even better with Cuba. We're gonna reopen the big casinos and put back the tables and the slots. Big new hotels with fancy restaurants and clubs."

"Vell, vell, vell! Cuba! You vill present me in one of the clubs, yes, Marco?" Her eyes sparkled with greedy anticipation.

"Sure, my little *kasha varnitchka*."

"I am tastier than *kasha varnitchka*. I vill knock them for a loop in Cuba. I vill sing in Spanish for them, 'Alla en el Rancho Grande.' I will also sing for them in French and German and Sanskrit. I know many languages. I am very bisexual!"

Suggi asked Marco, "When's the coup?"

"As soon as Fidel's brother, Raoul, thinks he's ready to betray him. That should be pretty soon. Raoul's afraid there's a revolution brewing. With no USSR to support them and China too busy with internal affairs to give a damn, Cuba's gonna explode, and that's when we step in and take over."

"Hey, Marco."

"Yeah, Pha'?"

"You want to go halfies on a Mars bar?"

Marco smiled, then placed the cigar back in his mouth, blissfully unaware of its overworked symbolism. "You can laugh all you like, Pha'. But I got apartment houses and a couple of mansions, while all you got is one crummy little walk-up in a brownstone, with mice and cockroaches."

"And when I sleep," Pharoah told Marco, "I don't have nightmares and wake up in a cold sweat."

Marco said to Suggi, "And he was such a smart kid, too. Maybe it was moving from Brooklyn to Manhattan that did him in. Natalya, how'd you like to be the queen of Cuban prostitution?"

Natalya stared at her beautifully manicured fingernails. "Is possibility. But, of course, must be equal-opportunity organization. I have had it up to here"—indicating her neck—"with oppression. Vill you maybe better make me movie star? They make movies in Cuba, no?"

"Oh, sure. Lots of porn." Marco winked at Suggi, who was mentally floating about in the never-never land of the future Cuba with himself as the Mafia puppet.

"Vot is porn? You mean dirty movies?" She feigned mock alarm. "You vould have Natalya star of dirty pictures?" She laughed.

"I'm only kidding." He leaned back, and his voice encompassed his audience of three. "Maybe we'll do the Catskills first. Been up there lately, Pharoah?"

"Been up there never."

"Most of the territory looks like it was hit by an atom bomb. When the Jewish families like Grossinger were reigning there, it was beautiful. The landscaping was a joy. The lawns were manicured; there were great tennis courts, indoor and outdoor swimming pools; the biggest acts played in their private casinos. But that was yesterday. Now there's today, and it's pathetic. The only big one left to carry on the tradition is the Concord, and they're struggling to survive. But it's a tough struggle."

"There's the Capri," Pharoah reminded him.

"Yeah, I suppose." He thought for a moment. "The Catskills was once big business. Real big business. Not just the summer, but all year round. Now the pools are abandoned and overgrown with weeds, the tennis courts have cracks in them, the elegant old hotels are now derelict and gone to seed." He grew expansive. "We're gonna fix all that. We're gonna take over the Catskills with gambling and prostitution. . . ."

"Sounds a lot like Cuba," Pharoah noted. "What fun we have to look forward to! A faux Roman Empire in the Catskills, and such a convenient location. A new breed of Borgias and de' Medicis with their special brands of poisons. Can I have the shoeshine concession?"

"Don't sell yourself short, Pha'. And while you're at it, stop sticking a finger in my eye. Or one of these days I'll stick a finger where you used to not like a finger stuck."

"Oh, you remember?" Pharoah was watching the entrance of another familiar Mafia figure accompanied by two bodyguards whose faces were remarkably devoid of intelligence. "Well, look who's here, Marco. Weeping Willie DiLuca with a small supporting cast."

"Is this Vee Villie. But vy he carries teddy bear?"

"He always carries a teddy bear," said Suggi. "It's his trademark. His security blanket."

"Is very childish, no?"

Suggi was getting up. "Willie is like that other Willy, Willy Loman. Attention must be paid." He excused himself and crossed the room to welcome DiLuca, however insincerely.

Natalya's voice was whipped cream. "Is very good-looking, Nicholas Suggi."

"You want him?" asked Marco magnanimously.

"Vot you mean, vant him?"

"You want him to screw you?"

Natalya said with indignation, "Vot you think I am? Public toilet?"

"What are you getting so upset about? You got the hots for Nick, then he's yours."

She said to Pharoah, "I must be going mad. I don't believe vot my ears are hearing."

"That's big-hearted Marco. Always willing to give you the shirt off somebody else's back." Pharoah was wondering if Marco was planning his usual Thursday night visit to Rita's. It was one of the two nights in the week that Rita's young ladies and young men made themselves up to resemble famous movie stars. There would surely be a Madonna imitator (easy) and a Marky Mark (Rita had an awful lot of those) and a Michelle Pfeiffer (though the kiddie who specialized in Pfeiffer, albeit still a blond beauty, was so far over the hill there was no climbing back up).

"Vell, Marco can keep his shirt."

"Come on, Natalya. Cool it. I was only joking."

"Some joke. Ha, ha. Here comes more joke. Your Veeping Villie. And look! He is veeping!"

Pharoah told her, "Willie weeps at everything. Movie credits, microwave instructions, you name it."

Willie's voice was hoarse and rasping. He arrived at the table between his bodyguards. "My condolences, Marco, my deepest sympathy, Pharoah. I know Herbie Marks was once your best friend. Was there no avoiding popping him, Pharoah?"

"No, Willie. Kismet." He referred to the bodyguards: "What's with the bookends?"

"I can't be too careful these days. Whoever's knocking off Marco's boys might also have plans for me." He stroked the teddy bear, and Pharoah wondered if it was ever dry-cleaned. "Ain't somebody going to introduce me to this gorgeous creature?"

Natalya, who'd been slumped in anger, sat up and aimed her bosom at Willie. "I introduce myself, Veeping Villie."

"Oh, so you heard of me."

"I am Natalya Orloff, of the Minsk Orloffs."

"Very impressive." He dabbed at his eyes with a multicolored handkerchief. "Say, ain't you the Russky singer I saw out in Brighton Beach a couple of weeks ago?"

"Yes, vas me. At the Vladivostok. I was costarred with the Ukrainian rock group the Leningrad Latkes."

"You're pretty damned good." Uninvited, Willie sat between Pharoah and Natalya. He stared at her breasts. "Yeah, pretty damned good. You quit Brighton Beach?"

"No, I still perform there. There," she said pointedly, with a side glance at Marco, "I am appreciated for what I am and not up for—how you crudely say—for grabs."

"Ah, come on, Natalya." Marco was chewing on the cigar.

Natalya favored Willie with a charming smile, one that promised much but would deliver little. "So tell me, Veeping Villie, if Mr. Salino takes over in Cuba and the Catskills, what have you in mind for yourself?" Marco paled. Pharoah stifled a guffaw. Suggi, who had come to tell Willie his table awaited him, froze. Willie DiLuca smiled, a thin, crooked little smile.

Willie said, "Mr. Salino's eyes have always been too big for his stomach."

Marco squashed the cigar in a tray. "You've always been in awe of my hearty appetite, Willie."

Pharoah stepped in swiftly. "Say, Willie, got any suggestions as to who's been deep-sixing Marco's boys?"

"I ain't big with suggestions, Pharoah. You should know that by now. You once told me it was easier to grill a piece of fish than to grill me."

"I don't suppose you've been crying over them."

"If I did, it was for their mothers."

Marco said, "They were orphans."

"Oh, yeah? Who deep-sixed their mothers?"

Suggi came to life. "Willie, your table is ready."

"Sure. My table is ready. Say, Marco," he said as he was rising, "the weather in the Catskills don't bother me none, but it can get awful hot in Cuba. See you again, Miss Natalya." He strutted away from the table, his bodyguards in his wake.

Natalya looked at her wristwatch. "Is time car take me to Brighton."

Marco said, "It's outside."

"You are angry vit me?"

A few beats were skipped before Marco answered her question. "It doesn't matter. Willie has his moles, and I have mine. We always find out sooner or later what's going on in each other's families. I prefer to learn sooner." He finally found a smile for Natalya, whom he genuinely liked. "Don't give it a second thought, baby. Willie's also got some territory staked out. You ever hear of a place called Tibet?"

Pharoah said, "There's a chauffeur in the doorway semaphoring this table."

"Ah, yes," said Natalya, "is my cousin Dimitri Popov." She said to Marco, "You should get to know Dimitri better. He was exiled to Siberia for six, maybe seven, years. He first-class fire man."

"What do I need with a fireman?" asked Marco, perplexed.

"To burn down factories for you, vot else?" She stood and patted Pharoah's cheek. "I like you very much, Mr. Pharoah. You are, how they say, one cool detective."

"I like you too, baby. We'll meet again."

"But of course." She zero'd in on Nicholas Suggi. "Marco says if I have hots for you"—Nicholas tugged at his shirt collar—"he will make arrangement. But you read about the Pilgrims, yes? Priscilla and vot'is name, oh, yes, John Alden. Like Priscilla say to Alden, Nicholas Suggi, I say to you, 'Speak for yourself, John.'"

She swept away on a cloud of powerful perfume while an embarrassed Nicholas said to no one in particular, "Great sense of humor. I always thought Russians were more downcast and breast-beating."

Pharoah said, "I have an idea she's got a breast you wouldn't mind beating."

"I've had enough of this smart-ass dialogue," said Marco. "I'm going over to Rita's. Maybe there's a Shirley Temple. Can you believe it, guys, after all these years, I still got a yen for Shirley Temple."

"Don't be in such a rush. The night is young, and I am beautiful. What about Willie, Marco?"

"What about him?"

"Maybe tonight ain't the first he's heard of the high C's. Cuba and the Catskills."

"That's right. It ain't."

"You know for sure."

"For very sure."

"So maybe he's already giving you trouble."

"If I thought he was, I'd tear his face. But you ain't looking for Willie. I know for sure. It ain't Willie."

"Maybe the future would be easier if you thought of splitting the territories with Willie."

"Pha', there's only two people I ever go halfies with, and Herbie's dead. See you later at Rita's?"

"That's as certain as death and taxes."

He and Suggi watched Marco make his exit, arousing the curiosity of a few patrons who recognized him from seeing his picture in the tabloids on various occasions.

Suggi was lighting a cigarette. "Why do I get the feeling"— he cutely mimicked Natalya—Veeping Villie has an inferiority complex?"

"Because he's inferior. Do you like Marco?"

"That's from out of left field."

"Well, do you like him or don't you?"

Suggi exhaled smoke. "Am I on an informal hot seat?"

"Let's say I pulled it out of thin air on the spur of the moment. I got some murders on my hands, and they're beginning to get awful heavy."

"I can see Marco likes you. He's offered you Cuba."

"I'm second choice. I should feel hurt. You ever sleep with Marco?" said Suggi.

"Lots of times. Some nights at his house. Some nights at my house. Some nights at Herbie's house. We were always staying over at each other's houses. Sex never reared its lovely head, though occasionaly we'd play 'You show me yours, and I'll show you mine.' Marco and Herbie mostly preferred to play it with Dirty Muriel, local girl who made bad. Now it's your turn."

"Me show you mine?"

"Don't be cute."

"Marco's a generous boss. He's no sweat. Other then that, he's a pompous, arrogant, overbearing asshole. You saw the scene he went through with the chef. He doesn't know squat about cuisine, and I'm sure if I was ever at a formal dinner with him, I'd be watching him drink from the finger bowl. You can take the boy out of Canarsie, but you can't take Canarsie out of the boy."

"You hush your mouth, white man, or I'll wash it out with soap. Where you from?"

"Equal Brooklyn squalor. Brownsville."

"You know the Cicci Twins?"

"I was nuts about Annie."

Pharoah was genuinely startled. "Well, how about that. No flubdubbing around. Out with it like a shot."

Suggi shrugged. "Annie wasn't nuts about me."

"She crazy? A handsome hunk like you."

"Please, Pharoah. Don't make a pass."

"You've got nothing to worry about. My days of making passes have passed. Thanks to seven letters of the alphabet—HIV and A and I again and D and S. Put them all together, they don't spell mother; they spell martyr." Suggi was examining the ash on his cigarette. Pharoah wondered if it was some form of a crystal ball for him. "You in mourning for Annie?"

"I didn't murder those bums."

"You don't waste time, do you."

"Let me put it to you this way, Pharoah. Because I work for a capo, you assume I'm a lieutenant. Don't interrupt, I don't get the spotlight on me too often. I'm Marco's employee. He hired me from a résumé I submitted along with a lot of others looking for a manager's job. He liked my credentials, and he liked my name. And like you heard the man say, I do a damned good job for him, and he pays me a damned nice sum of money, and like you also heard him say, like any manager worth his salt, I skim some off the top, but I don't overdo it. Skimming goes with the turf. If you do too much, you get your hands slapped. If you do too little, you're marked as a schmuck. If you do just enough, you've got respect. I'm not a member of the gang, just like not every Italian restaurant owner plays footsie with the Mafia. Now if you want to hear about some Koreans I'm familiar with—"

"You got any theories about the killings?"

"How much you know about the twins?"

"Only what I learned from Rita Genari. That Juana Gomez was their godmother and she brought them up."

"Good lady, Juana. Very loyal to Rita."

"Loyal enough to kill for Rita?"

"As Juana might say, *Quien sabe?* I'm sure there's a lot of hot blood running through Juana's veins."

"Just like what's running through yours."

"I didn't kill those bastards. And you're right. I don't waste time. Like when Annie Cicci gave me the fish eye, I backed off quick. When I want a chick and it gets as far as she invites me up to her place for a drink, I don't waste time with the small talk. I like to cut to the chase."

Pharoah commented ingenuously, "Now that's what I call class."

Suggi looked at his wristwatch. "And now class is out. I'm off to Rita's. I'm so horny I could even fuck Roseanne Arnold."

"Oh, please don't. I'm still digesting. Maybe I'll see you there later if you ever come downstairs."

Suggi smiled, said, *"Ciao"* and left Pharoah to his thoughts.

Cool, thought Pharoah, real cool and real smooth. Meow.

chapter

6

Albert West was tooling along Sixth Avenue in an un-marked squad car when he spotted Pharoah on the corner of West Forty-fourth Street, waiting for the lights to change. West pulled over, rolled a window down, and shouted, "Hey, Pharoah!" He pushed the car door open and gestured to Pharoah to get in beside him.

Pharoah feigned mock horror. "Aren't you afraid of conta-mination?"

"Walt's left messages for you all over the place. I even went to Rita Genari's."

"It must be hip-hopping crazy there by now." Pharoah got into the car, pulled the door shut. West forced his way into the heavy traffic, and Pharoah closed his eyes in anticipation of the worst. The gods were kind, and West narrowly avoided being sideswiped.

"It's berserk time at Rita's. Like she's hostessing a United Nations convention. Something made up to look like Marilyn Monroe shoved her tits in my face."

"I don't see any bruises." He braced himself as West cut in front of a taxi whose driver bore down heavily on his horn while favoring West with a barrage of nasty obscenities. Pharoah rolled down his window, stuck his head out, and shouted, "Blow it out the other end!" He sent the window back up. "What's Walt want?"

"There's been another pair of murders." He shouted, "Son of a bitch!" An Oriental on a bicycle making a food delivery had cut in front of Walt. "It's an effing madhouse tonight!"

"Who got murdered?"

"Lino Sasso and Rudy Fauci. They mean anything to you?"

"Not until now. Marco's lieutenants?"

"Probably. Walt assumes so."

"Tell me about them."

"They were found in a crappy apartment in a tenement on Tenth between Thirty-sixth and Thirty-seventh. They've probably been dead a couple of days. The odor was reported to the building superintendent, who lives in the basement. He used his passkey and found them slumped over the kitchen table. On the table was a partially eaten pizza. The pizza is at the lab. The coroner suspects it was poisoned."

"What about the stiffs? Still at the table waiting for seconds?"

West ignored the flippancy as he wished he could ignore Pharoah. "They're refrigerated at the morgue waiting to be identified."

"Did you tell Marco?"

"How? By remote control?"

"Wasn't Marco at Rita's?"

"I didn't see him."

"Maybe upstairs with Shirley Temple."

"What?" West almost hit the car in front of him. Pharoah, with relish, explained the celebrity nights at Rita's. "Ain't that invasion of privacy?"

"No, sweetheart. It's invasion of privates. She got the idea from a famous Hollywood madam who thrived in the twenties and thirties. Her name was Madam Frances. She was to the West Coast what Polly Adler was to the East Coast. Madam Frances dressed her girls as movie stars. She didn't do males. You wanted to lay a facsimile Jean Harlow or Joan Crawford or Jeanette MacDonald, heaven help us, Madam Frances had a girl for every appetite."

"You pulling my leg?"

"Not when sober. So Rita heard about it and thought it was a cute idea. She only does it twice a week because she doesn't get that many movie buffs. Take me to the tenement. I want to talk to the super."

"Isn't it a little late?"

"For what?" Pharoah rubbed his chin. "I'll call the precinct and let MacIntyre know we're together." He added wickedly, "At last." It was too dark in the car for Pharoah to notice that West was blushing.

Once out of the traffic, West made the tenement in under five minutes. Pharoah said, "The lights are on in the basement. He's probably watching the news." Pharoah opened a gate that led down a short flight of stairs to the door to what he assumed was the superintendent's apartment. "Albert, you got a match? I can't find the bell." West produced a cigarette lighter and found the bell. After a few seconds of being ignored and feeling abandoned, Pharoah banged on the door. Finally, it opened a crack. Pharoah produced his badge. "Open up. We have to talk to you."

"I already told them other guys what I know." He had a trace of an Irish accent, rare in New York supers nowadays.

"Now tell *us*," said Pharoah forcefully. "Open up or I'll puff up my cheeks and stamp my foot."

The door widened, and Pharoah and Albert were confronted by a middle-aged man with a beer belly, brand unspecified, several days' growth of beard, wearing jeans fashionably torn at the knees and a tank top that had probably last been laundered the previous spring. The place smelled of stale beer, cigarette smoke, and defeat. The super, one Oscar O'Hara, indicated a slightly battered sofa for them to sit on. West worried about fleas and bugs and other forms of surface evil, while fearless Pharoah sat and looked at the wooden crucifix hanging on the opposite wall. The TV was on, but the sound had been lowered.

O'Hara explained, "The pictures keep me company when I'm reading the Bible. I always read the Bible and have a beer before I go to bed." He was sitting on a tired Morris chair next to which was a small table on which stood a lamp with a tasseled shade, a can of beer, a half-empty glass, and the Bible. Pharoah saw a door that probably led to the rest of the squalid apartment and wondered if O'Hara ever thought of suicide.

"You live alone?" asked Pharoah.

"Oh, yeah, a long time now. My wife's been dead about five years now, y'know, and my boys are away. I have two sons, and they're both up in Attica. Attempted robbery and assault with deadly weapons. A pretty frisky pair." The palms of his hands rested on his knees.

This, thought Pharoah, is no leprechaun, and he's nervous as hell. The eyes were blinking rapidly.

Pharoah reassured him. "You don't have to be afraid of us, unless you murdered those two upstairs." He asked West. "What were those names again?"

"Lino Sasso and Rudy Fauci."

"Right, Sasso and Fauci. You know them, Oscar?"

"Never saw them after the night they moved in a couple of weeks ago."

"Night? They moved in at night?"

"It was like three in the morning. Very secret. Very quiet. I waited up for them to give them the keys." He thought for a moment. "Them wasn't the names they give me. They told me their names was Smith and Wesson."

Pharoah smiled.

West told Pharoah he got their real names from their wallets.

"Did they rent the apartment from you?" Pharoah wished the eyes would stop blinking.

"No. I don't know who the apartment belongs to. When somebody's going to use it, some woman with a very fancy voice tells me they'll be moving in and to let them have the keys."

Pharoah said to Albert, "Fancy voice. Probably somebody's secretary." He thought, Possibly Marco's secretary. She had what somebody like the super would think was a very fancy voice. Very fancy Chana Isaacs from the very fancy Mosholu

77

Parkway in the very fancy Bronx. Now she lived in the very fancy Brooklyn Heights in the very fanciest section of Brooklyn with her very fancy lover, Michaela Moriarity, Big Mike to those who loathed and feared her but envied her her black belt.

"Sasso and Fauci never left the apartment?"

The super shrugged. "Not that I know of."

"What about food?"

"They sent out for it. Lots of Chinese and Italian. They had other stuff delivered, too, like booze and that. Sometimes they'd phone down and I'd go up and get the money they'd hand to me with the door open just wide enough for somebody's hand and do their other shopping."

"What about laundry?"

"I guess they did their own."

Pharoah said to Albert, "Mother would have thought they were treasures."

Oscar O'Hara was scratching his unshaven chin. "Anything that was delivered was left outside their door."

"Such as a pizza?" asked Pharoah.

"Oh, yeah. The lock on the front door is busted. Anybody can get in."

"Why don't you fix the lock?"

"Nobody's told me to."

"Who's the owner of the building?"

"Some company down on Orchard Street. They send me my check the first of every month. I even get a Christmas bonus."

"That's nice."

"Who else lives in this building?"

"Some spick families, some actor types. There's an artist on the top floor, but he's always trying to hang himself. I keep promising to show him how to tie a good knot, but it keeps slipping my mind."

"You got whores here?" asked Pharoah.

"You know a building in this town that ain't got them?"

"Yeah. Mine."

"You so sure?"

Pharoah didn't answer him. He wasn't so sure. There were those two girls in the basement apartment who claimed they taught aerobics and were always behind in the rent.

Pharoah was on his feet and pacing. "So anybody can get into this building. The night they died, they'd been eating pizza. Probably left outside their door."

"They wouldn't open the door to anybody but me. They always gave me money to pay for the pizza and the Chinese."

"So anybody could get in here and fiddle around with the pizza."

O'Hara screwed up his face quizzically. "I don't know what you mean by that."

"If somebody wanted to poison them, he'd just have to patiently wait for a delivery, follow the delivery in, and when the man delivering left, they could quickly doctor the food."

"That's possible. Sometimes I'd knock and knock and they wouldn't hear me, they had the TV on so loud, especially when they were watching sports. Like I said, anybody can get in here. I'm always catching one of the homeless sneaking up to the roof or trying the apartment doors to see if any are unlocked, which some of them are. I'm always having trouble with squatters, but I get rid of them."

Pharoah said to West jokingly, "Maybe we should get this building condemned."

"Oh, no! Please no!" protested the alarmed super, adding with a note of pathos, "Where would I go?"

"I was only kidding, Pop," said Pharoah. He asked West, "Any point in looking at the apartment?"

"If you need the exercise. It's five flights up. We dusted the place. There's nothing there."

"The smell's still there," advised O'Hara.

"That's a comfort," said Pharoah. "I'd like to use your phone." It was an old phone with a worn dial. Pharoah could barely make out the letters and the numbers. O'Hara probably didn't use it very much. Poor bastard. Pharoah dialed and listened. He heard Rita Genari say, "This is Paradise."

"Pharoah here."

"Hello, sweetie. Coming over?"

"Is Marco still there?"

"For sure. I don't think he's in any rush to leave."

"Well, in case he is, hold on to him."

Rita was alerted by the urgency in Pharoah's voice. "What's wrong?"

"How should I know? I'm not a philosopher. See you in a bit." He hung up, leaving Rita in a sudden unwanted state of anxiety. He wasn't about to tell her about the latest murders until he first imparted the news to Marco. He said to West, "Let's call McIntyre from the car. Oscar looks sleepy and ready for beddy-bye."

The super was standing, awaiting any further developments from the detectives. "It's okay. I'm not sleepy." Pharoah hoped he wasn't about to suggest they join him in a late snack. Pharoah had seen two black cockroaches scurrying under the couch and amused himself by deciding they were eloping.

"Thanks a lot, Mr. O'Hara. You've been a great help to us."

"I respect the law," said O'Hara staunchly. He added with pride, "I fingered my boys, y'know. I don't hold with armed robbery and assault with deadly weapons. I'm a God-fearing man"—his right hand was raised and pointing at the ceiling, and the two detectives were suddenly inundated with a treatment of hellfire and brimstone—"and who so offendeth the law shall be surrounded by a wall of flames and rendered unto ashes! The Lord giveth and the Lord taketh away! And the Lord shows no mercy to three-time offenders!"

"Neither does their father. Come on, Albert, before he thinks of beating us into ploughshares."

In the car, Pharoah called the precinct and was told his chief was out having a late supper and would be back in half an hour. Pharoah promised to call back. "I guess, thanks to Sasso and Fauci, Walt's planning on making a night of it. Poor Walt." West aimed the car toward Ninth Avenue and West Forty-fourth Street and Rita Genari's fun house.

"What do you mean, 'poor Walt'?"

"I don't think he likes his job."

"Maybe. I never think about that."

"He's a frustrated singer."

"You kidding me?"

"He studied opera before he became a cop."

Albert West was skeptical. "Where'd you hear that?"

"Straight from the tenor's mouth. Walt told me himself one night after one bourbon with beer chaser too many. He sang for me, and I'll never forget it. Suddenly, Mahoney's Bar went quiet when Walt started singing this aria. The only word to describe it is 'glorious.' I'm no opera maven, but I know a terrific voice when I hear it. It was glorious, and it was heart-breaking. There were tears in Walt's eyes when he finished and that gang in Mahoney's was giving him the kind of hand he envisioned getting at the Met. Except a career in opera had long passed him by. He had let his mother nag him into becoming a cop and stop wasting his money studying for the opera. The opera was 'for them East side swells' and not for the likes of Walter MacIntyre. Some mothers are geniuses at destroying their children and stealing their dreams, like taking candy from a baby. Didn't you ever have any dreams, Albert, other than to witness the wholesale destruction of the world's homosexual population?"

Albert didn't answer immediately. He was waiting for a screaming ambulance to pass him. Then he said, "I wanted to be a lawyer."

"No shit?" Pharoah wondered how a man as bigoted as Albert West could ever dream of succeeding at the bar. He didn't wonder aloud. This was the first time in the five years he'd known Albert that they shared a personal colloquy.

"I wanted to be Clarence Darrow. Years ago my father took me to see a play starring Paul Muni as Clarence Darrow. It was called *Inherit the Wind*."

"I saw the movie."

"Muni's performance got to me, and I thought, This is for me. I'm going to be a lawyer. So afterwards, having ice cream sodas, I told my father, who said something like 'That's great, son, but don't tell your mother. She has her heart set on you being a priest.'"

"A priest? You? Your mother must have been mad."

"She was," said West. "She died in an institution. She stabbed my father to death, and then she killed my younger brother. She said the devil was in them both." He turned into West Forty-fourth Street. "My brother was gay. She accused him and my father of sleeping together. I think she was right." He pulled up in front of Rita Genari's. "Here's Rita's."

"Thank God," said Pharoah, meanwhile telling himself Albert West might deserve a complete reevaluation.

chapter

7

West remained seated behind the wheel of the car. Pharoah asked, "Ain't you coming in?"

"You don't need me in there."

"Why Albert, inside that tall, dark and handsome detective there's a prude trying to get out."

"I don't like whorehouses or the people who populate them."

"Fair enough. When you get back to the precinct, tell Walt where you left me. Tell him about our rewarding visit with the super. After that, meditate on your terrible driving." Albert West pulled away from the curb, the tires screeching, Pharoah wincing. Poor Albert, thought Pharoah, if he had a personality, he'd be cute.

Juana Gomez greeted Pharoah at the door. "We're having a very busy night."

"That'll delight the IRS, should Rita ever get generous enough to file a return." Juana moved to ascend the stairs. "*Uno minuto, guapa*," said Pharoah, grabbing her elbow. "I need to swap words with you."

"Come on, Pharoah. Stop kidding around. I'm very busy."

"Tell me about the Cicci Twins."

"What about them?"

"They lived with you. You should have plenty to tell. Like who do you think murdered them?"

The twinkle had disappeared from Juana's eyes. Her face was stern. Pharoah worried she might wind up and hurl a thunderbolt at him. "The mafiosi. You know that."

"Who do you think's murdering the mafiosi?"

"A saint." She spat out the word.

"Any saint in particular?"

"Pharoah, if I knew who was killing them, I wouldn't tell you."

"I believe you."

"You better."

"Did you know the twins' parents?"

"No."

Pharoah winked. "You know. But you're not going to tell me."

"Their parents are not important. Once they give up their children, the parents are not important."

"And here I've been wondering if maybe they were your daughters."

"I always said you had a good imagination. You write sometimes, don't you."

"Hey, hey, babe, you remember that. Sure I write. And sometimes just about describes my output."

"Maybe you should write about the twins."

"Write *what* about the twins?" They hadn't heard Rita Genari approaching. She was smartly dressed, and Pharoah could identify her Paloma Picasso earrings. Where expensive jewels were concerned, Rita was a bird dog usually pointing toward Tiffany or Van Cleef & Arpels.

"Juana's trying to steer me back to the typewriter because I'm getting too nosy about the twins. Juana, that's what detective work is mostly about. Getting nosy and asking questions."

Rita said to Juana, "See if Marco Salino has satisfied his appetite and send him down to my apartment. Come on, Pharoah. The vodka is very chilled."

"Been telling it ghost stories?"

Juana watched them enter Rita's apartment and then hurried up the stairs. In the reception lounge, Weeping Willie sat in his shirtsleeves, mindlessly stroking his teddy bear. The door to the room he had been occupying stood slightly ajar. Juana asked, "What's wrong?"

Willie's eyes were misting. He pointed to the door and said with a snarl, "*She's* what's wrong. If she's Madonna, how come she don't sing?"

"Maybe she has a sore throat."

"She's soon gonna have a cut throat if she don't get her act together."

"I'll go talk to her." Juana entered the room. On the bed reclined "Madonna," her nose buried in the *Reader's Digest*. "Why won't you sing for Willie?"

The petite facsimile flung the magazine to one side. "How the hell can I sing with a full mouth?"

Downstairs, Pharoah sipped his vodka while waiting for Marco to materialize. "Is Nick Suggi still here?"

"As far as I know. What's with Nick all of a sudden?"

"Not all of a sudden. I got interested in him after dinner. We had a nice, friendly chat. He had a case on Annie Cicci."

"Lots of guys had cases on the twins. They weren't interested in romance. Their careers came first."

Pharoah placed his glass on an end table. "So? The only one I've met so far is Nick, so I'm concentrating on Nick."

"I don't see Nick as a murderer."

"I'm not seeing Nick as a murderer. I'm seeing him as a suspect like I'm seeing some others as suspects. I don't even see me as a murderer, but whether I like it or not, that's what I'm going to see when I shave tomorrow morning."

"Come off it. Herbie Marks wasn't your first hit."

"You're such a mother hen, Rita. You should be running a nursery school."

"What makes you think I'm not?" said Rita, jerking a thumb toward the upper floors. Pharoah laughed. "What's up, Pharoah? You don't make a special trip here just to see Marco unless you've got very important news for him." She sipped her vodka and smacked her lips with overexaggerated relish. "I suspect there's been another pair of murders."

"Rita, you're a witch, but I've got a soft spot for witches. I'll bet there's a lot you know that I wish I knew."

"That depends on what you wish you knew. Who's been murdered?" Her eyes commanded that he give her the information. There was a quick rap on the door, and Marco Salino entered without waiting for Rita's invitation.

Marco said, "I know neither one of you is in mourning, but you look it." He crossed to the bar and poured himself some Chianti.

Pharoah said, "You've got two more names to cross out of your address book. Lino Sasso and Rudy Fauci."

Marco slammed the bottle down. Rita said, "I was wondering where they'd disappeared to. They've not been around lately."

"No need to send them Christmas cards anymore, Rita." Pharoah watched Marco working his lips, but not a sound emerged from his mouth. He took a slug of the wine and put his glass down.

"Son of a bitch," Marco said in a voice unfamiliar to both of them. "Stinking son of a bitch. How does he find them? How does he know where they'll be so he can ice them?"

"You know, Marco, this murderer is some kind of an artist. I think he's a gifted phantom. First he knifes, then he shoots, and tonight, we suspect, he poisoned."

"How poisoned?" Marco asked.

Pharoah shrugged. "If you mean what brand, we don't know yet. But if you'd like to know how, the killer doctored a pizza."

Marco exploded. "A pizza! A poisoned pizza! Nobody poisons a pizza! That's sacrilegious!"

"The pizza wasn't poisoned. The poison was put in the pizza to kill Fauci and Sasso?"

"What's the big difference?" asked an exasperated Rita.

"Rita, by now you should know I'm a purist. Pharoah cross-es the i's and dots the t's and very neatly tidies his bed in the morning and always lowers the toilet seat. I loathe sloppiness. Like I know you watch *Murder, She Wrote* and have seen that sheet of paper in the typewriter on which Jessica is supposed to be writing her latest best-seller. There's a line on that sheet of paper, and it reads, 'Arnold came racing out the door,' and it kills me. If the show's renewed, I'm going to write the exec-utive producer, who just happens to be the star of the show, and tell Miss Lansbury that if her character is such a fine writer she should know that you don't come racing out the door. You come racing out of a house or out of a room or out the doorway, but you can't come racing out a door because it is a solitary, stationary object and—"

"Fuck off, Pharoah!" bellowed Marco.

"And that's another physical impossibility," stated Pharoah with impunity. "Anyway, my odds are on the pizza being sprin-kled with something cozy like cyanide or something as unimaginative as rat poison."

"I'll opt for rat poison, "said Rita, "because they were a pair of rats."

"Now Rita," Pharoah cautioned mockingly, "you mustn't speak ill of the dead. I'm sure your mother must have told you that."

"My mother told me a lot of things, none of it useful."

"You know, Marco, you're really something." As Pharoah sipped the vodka, Marco stared at him, waiting for Pharoah to continue. "There are so many things in this case you have left unspoken. Such as why didn't you tell me your lieutenants—

or were they shooters?—were holed up in a hole on Tenth Avenue."

"Not *that* place," Rita said, and Pharoah filed her outburst away in that section of his brain reserved for information to be investigated further. "Not *that* place." How did she know about the tenement on Tenth Avenue?

Pharoah said, "'That place.' You own the building, Marco?"

"*We* own the building. It's been safe until now. Sasso wanted to stay there. He's very sentimental. He was born in that apartment."

"How touching," said Pharoah. "He's come full circle. Not all of us are that fortunate. Marco. I've asked you before, and I'm asking you again, and I'm going to keep asking until you level with me."

"I've been leveling. Maybe here and there I forget something, but later, when I remember, I tell you." His defense sounded childish, and since childhood Marco frequently tended to whine. He complained a lot, and he ate a lot, Pharoah reminded himself, always whining and dining.

"You don't say a lot about the Cicci Twins."

"What's to say?"

"You own the Capri."

"*We* own the Capri."

"Who books the acts?"

"Some agent."

"*What* agent?"

"Manny Robinson," Rita told Pharoah.

"You know him?"

"Never met him. He handles my boy Gino Vinelli. You know, the one who sings under the name Carl Turner."

"He here tonight?"

"He might be back. He was on an outcall." She picked up the phone and pushed one of a variety of buttons. After a wait she asked, "Juana, is Gino back? Send him down. She listened. "I don't give a damn how tired he is. Tired comes with the territory." She slammed the phone down.

She heard Pharoah asking Marco, "Marco, maybe you were sweet on one of the twins?"

"No way!"

"Didn't you think they were adorable?" Pharoah persisted.

"They were traffic stoppers, but I wasn't part of the traffic."

"You didn't take part in the orgy?"

"Like I told you before, Pharoah, and may I remind you I don't like to chew my fat twice, I was in the back of the hotel in the conference room, and I got half a dozen witnesses who'll swear to that except I can't give you their names."

"See what I mean, Rita, he's always holding out!"

"Oh, put a cork in it, Pharoah. Their names will mean nothing to you unless you're doing investigations into garbage hauling and life insurance companies and teamsters and longshoremen . . ."

"Okay, Rita, okay! Enough! *Basta!*"

"Bullshit," said Rita with about as much charm as the word deserved. "Everybody knows the Mob has a finger in every kind of pie imaginable. Abortion clinics, organized religion, bakeries . . ."

Pharoah uttered a stream of "tsk tsk tsks." "So they're responsible for defiling the once-noble bagel. Marco, isn't it possible there's a fink nibbling inside your organization?"

"If there is, he'll be nibbling on a bullet." He poured more wine for himself. "I really can't stand spies. I got no respect for them. It's a very low profession. I can't stand people who snitch."

"You *mamzer*," said Pharoah. "Back in Canarsie you brought snitching up to a fine art."

"I was a kid then!"

Rita heard a light tap on the door. "Come on in, Gino!"

Gino Vinelli entered holding a bottle of imported beer. He nodded at Pharoah and Marco and asked Rita, "You want me?"

"I always want you, darling. You're my favorite; you know that." She smiled warmly. "Was it a good outcall?"

"Another Hollywood slob."

"There are so many of those," Rita informed Pharoah and Marco.

"Sit down, Gino," said Pharoah. "Then you can slip back upstairs and put a cold towel on your forehead."

"I've got a trick waiting," said Gino matter-of-factly.

"Two in one night?" Pharoah knew Gino didn't recognize he was being kidded.

"He's my fourth. I'm very much in demand."

Rita said with pride, "Why, Gino's practically a cottage industry."

"Gino," commanded Pharoah, "tell me about your agent."

"Manny?"

"Yeah. Manny what?"

"Emmanuel Robinson's his name. He's not in the big time, but his time is better than no time at all."

"He book you into the Capri often?"

"Yeah. They ask for me."

"Asked," corrected Marco, "past tense." He explained to

Pharoah. "Sasso and Fauci were double-gaited. They liked boys, girls, and each other."

Gino clenched the beer bottle tightly. "You saying they're dead?"

"You can't get any deader," said Pharoah. "You weren't mad at them by any chance?"

Pharoah expected Gino to burst into tears from the look on his face. "Mad at them? But they were wonderful to me. They bought me presents and took me to rock concerts. Last year they took me to the circus."

Pharoah stated flatly, "A real circus?"

"Oh, yeah. No funny stuff."

"The circus wasn't funny?"

"Pharoah," said Rita, "you're getting tired."

"No, I'm not. I've got too much to do tonight. Gino, the night the twins were killed, you were busy with Lino Sasso and Rudy Fauci?"

"No. They told me to go back to the city; they had other plans. They gave me a hundred dollars. I drove back in the Russian's car." Marco, looking uncomfortable, stared at Pharoah in expectation of an outburst. Pharoah met his gaze briefly and then returned his attention to Gino.

Pharoah still remembered how to torture Marco. Prolong the agony. "This here Russian," drawled Pharoah. "Remember her name?"

"Oh, sure. Natalya Orloff. Very big knockers."

"And you're another knockers maven."

Gino shrugged. "I can take them or leave them."

"Understood," acknowledged Pharoah. "Man does not live by breasts alone."

"Pharoah," Rita said softly, "Come on, wouldn't you like a nice pick-me-up?"

Pharoah ignored her offer. "And what did the lady provide by way of entertainment?"

"Oh, come off it!" Marco said while refilling his glass.

Pharoah chose to ignore Marco as well. "Does she juggle or swallow swords?"

Gino sensed the tension in the room and was feeling uncomfortable. "She's a singer. Very schmaltzy. You know, stuff like 'Dark Eyes,' you know, stuff like that."

"She any good?"

"She ain't no Dolly Parton, but I suppose you can say Natalya does her own Russian version of country and western. I like her a lot."

Pharoah mimicked Natalya almost perfectly: "Vot a vonderful voman, yes?"

"Hey, that's not bad!" complimented Gino.

"You think Manny Robinson might be interested in me?"

"He might be. He's always on the lookout for talent."

"Where do I find him? I'd look him up in the phone book, but I didn't bring my glasses."

"He's in the Sardi building."

"Oh, good. West Forty-fourth is so convenient."

"I don't think he'd be there this late."

"I don't think so either. You better get back up to your score or he'll think you've lost interest in him. Don't forget to use a condom," cautioned Pharoah.

"Sure." He turned to Rita who indicated the door with a quick movement of her head. Gino hurried out.

Pharoah said to Marco, "I have dinner with you and Natalya Orloff and do you once mention she was up at the Capri with the twins? But of course not. What does she know that I mustn't know?"

"She don't know nothing."

"Anything," corrected Pharoah. "She don't know nothing. Like Ol' Man River she just keeps rolling along."

"It slipped my mind."

"Did you hear that, Rita? It slipped his mind."

"Lots of things slip Marco's mind. Marco's mind is very slippery." Pharoah wondered what she had on Marco that was so potentially dangerous that she dared razz him. Marco had a very unpleasant expression on his face. Rita sat back in her chair, crossed her legs, and folded her arms. She was fearless.

Pharoah said to Marco, "I don't really think you want this killer caught."

"Damn it, I do! He's knocking off my best men!"

"You can always train others. You guys multiply worse then rabbits and are nowhere near as cuddly. Who else was on the bill that night?"

"I don't remember."

Rita unfolded her arms and reached for her vodka. "Yoyo was up there that night. Yoyo the clown. Your friend."

chapter

8

"I'm not even married," said Pharoah, "but I'm always the last to know. Who else was there? Luciano Pavarotti?"

"Too expensive," said Marco.

"Marco, I'm beginning to wonder if maybe I should think about driving a stake through your heart." Marco blinked his eyes. "A piece of wood, not a piece of meat." He looked at his wristwatch. "So much to do, so little time in which to do it." He paused, staring from Marco to Rita and back again to Marco. "And it's so tiring listening between the lines. Marco, you've got to do better than you're doing. I know it's tricky. You want me to catch the killer, but you have to be cautious about what you reveal about your family. Okay. Stay cautious. The mortuaries always welcome the business."

"Vodka?" persisted Rita.

"No, thanks. You, too, Rita. There's a lot you're not telling me."

"I'm doing my best."

"Rita, right now, you're an underachiever. Maybe I'll see the two of you later."

Exiting to the street, Pharoah heard a familiar voice. It was the Grey Ghost, sitting on the curb scratching his beard and staring up at a full moon. Pharoah expected him to howl and, while baying, turn into a wolf, with yellow eyes and saliva dripping from his deadly fangs. The Ghost suddenly twitched, and it was so violent a movement that Pharoah feared that the derelict might be an epileptic.

"You feeling okay, Ghost?" Pharoah was standing in front of him in the gutter. The Ghost wasn't quick to respond. He never was. Pharoah was reminded of the time he once shared an apartment with a struggling comedian who, unfortunately for his career prospects, was slow on the uptake. One morning Pharoah had asked him if he wanted another cup of coffee.

An hour later, the comedian said, "Sure."

Pharoah, startled, asked, "Sure what?"

"Sure I'd like another cup of coffee."

"The moon is not made of green cheese." Pharoah could see the moon reflected in the Ghost's eyes, the kind of trick shot favored by Alfred Hitchcock.

"What's it made of, baby?"

"Ohhh . . . whatever you want it to be. For some people, lemon custard. For some people, cream cheese. For some others, ricotta."

"What about you, Ghost?"

"The moon is sort of a wreath for the dead."

"Oh, yeah? How so?"

"The moon is so mournful. It makes me want to cry." Obscenities. They came machine-gunning out of his mouth, a strange compulsion that fascinated Pharoah, although he knew it frightened others. Must be some kind of mental illness. Pharoah had read an article that claimed people who cursed a lot caused small blood vessels to break in their brains. The Ghost's face was now composed and serene. Pharoah thought he resembled a religious icon. He could be Jesus Christ sitting on a curb in Hell's Kitchen and scratching his beard.

"When's the last time you bathed?" Pharoah couldn't help asking. Having done so, he was sorry, for there was no offensive odor emanating from the homeless man. Obscenities, and they abated slowly, like a mechanical doll winding down. "No offense meant."

The Ghost was on his feet. Behind him, the door to the house opened, and a shaft of light emanated and enveloped the Grey Ghost like a sign from heaven. One of Rita's most popular African-American ladies stood in the light for a moment, studying Pharoah and the Ghost. Her silver lamé dress might have been painted onto her exquisite body. Tastefully décolleté, it revealed a tempting swell of bosom. It reached to a few inches above her knees, revealing nice legs, not spectacular but nice. Artfully draped around her shoulders was a white fox stole. She carried a small silver handbag. She reached behind her and shut the door, and as she did this, she said, "What's the Ghost been up to? Has he been a naughty boy?"

"We've been discussing the moon. How come no mink tonight, Lily?"

"Mink is for hockey games," she said as she carefully descended the stairs, her stiletto heels making sharp, echoing noises. Lily Davis, on Rita's celebrity nights, usually stood in for Whitney Houston or Diana Ross. "You behaving yourself, Ghost?"

She was engulfed with obscenities.

"Ghost, you're so genteel." She smiled at Pharoah, who winked. Lily turned to say something else to the Ghost, but he was gone. "How'd he disappear so fast?"

"He's gone into the alley, Lily." Pharoah took her by the arm. "You've been around here a long time. I've seen you talking to the Ghost. He ever tell you where he comes from?"

"I've never asked."

"Why not?"

"Well, in the first place, I don't give a damn, because wherever he came from, he's not going back. You can't go home again, you know that, Pharoah."

"That's open to discussion."

"Well, discuss it with yourself. I've got a mission to accomplish."

"What's the second place?"

"The second place is, the Ghost wouldn't tell me even if he could remember where he sprang from." She said with warmth, "Feels nice."

"What feels nice?"

"A man taking me by the arm. They're usually taking me by something else." She was looking into Pharoah's eyes as they paused briefly under a lamppost.

"See something interesting?"

"I'm looking for your soul."

"Don't waste your time. I traded it in years ago for a badge."

They resumed walking. They were headed toward Ninth. Lily said to Pharoah, "I hear there's been two more killings."

"News travels fast in this neck of the woods."

"News travels fast in Rita Genari's."

"You've been working for Rita a long time, haven't you?"

"I'm one of the charter members."

"You've seen a lot, and you've heard a lot."

"See no evil and hear no evil." She kicked an empty soda can into the gutter.

"So you must have known the Cicci girls."

"Sweet kids."

"Were they turning tricks?"

"Don't be crazy, for crying out loud. Rita would sooner have seen them in their graves than have them working johns."

"They're in their graves."

"Circumstances beyond their control."

"They come to the house?"

"Up the alley and through the kitchen. Never through the front door."

"They must have known what was going on."

"They weren't dumb. They weren't blind. Juana never hid anything from them, and I was around when Rita laid it on the line to them. Juana and Rita loved those girls like they were their own kids."

"You know if Juana has any kids of her own?"

Lily was staring at the moon as they walked, trusting Pharoah to navigate safely. "I guess she might. Back in Mexico. And if she does, maybe she sends them money. I never heard her mentioning any children of her own. It was always the twins. Millie and Annie this. Millie and Annie that. They're taking dancing lessons. They're taking singing lessons. Juana dreamed of them starring in a Broadway show, score by Sondheim, choreography by Tommy Tune."

"What did Rita dream?"

"Rita bankrolled them."

Pharoah stopped walking. Lily retrieved her arm. They were at the corner of Ninth Avenue, and Lily was in no hurry to hail a cab. "Rita put up the money for the act?" Pharoah knew he was on to something, but he wasn't sure what.

"Everybody knew. She was the big impresario. She paid for their lessons, their arrangements; she paid the creep who devised and directed the act."

"Who was he?"

"Just another available queen. He was out of the picture months ago. Anyway, Rita liked the twins. I sometimes think she knew their parents. You talk to Rita, don't you?"

"I'm getting a lot of evasions from Rita."

"So what? Keep at it."

"I wonder why Rita let them do the gig at the Capri. She must have known it could be dangerous."

Lily mulled this over for a few seconds. "Everybody knew the twins were special. Rita probably thought they'd be safe. Listen, Pharoah, when you're breaking in an act, you try it out in as many places as will let you. Take it from me. I tried doing a single as an exotic dancer for months, and it took less then five dates to convince me I was no more exotic than a cockroach. Anyway, the twins were being handled by Manny

Robinson, who books the Capri exclusively. You know Manny Robinson?"

"The Sardi building."

"Ever met him?"

"Tomorrow."

"You're in for a treat. I got to get me a cab. I'm rolling high tonight. Beekman Place."

"Wait a minute. What about Nick Suggi and the twins."

"Oh, ain't he just dreamy? Honey, he could just melt in my mouth, not in my hands."

"He was trying to make points with Annie Cicci."

"I think he was told to lay off. Anyway, Annie wasn't interested, or so Juana told me."

"You know the oldie about still waters running deep?"

"Sure, honey, on a couple of occasions I almost drowned in them."

"The twins could have been still waters."

"Pharoah, there's young and there's young. Those kids were *very* young, *very* naive, *very* innocent. They were nuns without the habits. They wore crucifixes, for God's sake, no pun intended."

"That didn't protect them from the vampires."

"*Taxi!*" Lily shouted. As the cab pulled over, she said to Pharoah, "Rita couldn't protect them, either. She wasn't happy about their doing the Capri. She clucked like a mother hen. I heard it. I was in the living room with them borrowing some bread from Rita. I'll say this for those girls. They didn't back off. They held their ground. They were a very stubborn pair. They were determined to fill the date, and they did, and if they were alive, I'm sure they'd admit they regretted it." She patted Pharoah's cheek. "Why don't you take me to a movie some night, honey. I love that martial-arts crap. Lots of jumping around, lots of broken bones, and lots of blood." She told the cabdriver her destination and got into the backseat.

"Lily . . ."

"What?"

"You're a good lady, Lily."

For a moment, Lily Davis looked wistful. If she wasn't what she was and Pharoah wasn't what he is, might they both have been singing duets, she wondered.

As her taxi pulled away into traffic, Pharoah's attention was caught by his old friend Yoyo, across the street, waiting for the lights to change. He was shifting his carpetbag from his right hand to his left while Pharoah tried to figure out what it was that turned human beings into street people. He realized he had never seen Yoyo without his clown disguise. He didn't really know what he looked like. He could tell that the clown's natural features were clean-cut and that under the variety of colors painted on the face there was probably a very attractive man. His voice, too, was surprisingly cultured when he wasn't disguising it. He knew how to manipulate his audience. He obviously adored kids, and Pharoah was impressed by the way he captivated the theater crowds. He also wondered how well he had succeeded with the mafiosi that fateful night in the Catskills. Now he and Yoyo were eyeball to eyeball.

"I was looking for you," Pharoah told the clown.

"Providence is on your side. Here I am. I was headed for the Greek's"—he indicated a coffee shop a few yards down the street—"for a snack. Come on, my treat. I had a good night tonight. A B'nai B'rith benefit and a class reunion at two of the shows, and while benefit audiences are notorious for sitting on their hands inside, they can be beautifully generous outside."

A few minutes later, seated across from each other in a booth, having given their orders to a weary waitress, Pharoah asked Yoyo, "Why do you play the streets, babe?"

"The subways are too noisy."

"You should be doing more gigs like the Capri."

Yoyo's eyes lit up, and his hands were outstretched. "Fame at last! Recognition! He knows I played the Capri!"

The waitress brought coffee and prayed that the clown wouldn't sing. She was already coping with a headache, and she had two more hours to go before she could brave the subway up to the Bronx.

"Believe it or not, I wowed those mobsters." He lowered his hands. "They threw coins at me."

"Not very couth."

"They were so stinking drunk, the place could have been torched and they wouldn't have known they were about to be cremated."

"Too bad it didn't happen. The twins might have survived."

"Sweet kids. Really sweet kids."

There it goes again, thought Pharoah, sweet. How sweet could sweet have been?

Yoyo was continuing: "I gave them some pointers on how to do their makeup. Millie kissed my cheek."

"Sweet."

"You know them?"

"Only as a statistic."

"They didn't belong in the business. It was a pleasant enough act, but pleasant enough just isn't enough to make it in the jungle. They should have been married, living out in Islip or the Moriches, driving the kids to school, attending PTA meetings. . . ."

"You're such a sentimental slob."

"Yeah, under the cold, hard, painted exterior there beats a soft heart and an even softer brain."

"How much more can you take of the street?"

"I got nowhere else to go."

"You're good, Yoyo, you're real good. What you need is an agent."

"I've got one. I have to look real hard at him when I visit his office to make sure he's breathing. Aw, what the hell, Manny's okay. He's the best I could get, and he tries real hard for me, for all of us, but it's all he can do to meet the rent."

"Sounds like you're talking about Manny Robinson."

"You know Manny?" The waitress served them hamburgers accompanied by some limp french fries on an even limper lettuce leaf.

"I know he books the Capri."

"And some other places in New Jersey and Connecticut. Marco Salino likes him. I think it's because he looks a little like his namesake, the actor Edward G. Robinson." Yoyo smiled. "You know, at times he sounds like him, especially when he's gotten himself into a snit."

"Does Manny always do a package deal?"

"Mostly. That night was a first for the twins and for some nutty Russian diva named something Orloff."

"Take it from me, something Orloff is truly something. The name's Natalya."

"Yeah, that's it."

"She's Marco Salino's current interest. I had dinner with them at La Fontana."

"She kept asking what I had hidden under the paint." He nibbled on a fry. "I told her there was a very ordinary Anglo-Saxon face."

"You ever work with Carl Turner before?"

Yoyo chose another french fry. "You've done your home-work."

"I'm an egotistical pig. I'm teacher's pet or nothing."

"Yeah, I've done some other dates with him."

"You know he's one of Rita's boys?"

"Gino Vinelli, who boasts, 'I never saw a dick I couldn't handle.' By now he should be a millionaire."

"You take part in the orgy?" It was like a dart shot from a blowgun.

If Yoyo's face was betraying anything, it was camouflaged by the carefully applied paint. "I didn't know there was going to be one. The Orloff offered me a lift back to town, so I took it. The Orloff, Gino, and me."

"She didn't offer the twins a lift?"

"I didn't see them anywhere after the show."

"The Orloff was a little miffed that Marco Salino stayed behind. I think she wanted to spend the night with him. God, this hamburger is greasy."

"Marco might have suggested that the twins spend the night. After all, they could trust him, right? Being Rita's friend?"

"I don't know. All I know is what I read in the papers. And what I read in the papers was pretty nauseating." He signaled for the check. "I got to get going. I've got to do the discos downtown. The baby boomers and the yuppies, an uneasy mixture of unhappy failures."

"Where can I get in touch with you?"

"Manny Robinson takes my messages. What the hell, most of us use him as our answering service. He likes it. That way he knows what we're up to."

The waitress had placed the tab on the table, and Yoyo covered it with a ten-dollar bill. She went to the cash register for Yoyo's change while the performer refused Pharoah's offer to split the bill.

"You go ahead," said Pharoah. "I'll finish my coffee. I've got some heavy thinking to do. Thanks."

When Yoyo left the coffee shop, Pharoah asked for the phone. It was on the wall next to the men's room in the rear. He fished in his pocket for a coin and in a few minutes was talking to Albert West.

West said, "This must be ESP. I was hoping you'd call in."

"Miss me?" Pharoah asked with feigned coyness.

West cleared his throat. "I've got the autopsy report on the twins."

"I'm listening." He heard West read matter-of-factly, as though he were imparting information on train departures from Grand Central Station. Sexually violated. Multiple bruises.

"That wasn't what killed them," West told him. "They were drowned. They were still alive when they were put into the front seat of the car that was pushed into the lake. Pharoah? You still there?"

Drowned. They were drowned. Albert West heard Pharoah say, "You know, I'm beginning to hope I don't catch this killer. I'm really beginning to hope."

"Cheer up. Maybe you won't and Walt MacIntyre will begin to have second thoughts about his protégé."

"Any idea what his first thoughts are?"

West didn't reply.

"Who owned the car? What about the registration?"

"The Sullivan County boys did a thorough investigation. The car was a rental."

"Hertz? Avis? Who?"

"Doesn't matter. It was stolen. It's a dead end there."

"No leads from the car at all. It was clean," continued Albert.

"I may scream."

"Come off it, Pharoah."

"Be nice to me, Albert. Please try to be nice to me. I have fallen madly in love with the twins, and now they're dead and I'll never know if I ever had a chance to win the heart of one or the other. I might have gone straight for the twins, Albert, do you realize that?" He had no idea he had a spellbound audience in the waitress, the short-order cook, and a couple seated at the counter. "Oh, Albert, Albert, be kind to me. Albert," he entreated roguishly. "Albert, tomorrow would you take me dancing at Roseland? You can lead."

chapter

Pharoah sat at the end of the counter and asked for a cup of coffee. The counterman was fascinated by Pharoah's earring. Jesus and Moses with their arms around each other. Nice. A nice idea. He didn't realize he had mumbled something.

"You talking to me?" asked Pharoah.

The counterman looked perplexed. "Sorry. Sometimes I talk without realizing I'm talking."

"You mentioned Jesus. Friend of yours?"

"It's your earring. That's real good, Jesus and Moses with their arms around each other. I think if they had known each other, they'd have been good friends."

"It's possible. They were both Jewish."

"Except maybe, I was just wondering, would Jesus have

been jealous because God dictated the Ten Commandments to Moses?"

"I don't think Jesus was the jealous type."

"I wonder how come there's only Ten Commandments."

"Maybe God developed writer's block."

The counterman chuckled. "So maybe God was only human, after all."

"That's real cute. Why don't you send it to 'Dear Abby.'"

The counterman abandoned a grateful Pharoah to attend to a new customer. Pharoah stared into the coffee cup. In his mind he reran some of his conversation with Lily Davis.

"Rita would sooner have seen them in their graves than have them working johns."

"Juana and Rita loved those girls like they were their own kids."

"Rita bankrolled them."

"Everybody knew the twins were special."

The twins were special. Very special. Lily had also suggested that Rita might have known their parents. Maybe if she weren't in such a rush to make some money, she might have provided Pharoah with more information about Rita. He sipped the lukewarm coffee. He fished in his jacket pocket for some bills, peeled off a single, and placed it on the counter. Deep in thought, he went out into the street and slowly walked back to the corner of Ninth Avenue and West Forty-fourth Street. He stared down West Forty-fourth Street toward Rita's house, bathed in the unwanted glow of the full moon. Rita shunned spotlights. She was content to be the anonymous empress of her personal, unholy empire.

Only a select group of clients was awarded an audience in

her very private living room. She referred to the Hollywood VIPs as Very Impertinent People. Although they were heavy hitters, she had little use for politicians. She had told Pharoah there were two things that could walk under coffee tables without hitting their heads, dachshunds and politicians. She loathed Ross Perot. She told Pharoah he looked like the dormouse at the Mad Hatter's tea party, and Pharoah had to agree he looked as though Tenniel had sketched him.

Over the years they had known each other, Rita had told Pharoah a great many things, some enlightening, some amusing, some sobering. This was one smart lady. But now, as he slowly made his way back to Rita's, Pharoah was pondering her current sins of omission. She had told him a lot in the past, but now, in the troublesome present, Pharoah suspected she had not told him enough. The twins are the modus operandi behind the killings. There's a batty avenger on the loose, and Pharoah was warming up to this conjecture. Every so often he had entertained a gnawing suspicion that the killings were internecine despite Marco's protestations. Methinks the capo doth protest too much. Marco Salino a capo. Unbelievable. The little putz from Canarsie a Mafia godfather. Why not? Wasn't a very bad actor a very bad president of the United States? His reverie was interrupted by a small voice asking a small question.

"Excuse me, is this the Salvation Army?"

Pharoah turned his head and looked at the disheveled, middle-aged man with the frightened eyes. Pharoah said, "For some it is, but what you want is two blocks over on West Forty-sixth Street, between Tenth and Eleventh."

"Could I borrow fifty dollars?"

"Gee, man, you should have caught me ten minutes ago. I just gave my last fifty to a needy mugger."

The man sighed and said, "Some guys have all the luck. Could I have a cigarette?"

"Sorry, I don't smoke."

"You some kind of a religious fanatic?"

"No, man, I'm just a cop who's getting a little bored with this chat."

The man shrugged, buried his hands in his trouser pockets, and shuffled on his way. Pharoah ascended to the front door and pressed the bell. He stared at the moon while waiting for Juana to open the door. Custard? Cream cheese? Risotto?

He heard Juana ask, "Are you coming in?" Pharoah pinched her cheek, and she slapped his hand away.

"You're a little touchy tonight, Juana."

"It's her." She tossed her head in the direction of Rita's private domain. "Did you come to see her again, or are you looking for something upstairs?"

"Since when do you let Rita get to you?"

"She hasn't been easy since the girls were killed."

"Nothing's been easy since they were killed. You want to tell her I'm here? Or is she still with Marco?"

"He's gone, thank God."

"They have a little disagreement?"

Juana fielded his question with a shrug and then tapped on Rita's door, entering without benefit of an invitation. A few seconds later, she beckoned him inside. He winked as he walked past her into the inner sanctum. Juana didn't react. She shut the door, and Pharoah mused as to whether she was going back upstairs to count towels. Rita had changed into a dressing gown with lapels of faux monkey fur. Pharoah suspected she had just wiped a scowl off her face. The perennial champagne bucket in which chilled the perennial bottle of vodka was behind the desk.

"Joining me?" asked Rita. Her half-empty glass was on the desk.

"I'll pass right now." He sank into a chair. "Rita, I been doing some heavy thinking tonight." She sipped her vodka. "You've been worrying me, Rita." She leaned back in her chair and fingered the string of pearls hanging around her neck. "You've been telling me a lot about the twins, but I'm beginning to suspect you've been skipping sentences. I think you can tell me a lot more about those girls than you've been telling me."

"Such as?"

"Why didn't you tell me you bankrolled their act?"

"Didn't I?"

"No, sweetheart, you didn't."

"What's that got to do with their getting murdered?"

"Well, in detective work, you have to keep an eye out for little subtle nuances."

"Putting up the money for their act is a subtle nuance?"

"When you think like Pharoah Love, it's definitely a subtle nuance. You see, it just doesn't confirm that you liked the twins; it tells me you liked them a hell of a lot."

"I did it for Juana."

"You did it for Juana? Is she their mother?"

"She was their legal guardian."

"That doesn't answer my question."

"I never asked Juana if she was."

Pharoah now sat with his legs stretched out in front of him. "Did you know their parents?"

"What's that got to do with the price of beans?"

"There you go hopping over mud puddles again."

"Who you been talking to?" She made no attempt to disguise her annoyance.

"It's not just one person I've been talking to. It's everybody I've been talking to. You. Marco. Juana. Nick Suggi. Gino the singing whore. Lily Davis. And don't get mad at her."

"I'm not getting mad at anybody. I'm too mad at myself right now."

His interest was piqued. "Oh, yeah? Where'd you go wrong?"

"Come on, Pharoah. What's on your mind? We've always been on the square with each other. It was me who urged Marco to go to you."

"And that's why you're mad at yourself. You thought I'd be as superficial a detective as you think I am a man."

"No way. There's nothing superficial about a guy who ices a best friend when he can understand that's the way the best friend wanted it."

"That's nice, Rita. Real nice. You, too, Rita. You're one of my best friends."

"We better be. I need all the best friends I can get. The market in best friends is in a bad recession. And don't tell me I'm drinking too much." She was refilling her glass. "You know, a long time ago I knew Joan Crawford. Shortly before she died."

"Heart attack, I remember."

"You don't remember right. It was suicide. Anyway, one

night in her apartment, on the East Side. Old, alone, dying of cancer, she invited me up. I asked her why she was drinking so much. Vodka, big tumblers of vodka. And she said, 'Why not? It's all I've got left.' Me, too, Pharoah, me, too."

"Let the demons out, Rita. Stop hoarding them."

"Which demon in particular do you have in mind?"

He studied her face and the unhappiness etched there. "You really loved those girls."

"Yes, damn it, I really loved them!"

"Like a mother."

She tried to blink back the tears forming in her eyes. "Pharoah, you are really one mean son of a bitch."

"I'm a detective. I get paid for doing it. The twins were your daughters."

"Oh, shit." She was on her feet and pacing.

"Who's the father?"

"Unimportant. We parted, ha, ha, due to professional differences. Does it matter they were my kids, my precious babies? They didn't know I was their mother."

"Ashamed?"

"Hell, no! If you mean this place, I ain't never been ashamed. I deal in a service, and I deal some great hands. This is a clean establishment because it's the only way I know how to play the game. Clean. Honest. Aboveboard. My employees get all the benefits I can afford to give them. I told you once and I'll tell you again, this is an equal-employment establishment. And my doctor's on steady call."

"For crying out loud, stop defending yourself."

"Then what's the big deal knowing I'm the twins' mother?"

Pharoah said quietly. "It makes you a suspect."

Rita sank into her chair, wiping her eyes with the palms of her hands. "I see. Sure it does. I'm out there killing these bastards to avenge my daughters."

"You could have hired somebody to avenge your daughters."

"You're damned right. And I was working on it. But the corpses started piling up before I could arrange for a shooter."

"Did you ask Marco for help?"

"No way! Ask him to kill his own men? You crazy?"

"There are them what are positive I am."

"If you're crazy, Pharoah, then you're crazy like a fox."

"Weeping Willie DiLuca? Willie and his teddy bear? Whether they've buried the hatchet or not, I still think there's no love lost between him and Marco."

"There's no love lost between me and Willie, either."

"Why?"

"He tried to strong-arm me for a cut a long time ago. I did let Marco handle *that* one for me. Willie's family owns enough whorehouses and fag bars. They don't need to invade my tight little island. They got the teamsters and some movie action and insurance companies and the garbage haulers—"

"They've got a lot of garbage to haul," Pharoah interjected. "I don't want you for a suspect, Rita. You're my friend. In fact, I'm nuts about you. Why'd you let the twins play the Capri?"

"*Ha!*" The room seemed to tremble from the force of her voice. "I can say it now—they were their mother's daughters. Stubborn! Goddamn stubborn. There was no reasoning with them. They'd played a benefit, and show business tasted good to them. I chewed out Manny Robinson for booking them. This house is off limits to him because of that, and let me tell you, it does me good to know he's hurting where he don't enjoy hurting." She opened a desk drawer where she kept a box of tissues. She blew her nose, crumpled the tissue in a wad, and laid it to rest in an ashtray.

"Why didn't you ask Marco to cancel their booking?"

"I did." Their eyes met. "He promised me they'd be safe. I took him at his word. I had to because the twins suspected I would do just that, and they told Juana they'd hire a car to take them to the Capri no matter what I did. Besides, Pharoah. I had to back down. My Annie kept asking, 'What's the big deal? What's the big deal, for crying out loud?' Yoyo will be there and Gino and Marco's new friend, the Russian. What's the big deal?'" Her voice softened. "It turns out there were two big deals, and their names were Millie and Annie. Raped. Beaten up. Oh, my God, how it haunts me. I don't sleep, I don't eat, I just drink and drink and drink."

Pharoah had earlier decided not to tell her the girls had drowned in the lake. She was bearing enough invisible wounds.

"Does Marco know they're your daughters?"

"Only Juana and I know." She lit a cigarette. "Interested in the story?"

"Very. Are you up to it?"

"It's burning a hole in my tongue."

"Pour me a drink." Which she did, and brought it to him.

She resumed pacing. "A long time ago there was an aspiring young actress who realized early in the game that she didn't have enough talent. But she could draw a little and paint a little, so her sainted parents, and believe me, Pharoah, my parents were absolute saints, they convinced her to enroll in the

Art Student's League. I found a second home there." Her face was glowing for the first time in a long while. "I was so happy there. I made friends. Me, the innocent schnook from Worcester, Massachusetts. My folks were rich. They owned a hotel and a restaurant. Very posh. Good food. Good drink. I was an only child. And I was going to be a great artist, always tough for women. But I was going to be one of the exceptions. Anyway, some of us go down to the Village for an Italian dinner. Place called the Portofino. You know Elaine's?"

"Sure."

"She graduated from the Portofino. Anyway, I'm introduced to this very—" she paused for a moment, looking to Pharoah as though she were reliving this important moment in her history—"this very good looking man. Very smooth. I thought it was love at first sight. It wasn't. It was lust at first sight."

"I've suffered a lot of that myself."

"Suffer is an understatement. I went through hell. Like all of a sudden I'm pregnant. And he's not returning my phone calls. I won't get an abortion because I'm a Catholic and if I get an abortion I'll burn in hell and Rita is afraid of fire. So I think and think, and I tell my best friend at the League and ask her what I should do. She was Mexican."

"Juana?"

"Juana's cousin. She arranges for me to go to Juana, who was living then in San Juan y Allende. I told my parents there was an art school there and I wanted to take some courses. No sweat. No questions asked. They trusted their daughter. She was a good girl. So good girl goes to Mexico and gives birth to twins. I'm living with Juana and her family, and they were wonderful to me. Then I planned coming back to New York. My folks were getting a little impatient with me. I was staying away too long. And Juana, she wanted to come back with me and help look after the girls. She wanted out of Mexico. Her family wasn't exactly poverty-stricken, but they were having a tough time scratching out a living, and Juana had five siblings."

"Didn't her folks own a TV set?"

"Don't be funny. Before we could leave Mexico, I get word our hotel burned down. My parents were killed. And I had a big fat inheritance." She sipped some vodka. "And a big fat hatred of men."

"That hurts."

"You're special, sweetheart. I knew it that first time you came in here and tried to shake me down."

"I was doing no such thing! Now don't you go trying to turn that around! You tried to buy me off! Walt MacIntyre had just been appointed chief. He wanted to make himself a hero by closing every bordello in the neighborhood." Pharoah smiled. "I convinced him to lay off you. I told him you could come in handy."

"And I have, haven't I?"

"You have. So how'd you become the madam of the house?"

"Through a shrewd lawyer who arranged for me to have the custody of my daughters without having to reveal the truth about them. I set them up in a place with Juana and let the word out that Juana was their legal guardian. And hinted that maybe Juana was really a single mother. Juana adored the kids. Once we got into the business, the kids were shipped off to a convent school in Westchester."

"You ever run into their father again?"

After a short silence while she chain-smoked from one cig-arette to another, Rita said, "He showed up again."

"Where'd he been?"

"Italy. Visiting the home office."

"He was a capo?"

"Then he was an associate. A lieutenant. Whatever they la-bel themselves." She blew a perfect smoke ring. "Isn't this about time for me to say, 'But why am I telling you all this?'"

"A terrible cliché, Rita, but doesn't it feel good to get it off your chest?"

"I wish it was getting off somebody else's chest. Damn it, Pharoah, I'll never be a grandmother." She was in tears again. She found a tissue and held it to her eyes. She leaned back in the chair, staring at the ceiling. In control again, she said, "Why I got into this business has to do with a smart lawyer. A friend of the one who arranged Juana's custody of the girls. Frankly, I liked the idea almost from the minute he suggested it. Believe me, Pharoah, I didn't think I'd be this successful. But pretty soon I'm going to get out of it."

"Not too soon, sweetie. I don't like being lonely."

"Pharoah, in time you get used to it. More vodka?"

"A soupçon would be pleasant."

She crossed to him with the vodka bottle. As she poured, she said, "You realize, darling, ancient history remains an-cient."

"My lips are sealed. Now what about Marco?"

"What about him?" She was returning to the desk.

"Has he ever guessed the twins were his daughters?"

chapter
10

"You're out of your mind!" she snapped.

"No, I'm out of yours. Marco is perfect casting for the man what done you wrong. Marco doesn't have a conscience. He never had one. He doesn't know how to spell it. From the time we were kids, he used women like tissue papers. Wipe and blow, crumple up and throw away. You. His wife. His girl-friends. They all looked at him the first time they met, and it was also lust at first sight. And me, too. He was my first im-portant and painful frustration. Marco weaves a special mag-ic and casts a special spell. Even now I find myself looking at him and wondering what might have been." He paused and then snorted, "My God, I wouldn't have been a cop, I'd have been a housewife. Fat Pharoah!"

He laughed. She didn't. She poured herself more vodka,

and Pharoah found himself thinking a thought he didn't like entertaining: She's committing slow suicide. The twins are dead, so there's nobody and nothing for her to care about anymore. She can't still be in lust for Marco. It's twenty years later. With Pharoah, lust usually didn't last twenty minutes.

"Stop staring at me like that," Rita said huskily. "Don't you pass any judgments on me, Pharoah. The condemned woman drank a hearty vodka." She raised her glass. "We who are about to die salute you." She drank. "Okay. Full marks for you. Go to a hockshop, buy yourself a medal and pin it on yourself. Only don't you ever let on to Marco he was their father."

"Does it matter now?"

"Yes."

"There's a lot of meaning behind that 'yes.'"

"The orgy. Suppose he lied about it. Suppose there was no private meeting with the other capos. Supposing they all joined in and enjoyed themselves." She paused to see if Pharoah knew where she was heading. She helped him. "Supposing Marco screwed his own daughters. Beat up on them. Set them up in the car and sank it. You think he could live with that?"

"Yes." The word flew out of his mouth and crashed into her ear. "Like I said, he has no conscience. He's like the apocryphal bastard who murders his father and mother and then throws himself on the mercy of the court as an orphan. I'm beginning to wonder if Marco hasn't long suspected the twins might be his."

"No way." She was lighting a cigarette. "He always thought they were Juana's. Funny enough, they had her coloring. It was weird, but they looked a lot like her." She got out of the chair and walked to a door that led to the rest of her private apartment. "Come with me."

Pharoah obeyed with alacrity. He loved adventure, and this was a new adventure. He was being allowed at last a glimpse of the forbidden unknown. Rita led him to her library. It was a beautiful room, tastefully furnished, with bookcases filled with expensively bound art books. The walls were hung with a good percentage of Rita's wealth. Pharoah identified a Picasso, a Juan Gris, a Modigliani, a Jimmy Ernst, a small Renoir, and what he assumed was a Rita Genari. It was an oil painting of two lovely young women in their teens, obviously twins. To Pharoah they seemed alive. They were smiling, and he thought that at any moment he might hear their laughter. Pharoah felt that a comment was expected from him, but at the moment he couldn't speak. Words failed him. Here was a shrine, and he was an instant convert. He was like Dana Andrews, in the haunting film *Laura*, looking at the portrait of a woman he thought was dead and wishing she wasn't because he had fallen in love with her.

Pharoah found his voice. "I'm in love with them."

"A lot of guys were in love with them. Some I knew about. Some I suspected. I don't think anybody scored. I think they'd have told me if it had happened. Or Juana. They'd have told Juana."

Pharoah said jauntily, "You know what Rabelais said?"

"No, we weren't on intimate terms," Rita commented dryly.

"He said, 'The only proof of female virginity lies in its destruction.' Theirs was destroyed." He forced himself away from the painting. Rita led him back to the living room and refreshed both their glasses while Pharoah marveled at her composure in the face of the stresses pressuring her. The vodka didn't betray her. Her hand was steady as she poured. When she walked, she didn't falter. Her speech wasn't slurred. Her eyes weren't glazed. She was indeed a witch.

When they were once again seated opposite each other, Pharoah took the plunge. "Why do I suspect you know who's murdering these bastards?"

"Because it comforts you to think that if you're unsuccessful in unmasking him, there'll be me to fall back on. Forget it. I can't help you there. You're on your own. You and your buddies at the precinct. You and your forensics. You and your autopsies. I know the twins drowned."

The sharp intake of breath he realized was his own. "Where the hell do you get your information? I only found that out less than an hour ago."

"'My vine has tender grapes,'" she slightly misquoted. "You know that. You know I've got the best sources in town. You've made use of me often enough."

"Is the killer somewhere on that vine of yours?"

"If he is, I don't think he's ripe enough to be plucked."

"You won't rest until he's wiped them all out."

"That's right. The two tonight were a pleasant surprise."

"You knew about the tenement on Tenth Avenue," he accused her. "You knew it's one of their so-called safe houses."

"None of their houses are safe; they're just badly furnished. Go take a look at the lobby of the Capri. It looks like a Yugoslavian dance hall. The basement club where the orgy took place, very art drecko. The bedrooms are instant Walmart. The Mafia has a lot of money and a lot of power, but it ain't got no taste. They're so unoriginal they even have to borrow their saints." She sipped and then said, "If you're wondering when I visited the Capri, it was one Sunday afternoon last summer when Marco gave me the 'old times' sake' bit and I went for it because I thought it might cure a romantic hang-over I was nursing at the time. Would you believe he had a picnic basket sent up from Dino and DiLuca's—no relative of Weeping Willie's, by the way."

"I should think nobody would want to be a relative of Willie's."

"Good thinking, but no such luck. He's up to his hips in family, and it costs him a monthly bundle. His father is an asthmatic with pockmarked skin that makes him look like an elderly, overweight dart board. His mother is tall, skinny, and ugly and ought to shave more often. I think she chews tobac-co in her lonely bedroom. I know she looks at porn tapes, but try as she may, she can't wax nostalgic because I'm sure the only time she got laid was when they wanted bambinos, all of whom should have been suffocated at birth. Anyway, we day-tripped up to the Capri, we picnicked under a tree on a blan-ket of pure, extravagant chinchilla and over a second bottle of Piper Laurie—"

"I think you mean Piper Heidsick."

"Don't be a show-off. Anyway, Marco made his pass, and I passed it right back to him marked 'unwanted,' so he settled for taking me on a grand tour of his then-recent acquisition. Very depressing. It wasn't as gilded garish as the old Grossinger's or as Hollywood phony as the Concord. He showed me where they planned to build additional casinos to house the gaming rooms."

"He's so convinced the state will legalize gambling."

"Pharoah," she said with a sly wink of the eye, "Marco knows something we don't know. And in this case, my money's on him. There'll be gambling in the Catskills and a lot of other places very soon, now that it's legalized for Indian reservations. You think the family's going to turn a blind eye and not move in for their lion's share of the loot?"

There was a tap at the door, and Juana entered giving Pharoah a look that he interpreted as asking, You still here? "Weeping Willie is misbehaving."

"Now what?"

"He socked Bette Midler in the jaw, and now he's yelling for Sharon Stone. We ain't got no Sharon Stone; Shirley's on an outcall. So what do I do now?"

"How badly did he bruise Marie?"

"Well, since she's imitating Bette Midler, you can't really notice any difference."

"Is Lucy occupied?"

"I'm not sure. It's awful quiet in her room."

"Who's with her?"

"One of them TV anchormen. You know, the hair dyed with brown shoe polish."

Rita looked at her wristwatch. "Roust him and remind him he's due at the studio in a couple of hours. Tell Lucy to put on her red wig, the one with the bangs, and try to convince Willie she's Shirley MacLaine. She can remind him they knew each other a couple of centuries ago when they were rubbing elbows with the Borgias."

"Like Victor Borgia?" asked Pharoah innocently. Rita flashed him a look, and since Juana had never heard of Victor Borge, she continued to look oppressed.

Juana asked, "Supposing Shirley MacLaine's too old for him?"

"For crying out loud, Juana, Lucy's only twenty-two years old. Tell him it's MacLaine when she first signed with Paramount."

Muttering under her breath, Juana left the room. Pharoah watched her go. Rita watched Pharoah. "No way," said Rita.

"No way what?"

"I'm reading your mind. Juana's no murderer."

"She's got the build for it."

"She doesn't have the taste for it."

"Why can't I guess when you're lying to me? If I ran a list of names past your ears, would you at some point stop me and say, 'You got it. That's the killer.' Marco. No soap. Weeping Willie. Never uses soap. Nick Suggi. Too smart. Gino the singer. Too too."

"Me."

"Never."

"Why not? Least likely suspect."

"I got other candidates for that position."

"Such as?"

"Yoyo the clown."

She waved the suggestion aside with her hand. "Don't be dumb."

"He was there."

"So what?"

"He's a man. He has appetites. He could have joined in the rodeo."

"Have you asked him?"

"Not directly."

"So ask him directly and see what you get. I can tell you you'll get nothing. For crying out loud, you've got suspects all over the goddamned place."

"There's safety in numbers."

"What about your pet?"

"What pet?"

"The Ghost."

"I don't think he could stop twitching long enough to murder anybody. And that goes for that string of filth that comes pouring out of his mouth."

"The twitches and the obscenities go with the territory."

"What's the territory?"

"A strange and very awful disorder called Tourette syndrome."

"Oh, yeah? How come you heard of it?"

"I had a friend whose son has had it since he was a kid. The symptoms show up between the ages of five and fifteen. It was discovered by some Frenchman named Tourette over a century ago."

"Trust a Frenchman to discover something like that. Can girls have it?"

"Anybody can have it."

"Say, what about this agent Emmanuel Robinson?" Pharoah asked.

"If you think he's the killer, then you'd better hurry up and nail him because I'm thinking of killing the bastard for booking the girls into the Capri."

"You can't kill an agent. They're too thick-skinned. Rita?"

"What?"

"There are too many loose ends." She busied herself lighting a cigarette.

"You're so sure Marco doesn't know he's the twins' father?"

"A long time ago I told him I'd had an abortion in Mexico. I didn't want his kid."

"He believed you."

"Enough to bring down the wrath of God on my head. 'Putana,' he yelled. 'Whore! Daughter of a whore!' My beloved mother, how dare he. 'You will never be buried in consecrated ground! Dogs will piss on your grave!'"

"I had no idea he was so colorful. I mean, when we were kids, the worst I heard him yell was at some girl in our chemistry class who wouldn't let him experiment on her. 'May you grow two tits on your behind.'"

"He never cursed out you and Herbie?"

"Oh, yeah." He was grinning, and in that brief moment Rita thought he looked like a mischievous imp. "When Herbie told him he and me had tried it and Marco yelled, 'I hope your dicks turn to stone and strike sparks.' Well, they didn't have to turn to stone for us to strike sparks. Good old Herbie, he was always willing to try anything once. That one time, it frightened him shitless. It took me days to convince him he wouldn't be struck by lightning." Only by a bullet I fired into him, Pharoah thought, and suppressed a shudder.

Rita said, "Pharoah, too bad you're gay."

"Why? What am I missing? Now I'll quote from Chekhov's *The Sea Gull*, a line I love, it's so beautifully Russian. 'I'm in mourning for my life.' I used to think maybe I should have gotten married. Maybe I should have married Annabel Kress."

"Who in God's name was Annabel Kress?"

"Nice kid I knew at Tilden High. She lived on Eastern Parkway in what is now Crown Heights. We used to sneak off to the movies together every so often. Or we'd sneak off to the Brooklyn Museum and then go walking in Prospect Park or the Botanical Gardens. We did a lot of sneaking around."

"Why sneaking?"

"Me Tarzan, me black. Her Jane, her white. And this was back in the Dark Ages when black was black and white was white and never the twain shall meet. Annabel Kress. So say we defied convention and got married? An action marked for instant doom."

"Maybe not."

"Oh, no? If I'd had a lawn, there'd have been a cross burning on it. So I'm married, right? We live in some ghetto because they won't rent to us anywhere else. We have, what? Four kids?"

"Why not? Why be hard on yourself?"

"Okay, four kids. Two boys, two girls. Four halfies. Half black and half white. Four hybrids. So the boys become junkies, and the girls come to their Aunt Rita for jobs."

"Don't be so hard on the girls."

"And then there's Annabel. What a tragedy. She always wanted to be a dress designer. Instead, she's stuck with four freak kids."

"They don't have to be freaks. They've got a daddy who has big ambitions for them."

"Yeah, but society won't give them a break. So Annabel turns to drink. And because her husband's a cop and away from home a lot nights, she starts screwing around. And one night I come home and find her in bed with our priest, and I shoot the two of them dead."

"Oh, Pharoah, that awful temper of yours."

"I'm headlines. Big stuff. The trial makes me a celebrity. I write the book with some typewriter jockey, and it's an instant success. I'm booked on 'Hard Copy,' and it's turned into a Movie of the Week starring Denzel Washington and the ever-available Loni Anderson."

"Not Denzel. He's big time now. Strictly features, no TV."

"Rita, you've helped make up my mind. I'm staying gay. I'm staying gay just like I'm staying black."

"You know you could pass for white."

"Not on a clear day. I've got to get moving." His knees cracked as he got to his feet. "Hear that, Rita. I'm getting old."

"You need a massage. Want to drop upstairs and have a quickie? On the house."

"No, thanks, babe. It might give me an appetite that can't be fulfilled.

"Gino gives one hell of a massage. You might get lucky and he'll give you a tongue lashing."

"Don't be lewd, Rita. You're one hell of a lady; stay that way. Why don't you think about retiring?"

"And do what?"

"Paint."

There was a small smile on her face. "You think I'm any good?"

"If that painting of your twins is a sample of what you can do, then you're robbing yourself of a lot of fulfillment."

"Pharoah, I sometimes think under that handsome exterior of yours there's a Renaissance poet struggling to get out."

"Maybe you're right. Here's a little sample of my poetry: 'The Bronx? No thonx.'"

"Good night, Pharoah."

"Too late. I'm beginning to catch my second wind. Try this one: 'Oscar de la Renta/Is a Yenta.'"

"Pharoah?"

"Yes, baby?"

"You're very, very tired."

"Yes, baby."

"And remember. Marco knows nothing about being their father."

"The Chic Twins. I would have liked to have seen that in lights."

"You will. I've ordered a neon gravestone with perpetual care."

"You think of everything. Have you thought of what Marco would do if he ever found out the truth?"

"I think he just might kill himself."

"Now wouldn't you like that?"

Seated at his desk, working late on his report of the murders of Sasso and Fauci, Albert West was so preoccupied, he didn't hear Pharoah enter his office, the door to which was ajar in hopes of luring in some fresh air.

"Say Albert . . ."

"Oh, Christ!"

"Heavens, did I startle you?"

"You could have given me a heart attack!"

"I'm not that generous. What you doing there?"

"Writing up the report on the poisoned mafiosi."

"Have we positive proof they were poisoned?"

"How else? There wasn't a mark on them."

"They could have bored each other to death."

Albert groaned. "They're due to be autopsied in the morning. But the coroner said he suspects from the discoloring of their fingernails there's poison in their systems."

"Oh, dear, and poison's supposed to be a woman's weapon."

Albert couldn't resist. "Maybe the killer's a fag."

"Tell me Albert, and don't fudge. You ever been in a gay bar?"

"Sure," he blustered unconvincingly.

"How'd you make out?"

"That's not funny."

"It isn't, I agree with you. Cruising bars is very boring and very tedious and often very discouraging, and it has been known to drive some to suicide. I mean, even if you get the guy next to you to cooperate with a little conversation, it's never eyeball to eyeball unless you're so drop-dead gorgeous he can't wait to get you home and ravish you with everything available. But usually, while they're talking, their eyes are on the entrance hoping for some improvement to appear. Honest, Albert," he said as he took a comb out of his back pocket and began attacking his ponytail, "it's enough to make a girl so suicidal she might deep-six her Tom Cruise poster and stamp all over her Judy Garland albums."

Albert said quietly, "As long as you're here, I could use some help with this report."

Pharoah folded his arms. "Albert, why don't you do the first draft and in a few hours I'll read it and work on the rewrite. We'll share the billing, of course, in alphabetical order."

"Pharoah . . . ?"

"Yes, Albert?" Pharoah realized that Albert's eyelids were now hooded like a cobra's.

"The chief asked me to ask you, should you drop by the precinct tonight, where's your report on Herbie Marks?"

"Why Albert," said Pharoah as he started out of the office, "you are a bit of bitch too, aren't you."

Pharoah went to his office and slammed the door shut behind him. He wished he had a bottle stashed away in his desk, but he knew he didn't. There was a note stuck in his typewriter from Walt MacIntyre reminding him to turn in the report on Herbie Marks.

Herbie Marks, Marco Salino, Pharoah Love. The Three Musketeers. Sure. Athos, Porthos, and Pathos.

chapter

11

Herbie Marks was on the late news. Pharoah had a small TV set on a shelf in his office to keep him company in the wee hours. He was struggling with his report on Herbie's death, but the appropriate words were eluding him. He had phoned Herbie's wife earlier, and she had flatly told him the funeral services were to be private. Just family, the very immediate family. No friends, no curiosity seekers. Pharoah had never particularly liked Gracie, and now he loathed her. He almost asked her if after the funeral she planned to stay home and add up Herbie's assets. He wondered about sending flowers and if Gracie would buy an obituary for Herbie in the *Times*.

Channel Seven was giving Herbie more space than he deserved. They had dug out of the files some pretty good shots of several of Herbie's previous arrests. There was one of Herbie laughing straight into the camera. That was Herbie, always laughing. Then Herbie yielded to the commercials, followed by the tenement on Tenth Avenue where Fauci and Sasso had been slaughtered. There were mug shots of the two victims, and Pharoah was surprised at how handsome they were, even with the numbers across their chests. Gino the whore had liked them. He said they were generous to him. Gino a criterion of taste? Still, Pharoah had to admit, they looked like very pleasant fellows. He stared at the blank page in his typewriter. He'd filled out dozens of these reports in the past. Water off a dyke's back. The palms of his hands were damp. He rubbed them on his trousers. His nose was itching. He scratched it. His mouth was dry. Now his eyes itched. He got up for a drink of water and could hear Albert's typewriter. That one was going full steam ahead, like he was maybe Joyce Carol Oates.

Returning to his office, Pharoah treated his eyes with drops, then took his place back at the typewriter. He hated the typewriter. He hated the blank form that teased him and taunted him because he didn't want to write about having killed Herbie Marks. It wasn't self-defense, though Al Drexel and Moe Holding, his backup team, would swear it was. Cops are always protecting each other, even when they've murdered one of their own. Friendly fire, you know. Pharoah leaned back in the chair, interlaced his fingers, and stared at them. He needed a manicure and made a mental note to try and get one tomorrow. He massaged the index finger of his right hand, took a few deep breaths, and finally attacked the typewriter keys.

• • •

A QUEER KIND OF LOVE

The Vladivostok Club in Brooklyn's Brighton Beach was Sergei Paskudnyak's very personal turf. It stood as the proud symbol of Russian Gangster Makes Good. Sergei sat in the booth always reserved for him. It afforded a perfect view of the room, the bar, the entrance, the dance floor, and the stage. On the stage, Natalya Orloff was perched on a stool, bathed in a flattering pink light, strumming her balalaika and in a tear-drenched voice singing of her lover who had been killed in the Afghanistan wars when he accidentally stepped on a mine and had to be pieced together by the medics like a human jigsaw puzzle.

Natalya had her audience by the short hairs. She knew how to work a room, milk them for every last drop. It pleased Sergei to hear purses popping open as hankies were extracted and noses sniffled and the ladies let it all hang out. Natalya was wearing a gold sheath rumored to have been designed by Franco Moschino, a rumor begun and nursed by Natalya herself.

Several men seated at the bar were also overcome by emotion; they were all émigrés who had escaped Russia before the fall of communism and were now citizens of their adopted country. Whereas they once had been terrorized in the old country, they were now doing the terrorizing. They harassed Korean grocers, who already had their hands full dealing with the Chinatown gangs that had proliferated in that area's dark warrens and extorted their fellow Orientals with sadistic glee. They harassed the East Indians, who seemed to favor operating news kiosks, and they were a constant threat to the Greeks, who mostly operated coffee shops.

Paskudnyak nodded his head lazily in approval as Natalya acknowledged the applause of the sparsely filled room. She gestured graciously to the small band, the Leningrad Latkes, and although a drunk at the bar was shouting for an encore, she modestly and demurely left the spotlight and joined Sergei Paskudnyak in his booth. A waiter stood at the ready to satisfy her any whim. She ordered a cold beer and a ham and cheese on black pumpernickel, easy on the mayo. Sergei smoked a cigar that looked like a midget torpedo.

"Vell, Sergei!" Natalya said with a lavish smile. "I have triumphed again. I was vonderful, no?"

He patted her cheek. "You are always wonderful, even when you are not wonderful." He asked abruptly, "Are you falling in love with Marco Salino?"

"Don't be ridiculous."

"He has his own way with women."

"Maybe vith vomen, but Natalya Orloff is not vomen. Natalya Orloff is an artist. Unique. Distinct. An up-and-coming goddess. Vy you have no plans to occupy Cuba?"

Sergei made a face. "I do not like tropical climates. Who needs Cuba? It is useless."

"That is not what Marco claims. He vill put there prostitution and gambling casinos and make billions. Can you imagine this Pharoah person refusing his offer to run Cuba? Vy he doesn't ask me to run Cuba? Vouldn't that be a big blow for the voman's movement?"

"They found two more of Marco's shooters murdered."

"Oh, yes? Must be an epidemic." She snuggled close to Sergei. "Tell me, Sergei. Are you dark horse?"

He shrugged her away gently. "I am no kind of a horse. What do you mean, dark horse?"

She was delightfully blunt. "Are you responsible for these murders?"

"Don't be ridiculous."

"I am not ridiculous. I know you don't like Marco, and Marco doesn't like you, even if you're involved in a lot of schemes together."

"Who says Marco doesn't like me?"

"*You* said."

"When?"

"Ven you sent me to spend the night with him that first time."

"You talk nonsense. I sent you to Marco because I need to know how he is cheating me, how he is double-crossing me."

"Vell," she said with a weary sigh as the waiter brought her sandwich and beer, "all I have found out is he is insatiable in bed. So much huffing and puffing, I expect to see clouds of smoke pouring from his ears." She was examining the sandwich with suspicion. "I think next time in bed with him I wear my Valkman and listen to Shostakovich symphony. This ham looks like corned beef. Here, look."

He looked. "It's ham. Everything I serve here is fresh, you know that." She camouflaged the meat with a blanket of mustard.

"Tell me more about this Pharoah Love," Sergei continued.

Her voice rose an octave. "Vat more can I tell you? He and Marco were boyhood friends. Marco, like I already told you, asked him special to find the murderer. So he is looking for murderer." She bit into the sandwich and munched warily and slowly. Her taste buds would never betray her. If it was ham, she'd know it. "It is ham. Very strange ham, but ham. Must be cheap cut."

"So order something else," he said with exasperation.

"No. This is fine. It vill do. If I get poisoning, you vill also suffer. Pour the beer for me, please."

Sergei asked as he poured, "This detective, is he corruptible?"

She thought for a moment. "He is charming. Very handsome. He is built beautiful, and you know I can tell this no matter how much clothes a man is vearing."

"And I am a typical Russian peasant. Thick legs, thick arms—"

"Thick everything," she added warmly as she licked mustard from her lower lip.

"Nicholas Suggi."

"Vat about him?"

"He made a pass at you."

"All men make passes at me. I am irresistible. Look at the men at the bar. Every single one of them wants to fawk me. I can tell vatching them when I am singing. Oh, Sergei, ven vill you admit that I was born to belong to the vorld!"

"This Pharoah Love, you think he will catch the killer?"

"Perhaps. How should I know? Marco places great store in him."

"Is Suggi a suspect?"

Natalya gave the question more thought then it warranted. "Vell, maybe yes and maybe no. Ven Marco and I left the restaurant, Pharoah stayed behind, I'm sure, to get to know Suggi better."

"Perhaps Suggi is a suspect?"

Natalya's beer left traces of foam on her upper lip. Sergei wiped it off with a napkin. She abandoned the sandwich and lit a cigarette. "Sergei." Her voice was suddenly grave and dark. He removed the cigar from his mouth and contemplated the smoldering end. He suspected what was coming. She had asked the question before. "You promise me you had no part in the orgy? You had no hand in killing those poor things?"

"Natalya, you can be very annoying. I was in the back of the hotel with Marco and the others planning how to bleed more money out of Russia. How to increase the illegal export of goods from there through the Arctic Circle and across the northern boundaries into Finland. It is a billion-dollar operation. Billion dollars."

That didn't answer her question, and she told him so.

"Natalya, I have a one-track mind, so I cannot indulge in orgies. And you know I have difficulties remembering names. How can I be in an orgy if I don't know who I'm fawking? I told you many times, and I will tell you now for the last time, and never ask me again. When our meeting was over, all was silent. There was no one in the cellar bar. Marco was angry that we had been left unprotected, that the others had gone without his permission. Then poof! All of a sudden! They are back! *Now* we know where they were. Down at the lake taking care of the twins in the car." He suddenly waxed indignant. "How dare you even consider that a man in my position would be a party to something so common and vulgar as an orgy!"

She said with a smirk, "In Moscow, we met at one. How quickly you forget."

"Pah! You call that an orgy? Nobody was taking their clothes off!"

"It vas very sedate, I admit. I am tired. Take me home."

"Oh? And Marco does not expect you?" The cigar was back in his mouth.

She mimicked him viciously. "'Oh? And Marco does not expect you?' Who handed me to Marco in the first place?"

"I don't remember you objecting strongly."

"Vy should I? You said you need a spy there—like mole—and I said sure, I'll be your mole. Vere they find such vords as mole? Mole is a spot on the skin, a nasty animal. *Oy!* Now I understand! I am a spot on the skin! A nasty animal!"

He put his arms around her and kissed her passionately. "You are my Natalya," he whispered steamily, "and someday, I promise you, we will return to Russia in triumph."

"Oh, yes?"

"These billions we are taking from Russia. They will finance my plan to overthrow their so-called democracy, and with the army I plan to recruit with the help of China, we will storm into Russia, and the poverty-stricken populace will greet us with open arms. I shall be Emperor Sergei Paskudnyak the First and you, Natalya Orloff, shall be my empress!"

"Sergei! Sergei! Is this the truth? Is this a dream, or is it a nightmare?"

"It is a reality. And don't you breathe a word of this to anyone!"

"Are you sure Marco Salino doesn't know about it?"

"I am positive. He wants Cuba? He can have Cuba. I'll throw in Haiti and the Dominican Republic. Trust me, Natalya. Believe in me. Believe in me." He whispered softly, seductively. "Today Brighton Beach. Tomorrow the world!"

"Sergei?"

"I hope these valls do not have ears." He laughed.

He wasn't sure, but he didn't say so. He just smiled a very enigmatic smile. He lifted her in his arms and carried her up the back stairs to his apartment. Both were breathing heavily, Natalya with passion, Sergei from exhaustion. Carrying her up the stairs was a serious error in judgment, and he prayed he hadn't exhausted his supply of backache pills.

At eleven o'clock the next morning, Pharoah Love stood looking up at the Sardi building on West Forty-fourth Street between Seventh and Eighth. It would be an hour before the restaurant would be open for lunch. Pharoah remembered how, as a teenager, he'd been brought here for lunch by his cousin Roscoe, who at the time showed some promise as a pop singer. Pharoah had worried whether blacks were permitted in Sardi's, having heard they were barred from many restaurants in Manhattan. But Roscoe had reassured him that there was no racial discrimination at Sardi's. It was home to actors from the world over. The walls were peppered with framed celebrity caricatures, and Roscoe took joy in pointing out to Pharoah the celebrities who were lunching. However, that was now over two decades ago, and Sardi's had suffered severe reverses. The quality of the cuisine had deteriorated, as had the quality of the patrons. The celebrities had abandoned Sardi's for other, more intimate locations in the neighborhood. Thanks to tourists, the restaurant survived, but barely.

Pharoah loved the forties, better known as "Broadway." He loved the Shubert Theatre and the adjoining Broadhurst and the Majestic. To his right was the St. James Theatre, where *Oklahoma!* had had its spectacular world premiere. To his left was the Helen Hayes, first known as the Little Theatre because it had the smallest capacity of any theater along the Great White Way.

His wave of nostalgia receded as he entered the building, studied the directory, and a few minutes later was in Emmanuel Robinson's waiting room. There a small woman with a large nose, thick lips, and suspicious eyes presided behind a desk. On it were three telephones, a Rolodex, an appointment book, and a pile of unopened mail. There was also a paper cup containing black coffee and a paper plate holding a prune danish that looked as forlorn as the woman who planned to demolish it.

Pharoah sized her up swiftly, professionally. No wedding ring, and there probably would never be one. Designer-framed eyeglasses, one of an occasional extravagance. A red AIDS pin was fixed to her indifferent bosom. The hair was hennaed and stiff with spray; the fingernails were obscenely long and artificial. She was one of a small army of single women who drifted into show business as secretaries, receptionists, personal assistants to demanding employers, with no hope of any gratification other then meeting celebrities and occasional free theater tickets. Some managed to live alone. Some shared apartments, despising or envying the roommate who had a boyfriend. Most lived with their families and commuted from

Brooklyn, Queens, Staten Island, Long Island, or some mis-begotten community in some woebegone area of New Jersey. Most were easy lays but rarely got laid; they mostly got mis-laid. They were privileged to call their employers by their first name. Usually Don, Irving, Matt, Mack, or Manny. This gave them status. All were clones of Cerberus guarding the gate.

Pharoah could hear Robinson shouting behind his closed door. Maybe making or losing a deal or more probably stalling a creditor. The empress behind the desk asked, "Yes?"

"I'd like to see Mr. Robinson."

"Do you have an appointment?"

The appointment book was open, with the day's date written large across the top of a page. The page was blank. Robinson didn't seem to be either terribly busy or terribly popular.

"No, I don't. I'm a detective." He showed her his identification. She was not impressed.

"What is this in reference to?" Very, very cool and very, very indifferent.

"Murder."

She folded her arms and regarded him sternly. "And who is he supposed to have killed?" She screwed up her face. "Who or whom?"

"Beats hell out of me."

"I never could get them straight. Anyway, you hear him yelling. He doesn't like to be interrupted when he's yelling."

"Am I in for a long wait?"

"Why? You got something better to do?" He smiled. "Why don't you take a seat. He can't escape. The front door's the only way in or out."

Pharoah sat. "Your coffee's getting cold."

"Serves it right. It's rotten coffee. It's from the dump on the corner. What was your name again?"

"Love. Pharoah Love."

"Pharoah like in pyramids?"

"Almost. In Egypt it's spelled pee-aitch-ay-arr-ay-oh-aitch. Mine is oh-ay-aitch."

"How come?"

"My mother couldn't spell." She smiled. He could tell she liked him. "What's your name?"

"Edna. Which murder?"

"Is he touching base with a lot of them?" Emmanuel was screaming and it was jarring Pharoah's nerves.

"Well, a couple of months ago the male half of a dance team was knifed to death in the men's room of Blooming-dale's. I haven't heard of that one being solved. At least I don't think Manny has. If he had, he would have told me. Then we had a ventriloquist whose skull was crushed with his dummy in his dressing room in some club in Yonkers." She said mat-ter-of-factly, "Nobody should play Yonkers. Very bad show town."

"Especially for ventriloquists. You forgetting the Chic Twins?"

"No. I was coming to them. I had an idea that's why you're here."

"Is it written on my face?"

"In a way it is. The other detectives who came around were the ordinary movie stereotypes. No class at all. You've got some style, I think." Pharoah smiled. "I mean, the way you're dressed I wouldn't let you take me to lunch unless it was someplace obscure on Eleventh Avenue. I mean, really. Torn jeans, corduroy jacket, those boots. Don't you think you're a little old for grunge?"

"Everything else I've got is at the cleaners. Did you like the girls?"

"What girls?"

"The twins."

"Oh, them. Did you think they were something special?"

"They are now that they've been murdered. I never knew them. I saw a painting of them. They were sure a pair of lookers."

"I suppose you could say they were."

"You handle all the paperwork around here?"

"I'm all there is and have been for close to fifteen years."

"That's a long time for servitude."

"It isn't servitude. It's called earning a living." Suddenly, she raised her right hand. "Hark! Don't you hear it?"

Pharoah leaned forward. "Hear what?"

"The silence. It's deafening. Himself has stopped yelling. I shall announce you. How about that?"

She picked up a phone and pressed a button. "Manny, there's a Pharoah Love to see you." Pause. "No, he's sort of black. Coffee colored. Oh, yes. Nice looks." Pause. She asked Pharoah, "Do you tap-dance?"

"Well," said Pharoah, "I used to do a kind of a time step. How'd he know I was an African-American?"

"With a name like Pharoah, did you expect him to think you were a Lithuanian?" Back into the phone: "Manny. Stop horsing around. He's a detective. The Chic Twins." Pause. "Manny? Manny? My God, I hope he didn't go out the window!"

Emmanuel Robinson flung his door open wide and stood in the doorway. "I knew it! I knew it! It's going to be one of *those* days! It's started already! There's a full-moon hangover! Okay, Detective Love. Come on inside and give me a hard time. I'm a masochist. I'll love it!"

chapter 12

"Murder! What the hell do I need with murder on a nice day like this?" Pharoah was watching an anachronism. Emmanuel Robinson was lighting a pipe. An agent smoking a pipe, not a cigar. Might be a Yale man. Robinson also had manners. He asked Pharoah if the smell of pipe tobacco bothered him.

"As long as you don't blow it in my face."

"So tell me, young man, how long have you been with the police force? Do you really like the work? What fascinates you about police work? The danger? You certainly don't meet a better class of people. I had two uncles who were cops. Unusual. We're not Irish. My uncle Nate, who's dead, and my uncle Izzy, who might as well be. Alzheimer's. Be careful. Lots of cops end up with Alzheimer's. Did you want to be a cop when you were a kid?"

Pharoah was fascinated. The stream of consciousness was engulfing and threatening to drown him. The voice was flat and nasal. The face was round and tired, with circles under the eyes deep enough to accommodate a couple of beds of vegetables. The hair was thin and drab looking, in desperate need of treatment. There was an unhealthy pallor to his skin, a professional hazard. Only in Los Angeles did agents have bronzed skins. He wore a thin wedding band, and around his left wrist was an imposing Rolex. Possibly a fake; there were lots of them being vended in the streets. There seemed to be no way to dam his stream of consciousness. A middle-aged man who had long ago seen the parade pass him by.

"So? Am I a suspect? If I killed those two cuties, I had to do it by remote control. The night the girls were at the Capri, I was home in bed with my wife, trying to convince her I had a terrible headache and she should stop poking me in the ribs for some action. She's always horny when she's lost too much on the ponies. I'd be well off if it wasn't for the ponies. Rachel is ruining me. That's my wife, not a pony. Nice woman, though, if you like nice women. I know, I talk too much."

"I haven't heard anything useful."

"We hardly know each other a few minutes and already I'm boring you?"

"Maybe I should talk to Rachel."

"It's not a bad idea if you want a recipe for chocolate chip cookies, but if you want to learn anything about the Cicci girls, you better stick with me. Want some coffee? Tea? Diet anything?" He sucked on the pipe. "Shall I tell Edna to hold my calls?"

"Is it necessary? You don't seem to be getting any."

"It's too early. My clients are night owls. They've forgotten what breakfast is."

During the run-on monologue, Pharoah looked at the walls, which were covered with autographed photographs, presumably of clients, none of whom Pharoah recognized or had heard of.

"There's no picture of the twins."

"The Chicsers?" He waited for a reaction from Pharoah. Pharoah offered none. "Don't you get it? Chicsers? *Shiksas?* You know, *shiksa,* Yiddish for a Gentile woman. Don't you know any Yiddish?"

"I know the dirty words." Pharoah crossed his legs.

Robinson knew he wasn't scoring points. He knew he was a bore and tiresome. He was reminded of it at least once every day when he lunched, usually alone, occasionally with a grateful Edna at the Russian Tea Room. There he would table-hop, working the room like a UJA fund-raiser. A perennial optimist, he viewed the world of his betters through rose-colored glasses. Someday, someday soon, before being felled by the stroke or the heart attack that lay in store for him, a celebrity would smile, punch his arm playfully, and say, "You're looking good, Manny, you're looking real good. Hang in there!"

"Hey, Robinson!"

Pharoah shattered the agent's doleful reverie. "What? What is it?"

"I don't have your undivided attention. I need to ask questions."

"Shoot. From the mouth that is, not the hip." He winked.

"I'm sure you've been reading in the newspapers and seeing it on the news that somebody's decimating the Salino family."

"I'd have to be deaf, dumb, and blind to miss it." He indicated a tabloid spread out on the desk. "Look at this headline. 'Poisoned Paisanos.' Very racist. The girls didn't rate such a spread." He sucked on the pipe. "This is mixed up with the girls, isn't it?"

"You know it is."

Robinson was nervous, playing with some pencils on his desk. "Yeah. I guess I know it is. I wish I didn't, but I do."

"You booked the girls into the Capri."

"Yes."

"Why didn't you come to us and tell us the girls had done a gig at the Capri, less then a mile away from the lake into which they were dunked?"

"Dunked. That's not a nice word."

"Those were not nice deaths. Why didn't you come forward with the information?"

"Because I . . . I"—he fumbled—"didn't think there was a connection."

"Bullshit."

"Listen, Mr. Love, you don't screw around with the Mob. You could get your kneecaps broken or find yourself swimming against the tide in the East River. That's if they dump you in alive. I'm a lousy swimmer."

"You didn't want to lose Salino's business."

Robinson parked the pipe in an ashtray. "He's been very good to me. I book the Capri exclusively, and thanks to him, I've picked up a couple of Russky clubs in Brighton Beach."

"Like the Vladivostok."

"How'd you guess?"

"Natalya Orloff."

Robinson's face brightened. "You've met Natalya?"

"Vot a Voman." Pharoah's unexpected smile relaxed Robinson.

"Smart cookie, Natalya. She's coming by soon for a little powwow. I'm going to line her up a recording contract. She's no ordinary singer. Never hear her? A real original. You know, like Tiny Tim."

"Salino's got a finger in some record companies."

"Gee, that's right! I'll have to have a talk with Marco." He coughed. "How could I forget he's got a big chunk of recording companies?"

"That's right. How could something like that slip your mind unless your mind is very slippery. So you book the Capri exclusively."

"Like I told you."

"Who chooses the acts?"

"I do."

"Marco gives you carte blanche? He never specifies he wants a particular act up there, like maybe the Chic Twins?"

"No, no. Sometimes he asks me to give some ambitious Italian kids a break, and so I book them. He had nothing to do with the twins. They were my idea."

"Did you know Rita Genari was bankrolling them?"

"I assumed as much. They were her protégés. She gave me hell for booking them into the Capri. I couldn't understand what she was so upset about. It was their first paying job. They'd only played a benefit, and they're always for free. I never had any trouble at the Capri before, and I've been booking it ever since Marco bought it. I been booking the acts the way I book acts for smokers. I mean, for crying out loud,

Rita sends up some of her hookers every so often, of both sexes." He raised the tabloid on the front page of which were grainy photos of the late Fauci and Sasso. "These two used to three-way it with Gino Vinelli, one of Rita's hottest numbers."

"So Gino told me."

Robinson put the newspaper aside. "Bet you didn't know there's gays in the Mafia."

"Sure. Like I didn't know there were gay athletes and gay servicemen. You've known Rita a long time?"

"A couple of years. Met her through a gal who used to be a lounge singer. Lily Davis. Maybe you know her."

"Smart lady."

"Doing damn well for herself working for Rita. She just bought an apartment house in the Bronx."

The Bronx?/No thonx.

"Was Rita there when you auditioned the twins, assuming you auditioned them?"

Robinson bristled. "Of course I auditioned them. I hold auditions twice a month." He mentioned a rehearsal hall he rented on lower Broadway. "I don't book my acts blind. I don't book any act that doesn't meet my standards. I mean, look at all of them." He made a sweeping gesture that encompassed all the autographed photographs decorating his walls. "You see these autographed pictures? They represent gratitude. I book them all over the country. Vegas and Reno, and I do a lot of business with cruise ships. You name the place, it is one way or another an outpost of Emmanuel Robinson. The sun never sets on Manny Robinson!"

Pharoah was tempted to ask, So with all these lucrative

bookings, how come you're in this seedy rat trap, and how come the phones aren't ringing?

Robinson continued to gather steam. "Go ask Edna to show you my files and all the bookings. Go ahead! You'll see how active I am. Maybe I'm no William Morris or ICM, but I do damn good. Do you know how often I get offers to sell out, give up my independence, and let myself be swallowed up by one of those octopuses?" Pharoah considered patting him on the head. Robinson blinked. "I mean, the idea, the idea I'd book an act before auditioning it. Jesus Christ!" He applied a match to the pipe bowl.

"How much business does Marco throw your way?"

"A lot. He's got a great pitching arm." It reaches across the country. He's got show-business connections up the kazoo. When Marco yells in New York, the Hollywood sign short-circuits."

"Do you work for Marco exclusively?"

"No, of course not. I book lots of places."

Pharoah wondered when he'd finish drawing on the pipe. The cloud of smoke above his head was beginning to look like the result of a tiny atomic detonation. "How deep are you into Marco?"

Robinson's eyes widened. Blood had rushed to his cheeks. "Deep? What do you mean deep?"

"How big's the marker Salino holds on you?"

"What the hell are you talking about?"

"The ponies."

"Ah, come off it! Rachel and me, we take an occasional flutter, nothing serious."

"Marco Salino makes another fortune loan-sharking. You're

in so fucking deep to him it'll take a steam shovel to get you out."

"Say, what the hell is this all about?"

"What it's all about is you've been told to keep your lips hemstitched or you'll be ripe for instant retirement. The twins were murdered, and because of that, some nut case is out there knocking off Salino's shooters in pairs. Nice touch, I might add."

"I don't know anything, I tell you!" he shouted. "I'm telling you what I know, and that ain't more than I booked them and I'm sorry I booked them because it's bought me more tsuris than I need right now. God, I've got enough miserable weight on my shoulders. Who the hell needs more?"

"Maybe I should be questioning Edna."

Robinson exhaled some smoke. "Edna's a nymphomaniac, and from looking at her you can understand when I tell you she ain't had much practice lately."

"We are not amused." Pharoah looked ready to pounce on the besieged man. Robinson was a mess, nearing the end of his rope. He was the last of a dying breed, the independent theatrical agent. They began to be phased out when vaudeville disappeared. They had a brief reprieve when variety shows were popular television fare, and when viewers grew bored with them, dinosaurs like Emmanuel Robinson fought for survival by booking stag parties and smokers and weddings and bar mitzvahs and fraternal organizations, and soon these bookings would suffer a severe decline.

Robinson was speaking so softly that Pharoah had to strain to hear the words. "I'm up to my chin in debt. I owe Marco too much. It's obscene. I'd be ashamed of myself except I put my morals into hock years ago. I kick back to him half of what I collect from the clients. I survive because my Rachel is one hell of a poker player. She makes plenty on games with lonely widows and spinsters who don't give a damn how much they lose as long as they've got company for a couple of hours. We're neither one of us proud of what we do, and if Edna was in this room, I'd apologize to her. Edna's my sister. You interested in marrying her?"

"Meanwhile, back at the Salino ranch. How long's Natalya been his girl?"

"He's got a slew of women."

"How long's Natalya been his girl?"

"Not long. She's on loan."

"Go on."

"Sergei Paskudnyak. He owns the Vladivostok, where Natalya's working. He's Russian Mafia."

"Very generous lending him Rita."

"It's your turn to use the gray matter, Mr. Love. Paskudnyak is an Einstein compared to Marco. True, he's in on some deals with the Eye-ties, but of course they don't trust each other. Natalya's no sacrificial offering. She's with Marco to learn anything that Paskudnyak will find of value. It's been done before. Rita's kiddies, as she so quaintly refers to them, are trained to get information and turn it over to Rita. Likewise, some of my acts."

"The twins?"

"Hell, no. They were just beginning. It was too soon to use them that way."

"Who told you to take them on?"

"Nobody told me anything. Gino suggested I audition

them. It seemed innocent enough at the time. He said they were living with Juana Gomez, and I knew Gomez and Rita were attached at the hip. I auditioned them. They were cute. They needed a lot of polish, savvy, maturity. But they danced okay, and they certainly looked terrific, and I was helping provide acts for an AIDS benefit, so I let the girls perform."

"When was this?"

"A couple of weeks before I put them into the Capri."

"Where was the benefit held?"

"At another of the Mafia's venues, the gay joint, the Fountain of Youth. You know, on East Fourteenth Street."

"I know it well. It was once my home away from home."

That brought a raised eyebrow. "Oh, really?"

"Oh, really. I liked their pizzas."

"It was practically the same package I put into the Capri. Natalya, Gino, and the twins. The other performers weren't mine. Drag acts, lip synchers. I don't do them anymore. Just when they're getting hot they catch the plague. Either that or the paraffin in their tits melts."

"Yoyo wasn't on the bill?"

"He didn't want to do it."

"Don't tell me he's a homophobe."

"No, he just doesn't perform well in front of gay audiences. I can understand it. They can get very raucous and bitchy, especially when they've had too much to drink. I mean, just because the plague is thinning the herd doesn't mean they're saints."

Pharoah agreed. "My sisters can be very embarrassing at times."

Christ, thought Robinson. I'm being intimidated by a fag

cop. Wait till I tell Rachel. She won't believe a word of it. He was worrying his pipe again. "It might interest you to know who ran the benefit. Adelaide Benarro."

"Why do I get so many names thrown at me that end in vowels?" Pharoah clucked his tongue and shook his head from side to side.

"It's the stereotype casting."

"So who is Adelaide—"

"Benarro. You'll be happy to know her maiden name doesn't end with a vowel. Years ago she was a pretty popular club singer, Adelaide Gibson."

Somewhere it rang a bell in Pharoah's head. "Adelaide Gibson. Yeah, I remember her. She worked the fancier cribs. The Persian Room. The Rainbow Room. Café Society Uptown and Downtown. She was billed as 'the Society Singer.' 'The Philadelphia Main Liner.'"

"She never mainlined!"

"I'm talking about her origins, not her hobby."

"Addie's a terrific gal. She lost one of her sons to AIDS. Michael. The money's for the Michael Benarro Memorial Fund. She gives to AIDS research, hostels, Gay Men's Health Crisis, you name it, Addie's giving them money, and a hell of a lot of it is her own. She's loaded but not ostentatious. I mean, she leaves the jewelry displays to Elizabeth Taylor. She's Salvatore Benarro's widow."

"Salvatore Benarro." Pharoah looked at the ceiling, which was peeling, and there materialized a newspaper headline. "Of course. Salvatore Benarro. Murdered in an East Side chop-house while attacking a T-bone steak. An ice pick shoved in his ear. Ice pick, very old-fashioned. The perp was a pigeon dishwasher in the kitchen. I seem to remember Marco Salino was questioned." Robinson's mouth idled in neutral. "Something about somebody moving in on somebody's exclusive territory."

"Well, you know, there's always a lot of that going on. One of Salino's lieutenants picked off the perp with one shot."

"Stupid. The trigger-happy bastards always shoot before they leap. Should've just winged him and turned him over to us. We'd have found out who ordered the rubout." Robinson seemed to have the pipe under control and was puffing away with what might have passed as a beatific expression on his face. Pharoah wondered why losers were so simpleminded. He marveled at how he could drive them to unburdening some of what remained of their souls. Poor Emmanuel. Poor Rachel. Poor Edna. "So Benarro left behind a grieving widow."

"Oh, sure. Real begrieved. Up to her knees in a pool of crocodile tears. Some girls have all the luck, as my Rachel said at the time. Benarro left her a fortune. A mansion on East Sixty-eighth Street the size of a minihotel. With an indoor swimming pool that could pass for a lagoon. There are rooms in that place that she has yet to set foot in. Then there's the platoon she calls a household staff." He was reaming the ashes out of the pipe bowl, and they gave off an unpleasant smell. This time Pharoah made no effort to interrupt. He realized that there was more to learn from Robinson by letting his geyser gush uninterruptedly. "God knows how much a month it costs her to run that place. Mind you, I don't begrudge her." He emptied the ashtray into a wastepaper basket hidden under his desk. "She earned her stripes. Almost three decades as Benarro's wife. As far as I heard, she never gave him any cause to weep except Michael, the son. Poor Salvatore wanted a son who was macho, and instead he got a son that was mucho. Fate can do some wicked things with her fickle finger. Clever kid, Michael, he wrote music. Even had a couple of his songs recorded."

"By singers whose names ended in vowels."

"Yeah. How'd you guess?"

"Sometimes I get lucky," Pharoah responded wryly.

"After Benarro bought the one-way ticket, Adelaide was in line for every fashion award for her taste in widow's weeds. Geoffrey Beene, Oleg Cassini, Eva St. Laurent . . ."

"Yves," corrected Pharoah.

"Is that how you pronounce it?" He was refilling the pipe bowl. "You live and learn. She's quite a lady, Adelaide. Real class. Stayed away from any involvements with men for about a year. Marco Salini broke her fast."

"Marco's pretty good at that sort of thing. We know each other since we were kids."

"No kidding! Is that a fact! Knew each other when you were kids!"

"In Canarsie."

"Canarsie! Well, what do you know! I knew we'd find something in common! I come from Brownsville, a short trolley ride from there."

"Emmanuel, believe me. The only thing we've got in common is that we've got nothing in common."

"Ah, come on, Pharoah, loosen up. I ain't such a bad sort. Dogs don't chase me in the street, if you know what I mean."

"You're okay, Emmanuel," Pharoah lied, "real okay. Tell me more about Adelaide. You seem to have done a lot of homework on her."

"I cannot tell a lie. I was her strong right arm helping to put the benefit together. When we weren't lunching, we were on the phone with each other five times a day. She's very open about herself; at least with me she was." He winked. "Rachel was getting a little jealous. I told Addie, and she made me bring Rachel to lunch. You want to know something? Ten minutes into the lunch they forgot I was there, they got so wrapped up in each other." Pharoah almost told Robinson he was the forgettable type but decided the man had been stepped on enough in his lifetime. "Yeah, I suppose I know more about her than anybody else, including the gossip columnists. Adelaide never got herself written up like Ivana and Marla and the rest of them bimbos. Adelaide's a class act."

"She still seeing Marco?"

"Not too much socially, I don't think. They've both got other fish to fry. But don't get me wrong. They're still friendly. They talk on the phone every so often, I guess."

"I suppose it takes a special kind of upbringing to be a classy widow."

"Where Adelaide's concerned, you spell class with a capital K. Like when she found out her son had AIDS. After thanking God Salvatore hadn't lived to see his boy afflicted, she took him all over the world looking for a cure. Shinto priests prayed over him in Japan, and in India holy men dosed him with special herbs and bathed him in the Ganges. You know AIDS originated in Africa, so she even found some witch doctor with a degree in medicine from Johns Hopkins. That poor guy got so frustrated trying to concoct formulas from his medical books, he finally broke down and took to

burning chicken feathers and slitting goats' necks and string-
ing shells and beads together which he'd shake over Michael's
head. All the time, the way Adelaide described him, the poor
kid is wasting away. Only twenty-four years old." He shook his
head from side to side sadly. "The incredible shrinking son.
After giving up on darkest Africa, she made one last pilgrim-
age to try and save Michael's life. She flew him to Lourdes."
He was shaking his head again. "That turned out to be a terrible mistake. It was so damp in the grotto, Michael caught
cold, and by the time she got him back to the mansion, he had
developed pneumonia, and then it was curtains. She gave him
a real big send-off. She held the services in the grand ballroom
of the mansion. There were over fifteen hundred in atten-
dance, or so she claims. I hadn't gotten to know her yet or I'm
sure I'd have been invited. She has a teletape she used to run
for me a couple of times a week. What a service. It should
have been a network special. Aretha Franklin sang spirituals.
Paul McCartney did some Beatles' tunes. Itzhak Perlman
played a special violin version of Ravel's "Pavane for a Dead
Princess," since I suppose you could stretch a point that
Michael was both a dead prince and a dead princess. She
showed me pictures of him in drag. He looked just like that
actress Molly Ringworm."

"Ringwald."

Robinson chose not to hear him. "And oh, yeah! Yoyo did
his act. Lots of pathos mixed in with the laughs. You know,
laugh, clown, laugh stuff. That's the first time I saw him, on
the tape."

"There must have been a lot of gays at the service."

"Adelaide said if a bomb had dropped on the mansion there'd have been no more sex below Fourteenth Street. Gay sex, that is."

"Yoyo has no trouble performing in front of gays at the service but balks at doing a benefit at the Fountain of Youth."

"That's easily understood. At the service they were on their best behavior. In a gay club, it could be another matter."

"True. Too true. Ever see Yoyo without the makeup?"

"Now that you ask me, no. No, I haven't."

"Know anything about his background? Where was he born? Where does he live?"

"All I know about him is Edna takes his messages. He drops by every day to pick them up."

"What kind of messages?"

"Mostly bookings offered for kiddie parties. He runs an ad in *New York* magazine and the *Village Voice*."

"Those ads aren't inexpensive."

"I figure Yoyo does okay for himself."

"Maybe Yoyo has friends in the family?"

"You mean Marco's family?" Pharoah nodded. "Well, he's played some kiddie parties for them. I've been trying to get him into the Ringling Brothers circus. I think he's real ready for the big time under the big top. I think he's terrific."

"I'd like to get to know more about him."

Robinson was suddenly puffed up. "I'll see if I can help you there."

"That's mighty white of you."

"Yoyo likes me and trusts me, and Edna bakes him brownies. I'll try to corner him and do some real probing." Pharoah had a vision of a special kind of root-canal work as perfected by Emmanuel Robinson.

"You do that. Could you write Mrs. Benarro's phone number and address on a piece of paper for me."

"Well, gee, Pharoah, I don't know. All that's very private." Pharoah stared at him. He said nothing. Robinson placed the pipe in the ashtray. "I'm sure Addie won't mind my giving it to you. You're someone special. I think Addie and you will get along great." He was twisting the Rolodex with the look of a man who meant business. In a few minutes, Pharoah had pocketed a slip of notepaper with the information he wanted.

"You've been a real help, Emmanuel."

"Anytime! Anytime!" Pharoah was sauntering to the door, a very short saunter owing to the very cramped office. Robinson rushed to the door and held it open for Pharoah.

"I'd tip you, but I'm fresh out of coins," Pharoah said.

chapter 13

As the door to the elevator reached the ground floor, Pharoah heard shrieks and yells coming from the street. He drew his service revolver and hurried through the lobby. It sounded to him as if someone were being mugged. What idiot would make a pass on a street as busy with traffic as this one? It wasn't an idiot; it was two idiots. Pharoah recognized them. Two Hispanic teenagers were trying to carjack a Cadillac. They both held Raven MP-25s, small but dangerous, mostly used by school kids. The Cadillac's chauffeur was pleading with them not to shoot while from the backseat Pharoah recognized a familiar female voice cursing in Russian, "*Ybitvayamot!*"

Pharoah shouted, "Freeze, you pricks!"

They froze. They recognized the voice. They knew it well.

It was the voice of a cop who took no prisoners. "What the hell are you little sons of bitches doing so far downtown?"

Their names were Castor and Pollux Hernandez. They were brothers. Castor whined, "We found some tokens. Come on, Pharoah, we aren't serious. We're just practicing."

Natalya stared out the window at Pharoah and crossed herself with relief.

Pollux, a certifiable idiot, asked in a piping voice, "Can I wipe my nose with my sleeve, Pharoah?"

"Drop the guns!" commanded Pharoah. "Hey, you," meaning the quivering aspen of a chauffeur, "pick them up!"

"They ain't dropped them yet!" the chauffeur responded.

Natalya was out of the car, confronting the two thieves. "Natalya pick up guns! And maybe Natalya shoot their balls off!"

"Please, lady," pleaded Castor, "don't take us too serious." Natalya picked up the guns and pointed one at Castor's crotch. "Please, lady, please! I can't stand pain!"

Natalya waved the guns under their noses ominously. "When Natalya much younger recently, she serve in Russian army. She how you say, shop shooter?"

Pollux gambled and wiped his nose. It didn't improve his appearance. Pharoah saw a patrol car turning into West Forty-fourth Street from Broadway. "Bring the guns to me, Natalya."

Castor yelled, "Jesus Christ, the broad knows the dick. It's an ambush!"

"Vot bush is ambush?" Natalya asked Pharoah.

Pharoah didn't take his eyes off the boys, much as Natalya's eyes pleaded for an explanation. He had dealt with them before; they were two kegs of gunpowder that could detonate at any moment. They were always caught. They were always released. Their mother could have been a great dramatic star. Her pleas for their release had dissolved many a judge in tears. She was in her early forties, had a voluptuous body and an exotic face, and had long been suspected of being an important drug dealer. The patrol car pulled up, and the two officers emerged with guns drawn.

"What have we got here, Pharoah?" asked one officer whose diction was execrable.

"Attempted carjack. Don't you recognize the schmucks?"

"Oh, for crying out loud," said the second officer, who was prematurely bald and developing a potbelly. "I'm getting very bored with these two."

"Come on, hands behind your backs!"

"Ow!" yelled Castor. "They're too tight."

"They should be castrated!" insisted Natalya, who, having retrieved her handbag from the backseat of the car, was examining her face in her compact mirror. Pollux drooled at the sight of the bejeweled compact. They should have tried to hijack her instead of the Cadillac. Pharoah holstered his gun and asked the chauffeur, "You all right?"

"Sure, sure." He was mopping his brow with a soiled handkerchief.

Natalya glared at the chauffeur and murmured, "My hero."

Castor and Pollux were deposited in the backseat of the patrol car, and with sirens blaring, the officers disappeared with their first catch of the day.

Natalya returned the compact to the handbag, snapped the clasp shut, and favored Pharoah with what she was sure was her most bewitching and enchanting Slavic smile. "If providence not send you, Natalya might be lying in street in pool of Russian blood like beet soup." Her eyes widened. "How come you here? Vot brings you?"

"I was interviewing your agent."

"Manny? My Manny? Of vot are you suspicious from Manny?"

"Routine investigation."

"Oh, yes?" Coquettishly. "You like maybe give me routine investigation?"

"It just so happens there are some questions I'd like to ask you."

"Vell, as they frequently say in Odessa, there is no time like the present. I vouldn't mind glass of tea."

Sardi's doorman had taken in the scene of the attempted crime from the vestibule and had swiftly called the police. He recognized Pharoah and was standing nearby waiting to see if he could be of any assistance. He heard Pharoah say, "I'll see if Sardi's has started serving."

"Vy not serving? Is restaurant, no?"

The doorman said, "It's okay, Pharoah. Go right inside. I'll keep an eye on the car."

"Is not car, is Cadillac," said Natalya haughtily. "Is big difference. Like difference between diamonds and zircons." Her eyes swept the doorman from head to toes. He was big. Natalya liked them big. She asked him as her eyes smoldered, "Is perhaps bass baritone?"

"No, ma'am. I can't sing."

"Vot a vaste." She swept into the restaurant. Pharoah winked at the doorman and followed her in. They were seated just inside the doorway. A waiter promised prompt delivery of tea and coffee, but Pharoah knew better. Natalya was absorbed briefly in staring at the myriad framed caricatures on the walls. "Very clever, these—how you say . . . ?"

"Caricatures."

"*Da*. Caricatures. Are you *peut-être* also here on the vall?"

"I'm not a celebrity."

"No?" She drew the simple word out into six musical syllables. "But verever I look, everyone seems to know you."

"This is my turf. I've been working Broadway ever since I was a young Turk with big ambitions."

"And you have no more ambitions?"

"Some of them are simmering on the back burner."

"On whose stove?" she purred.

"Mine."

"Tell me about your ambitions."

"The idea is for me to do the questioning and you to supply the answers."

"Ve vill do both."

"What about your appointment upstairs?"

"Manny vill vait. It is vot he does best. Vot ambitions you have?"

"I've been working on a novel."

"A novel! Like maybe *Var and Peace*?"

"Not so ambitious."

"Vy not? You must not be modest. You must vish to be giant like Dostoyevski, like Tolstoy, like Pushkin, like Jackie Collins!"

"I'm a very simple man, Natalya. I have no pretensions."

"No? An earring with Jesus and Moses making cozy is not pretentious? Where is the other earring?"

"I gave it to a guy with one ear."

"Now you make fun vit me."

The tea and coffee were placed on the table. The waiter had brought both lemon and milk.

"Thanks," said Pharoah. The waiter nodded and drifted away quietly.

"So vot kind of novel is your novel?"

"It's a detective story."

She clapped her hands together. "But of course! You are writing from experience. Is very vise. They tell me Ivana Trump's writer ghosts book from Ivana's experience."

"No sweat there. The lady is a Trump."

"Vell, tell me, Pharoah, your novel. Is it maybe perhaps about the murder of the mafiosi?"

Pharoah thought fast, one of his strongest assets. She was offering him the opportunity to get her back on the track he wanted to pursue. "How'd you guess?"

She favored him with a sly smile. "I guess to please you. You vant to ask me questions about Marco and Sergei Paskudnyak and other things, and I am voman who likes to please man." She leaned forward seductively. "Especially man she vants to please." She ladled sugar into her tea as though she'd been tipped off to expect a shortage. "I love sveet tea. It is so good for my disposition. Vell, Mr. Pharoah Love, begin. Natalya is on, how you say, the hot seat? *Da*? Vell, I have a very hot seat." She sampled the tea, made *mmm* noises, and decided it was just right. "You mind if I smoke?" She didn't wait for an answer and fished in her handbag for her cigarette case and lighter, both matching her compact, all three purchased for her at Tiffany's by Sergei Paskudnyak. "If you are vondering, I have no fear of lung cancer. By the time it should ever attack me, they vill have found a cure. So, vere do ve start?"

"Why didn't you tell me you were at the Capri with the twins?"

"I didn't? I could svear I did. So vat does it matter? I tell you now. I vas at the Capri that night, yes. Very disorderly audience. They did not appreciate my balalaika. Vas also the singer and the clown. I give them lift back to city in Cadillac that is outside."

"Did you offer the twins a lift? There would have been plenty of room. They would have accepted, I'm sure, and still be alive today."

"But I *did* make offer. But the Millie tvin, I think it was Millie, she thank me sveetly but say they already have lift home. They vere vaiting for Marco's meeting to end. One of his gangsters offered them a drink downstairs vile they vait, and ven last I see them, they are descending the stairs—" her eyes darkened, her voice lowered—"to their destiny." She paused. "I have theory about life and death." Pharoah knew he was going to hear it whether he wanted to or not. "My theory is, people die ven they are supposed to die. The tvins died young. It was their fate. It vas written in the stars. Before show, I ask them their birth sign. Of course it is Gemini, the tvins. Kennedy, Garland, Monroe, also Geminis. Vot vastes."

"Did they say who had offered them the lift back?"

"Oh, yes. Vas handsome devil from La Fontana."

"Nick Suggi?"

"Such a gorgeous creature. Ve have nothing like him in

Russia. So slim, so svelte, and those eyes, so seductive, so hypnotic. Vy, I wonder, is he not movie star?"

"Maybe he can't act."

Both her arms were outstretched. "So who can?"

Pharoah's brain was spinning like a Catherine wheel, emitting sparks that generated juices that had been lying dormant, waiting for a sudden stimulus, such as the information that Suggi had been at the Capri that night. He hadn't mentioned it last night. But he had made it clear he was Marco's employee, and only an employee. Not a shooter. Not a lieutenant. Not in thrall to the family.

Natalya was reclining on an invisible cloud of ecstasy. "Perhaps Natalya will taste a sample of Nick Suggi."

Pharoah was thinking, Or perhaps Pharoah vill. He looked at his wristwatch. La Fontana would be serving lunch by now.

"Vy you look at wristvatch? You grow tired of Natalya?"

"I could never grow tired of Natalya."

"You are a very interesting-type cossack, Pharoah Love. Ve do not have many people your luscious color in my country. You like being detective?"

"I like being detective."

"It pays vell?"

"I survive."

"Pooh," she said. "Survive. This is a vord for the underprivileged. You should be more ambitious. You should vant vealth. Vy you not corrupt and make deals in drugs like other detectives?"

Pharoah refrained from wincing. "You got some names?" It was common knowledge there were rogue cops on the take.

Pharoah wondered which ones Marco and Sergei had on their payrolls and then elected to wonder aloud.

Natalya smiled. "I do not know names, and if I did, I vould not betray. I am, how you say, a straight shooter. *Da?*"

"*Da.*"

From out of left field she asked, "You think maybe Nick Suggi is murderer?"

Pharoah gave a Gallic shrug and then said with a twinkle in his eyes, "Who knows what dark deeds lie smoldering in the underbellies of men."

She rubbed out her cigarette and said, "Pharoah, that is one big load of crap."

"Why haven't you asked me if I suspect Sergei might be the mastermind behind the murders."

"I vould ask if you ask me questions about Sergei, but you ask nothing."

"Marco and Sergei don't really like each other."

"This is statement or question?"

"Either or."

"Shall ve say they are like politicians who are strange bedfellows. Ven they need each other, they make believe they like each other. Obviously they are involved in some kind of deal. Ven deal is finished, then maybe they var with each other."

"Probably. Lots of blood has already been spilled in the corridors of power."

"It's like Marco and Veeping Villie and his teddy bear. They despise each other. It is so obvious. But for appearances they make nice with each other because for the moment it is to their advantage. You mark my words, vun day they vill all be extinct like dinosaurs. You know, some of the families are hurting bad. You know, no money. Some are selling everything but their wives and retiring to maybe Fort Lauderdale. Pharoah, keep in mind the capos are getting old. And there are not many young ones who vant to replace them. The few that are just aren't ruthless enough. There's no blood in their eyes. These killings trouble Marco not so much because he is losing trusted shooters but because no employment agency exists that supplies young gangsters.

"These little bums who try to steal my Cadillac, perhaps, they might be possibilities. But vat are they? Teenage animals! Animals do not make good mafiosi. My Sergei has same problem as Marco. Vere to find fresh recruits. Maybe import them from Russia. Lots of young gangsters in Russia, but very unsophisticated. They pick their teeth with their fingernails." She selected a cigarette from her Tiffany case.

"Could I have one of those, please?"

She looked at him with surprise. "You smoke?"

"Every once in a blue moon." He helped himself. It was like no cigarette he had ever seen before. Both the tobacco and the paper were black.

"Turkish. Very potent." She held the flaming lighter for him. "Inhale very gently or you will damage the lining of your nostrils." He tried it. The stuff had to be refined camel dung. "You do not like it?"

"I just hope it's not lethal."

"Is same taste as marijuana." She was lost in thought for a moment. "I read about your murderer this morning with my breakfast of triscuits and goat cheese. He kills in pairs. Very symbolic, yes?"

"Very."

"The twins were a pair. Very obvious, no?"

"Very obvious, yes."

"It should not be so easy to kill two mafiosi at a time. And yet this person succeeds. Poison, knifing, sniping. He knows vere to find them no matter how securely they think they hide themselves. So is person who is—how you say?—privy to—how you say again? Oh, yes, classified information. So, this person is very close to Marco's organization?"

"That's right. Or very close to someone who's very close to Marco's organization."

"Could be me, maybe?"

"No."

She smiled. "Then who?"

"You're familiar with Gilbert and Sullivan's *The Mikado*?"

"Oh, yes. Plays many times in Minsk ven I was stunning little girl." She lustily la-la-laed "Three Little Maids from School Are Ve."

"The song I had in mind is the one that includes the line 'I've got a little list.'"

"Ah, yes. Is very clever. So, Pharoah Love, you have a little list. That is a good beginning, yes?"

"The trouble with my little list is that as new events surround me, my little list contracts and expands, like a hopeless dieter."

"I do not diet ever, of course. I have perfect body. You admire my breasts? They are very unique. Very original. I come from a long line of vunderful breasts. It's in the genes. Oh, Pharoah Love, I'm embarrassing you!"

Pharoah said wryly, "You have the undivided attention of

the entire room." They hadn't noticed that the place was filling up with tourists, some local businesspeople who still had expense accounts, and a few theater people who dropped in for nostalgia's sake despite the decline in the quality of Sardi's cuisine.

"So vy they do not applaud?" She laughed. "I adore to shock people. You are not so easily shocked, yes?"

"Natalya, I've seen it all and I've done it all, and sometimes twice."

"Oh, yes? But you have not yet done Nayalya!"

"Who knows? Stranger things have happened." He signaled for the check but was told it was on the house. On the way out, Pharoah thanked Vincent Sardi, Jr., who stood guard at the door, introduced Natalya, waited patiently for the exchange of amenities to conclude, and then escorted Natalya to the street.

"Have you learned something valuable from me?"

Pharoah nodded. "It's been profitable."

"Vould you like the Cadillac to take you someplace? I vill be a vile with Robinson." She heard a string of obscenities. "*Borgiamoy*! From vere comes such filth?"

The Grey Ghost had materialized as though summoned by an arcane imprecation. Natalia eyed his improbable getup with a mixture of distaste and perverse amusement. "This is man, or this is ectoplasm?"

"This is my friend, the Grey Ghost."

"Oh, yes?" She asked the Ghost, "Vat is your real name, dolling?"

"I am Everyman. I am saint, and I am sinner."

Pharoah asked the homeless man, "What you up to, Ghost?"

"A little of this, a little of that."

"Have you had any breakfast?"

"It's too late for breakfast."

"Here's ten bucks. Get yourself something to eat."

A gloved hand snatched the bill from Pharoah. "It won't be Lucullan, but it will be sufficient unto the day," he intoned, followed by the usual muttered curses as he lurched and dodged through traffic, weaving his way into Shubert Alley and then disappearing from sight.

Natalya watched him go, mouth agape with amazement. "He is unbelievable. Those bad vords!" Pharoah explained about Tourette syndrome. "How tragic! He vill die soon?"

"Who knows. I guess if the disease doesn't get him, the street will."

"But under all those filthy rags I suspect he's very young man!" She clucked her tongue. Minsk was never like this. "Anyway, you vill use the Cadillac?" Pharoah accepted the offer. He'd be at La Fontana that much sooner. Instructing the chauffeur to return as soon as he dropped Pharoah, Natalya grabbed Pharoah's hand. "Perhaps I vill be of more use after tonight."

"What's on for tonight?"

"Marco takes me to early dinner in Chinatown with the head of Chinese gang. Should be very interesting. Very special dinner. Tell me, Pharoah, vot is a vok?"

"A wok? That's a Chinese Italian."

chapter

14

Albert West was in Walt MacIntyre's office. The previous day's inexpensive but sober Bond Brothers brown suit had today given way to a devil-may-care striped sports jacket and slacks. The chief of detectives commented slyly, "That's the sort of getup I expect Pharoah to wear."

"This? It's been hanging in my closet for so many months, I decided it was time to give it an airing. Er, you read my report?"

"Yeah. Good. Read Pharoah's and the coroner's, too. Poetic justice, those rats being poisoned with rat poison. By the way, where the hell *is* Pharoah?"

"I don't think even a crystal ball could supply that answer."

MacIntyre picked up a phone and pressed a button. "Eddie? You hear from Pharoah?"

Eddie, the sergeant on duty at the front desk, told him, "He was seeing some agent in the Sardi building, after which he expected to drop by here."

"What else has he got on his plate today?"

"Your guess is as good as mine."

"My guess is better then yours. Phone Rita and see if he's there or if she's expecting him." He replaced the phone and stared at it as though, if given time, it would reveal Pharoah's secrets.

West said peevishly, "Pharoah gets away with murder around here."

"Correction. Pharoah investigates murder around here, and he's the best I've got. I suppose you don't like working with him, his being gay and all that crap."

"He's not bad to work with—*if* I'm working with him. Pharoah's a one-man operation despite the fact we're supposed to be a team."

"I repeat, he's the best I've got. And they also like him a lot downtown. Pharoah doesn't waste time. This mafioso investigation is a ball-breaker. We're taking a lot of heat from the media. How come we're expending so much energy on a bunch of wasted mobsters? How come, indeed! I admit I was very surprised when Marco came to Pharoah and asked him as a personal favor to try and track down this killer. After all, the Mob usually does its own dirty work, and you know the old expression 'They only kill each other.' So this one had Marco stumped! The killer's a lone ranger; nemesis with blood in his mouth. Damned good killer, too."

West was confused. "Is there such a thing as a damned good killer?"

"You bet your ass there is. You ever check the statistics on unsolved crimes in our beloved city? Believe you me, Albert, there's a lot of killers out there getting away with it. Until AIDS struck the fear of God into gay hearts, do you know how many fags were murdered and their killers never caught? Pharoah can tell you. We used to assign as many of those to him as we could. It wasn't nice of us, because it was like rubbing his face in shit. But that's when we learned and appreciated that Pharoah was an old hand at flinging down the gauntlet. And without realizing it, it was one of the smartest moves I ever made." He was lighting a cigar. "You see, the majority of gay sex is anonymous. Serious cruising for a casual pickup. No names exchanged, at least not any real ones. The majority of these murders were S and M. But the sadist gets carried away—you know, they get very emotional. So then they beat the maso into unconsciousness and for dessert indulge in a little strangulation. Which is followed by the distasteful game of follow the scent to the scene of the crime. Usually some dingy room in a run-down hotel no self-respecting flea would inhabit. Sometimes, too, it happens in a first-class hotel, like the case of a famous playwright who they claimed died choking on a medicine-bottle cap. For crying out loud, what was he doing with it, gargling?"

MacIntyre paused to take a call, studying Albert West, who was himself studying a fingernail on his left hand. Albert was uncomfortable, MacIntyre could tell. Serves the prude right. Teaming him with Pharoah was another act of sadomasochism on MacIntyre's part. He, of course, was the sadist; Albert, the masochist.

But MacIntyre salved his conscience with the assurance

that Albert West would emerge from the experience a better man. Or else he'd switch his profession to serial killer, with homosexuals as his victims. When Albert heard the chief hang up, he abandoned the nail examination, which was very boring, anyway.

"Where was I?" growled MacIntyre. "Oh, yeah. So anyway, you know what Pharoah does without me or anybody ordering him to do it? He lays himself on the line. He goes out into that jungle on the prowl for just those likely sadists. Pharoah's not even a little worried because, like Fearless Fosdick, nothing ever seems to frighten Pharoah. And so he catches himself a murderer. And you know something? The guy's an accountant from Hoboken. Married with three kids. Confesses to over a dozen killings. You know what his wife says when the news catches up to her? 'I thought he'd been acting funny lately.' How's that for a laugh?"

Albert unwrapped a stick of gum, popped it in his mouth, and slowly mashed it to a pulp. MacIntyre was saying, "After that, Pharoah was aces with me. Like pleading with me to send him out after Herbie Marks. His old pal. His old buddy. What he was doing was a favor to Herbie. Pharoah knew he'd have to kill him; Herbie would never surrender. Old pals can't help but know that sort of thing. They just understand it. It's like the Corsican Brothers, Siamese twins at birth, and after separation they could still feel when the other one was hurting. Pharoah knows when his brothers are hurting." He paused, looked at the ceiling which needed a paint job and then said, "He knew Herbie was hurting, and now he knows Marco is hurting."

"Sounds to me like he couldn't be more prosperous."

"Money, yes. He's rich. But these murders are loosening the underpinnings of his organization. So Marco's on the spot. Now he's lost six shooters, and he's going to lose more unless Pharoah moves in on the perp sooner rather than later. A lot of the families are hurting. Not for the same reason as Marco, but for reasons equally bad. You see in the paper this morning about this upstate capo looking to auction off the family assets? That means he's in real serious trouble. And he can't look to Italy for any help. They've got problems of their own. Oh, boy, have they got problems, the way the government's cracking down! Talk about genocide! Marco's not in good shape. He puts up a good front, but it's all bluster. Marco's marked, he knows it, Pharoah knows it, I know it, unless by some miracle he can start shoring up his shaky organization. Like Gotti got his, Marco's due to get his. Aren't you glad you're a cop?"

Pharoah and Nicholas Suggi sat alone in a secluded booth in La Fontana's rear dining room, the one rarely used for lunch. Suggi was quickly on the defensive, Pharoah having slugged him verbally with why he hadn't told Pharoah he was at the Capri.

"It didn't seem important I was there!"

"You told me last night you're not part of the family."

"I'm not! I didn't lie! I been to these meetings lots of times. I run this restaurant for Marco. You know he's got lots of other restaurants in his chain. He's the McDonald's of the Mafia! That meeting was about widening the expanding. Marco respects my expertise. I was raised in the restaurant business. For crying out loud, I'm even an Escoffier graduate!"

"Scrub that. Let's get down to the bare bones. Natalya says the twins were hanging around waiting for you to drive them back to town."

"Listen, Pharoah, and you're hearing the truth. The twins didn't want to go back in Natalya's car. They wanted to hang around and have some fun."

"Come off it!"

"Okay, so don't believe me. What I'm telling you is the truth. What I did say to them was if they were still downstairs with the boys when the meeting was finished, I'd come looking for them and give them a lift back. Well, the meeting was long—so damned long that Marco and some of the rest of us were thinking of going ahead and spending the night. It was a hard, long grind, and by the time we finished, which was like maybe three in the morning, my brains were mashed potatoes. Still, I went looking for the twins. Not a sign of them. The shooters weren't there, either. So I figured they found some other means of transport."

"They did."

Suggi went quiet for a few seconds. "I had nothing to do with any of it, I swear to it. Marco's boys suddenly returned, and when I asked who drove the twins back to the city, they threw a name at me that meant nothing to me because all their names meant nothing to me. They *continue* to mean nothing to me! I was so beat, I was afraid to drive back, afraid I'd fall asleep at the wheel. Marco didn't trust his driver, either, so we chose rooms and went beddy-bye. Anything else I can tell you, you already know."

"What about the twins?"

"What about them?"

"Wanting to hang around and have some fun with the boys."

"That's what I said, and that's what they wanted to do. Look. For a while there I had a yen for Annie. But she discouraged me real quick. Look at where'd they'd been cooped up for years. In a convent school, for crying out loud. Years of discipline and sexual repression."

"My mama told me when I was a kid what you ain't ever had you don't miss."

"Pharoah, Millie and Annie Cicci were time bombs. They wanted to be in show business because they heard that's where all the action took place. Kids grow up faster today than they used to. Come on, you're no innocent. You know what's going on! The drinking, the drugging, the screwing around, it's epidemic."

"Okay, okay." Pharoah held up his hands. "Peace. Then you didn't shed any tears for them, did you?"

"Have you? I got nobody in my life to shed any tears for. When my grandmother and my mother went, I was all short on tears. They were two terrific ladies, and let me tell you, they kept me in line. They said, Nicky, you learn the restaurant business, so Nicky learned the restaurant business. Everything. How to run the kitchen, the bar, how to buy the booze and the groceries, how to carefully screen for waiters and washroom attendants and bartenders. How to study a busy bar and be able to tell the hookers from the schoolteachers, and that isn't always easy. And like I told you last night, how not to skim too much and how not to skim too little."

"And so soon you may have Cuba in your back pocket."

"That's bullshit, too. It won't happen. I play life by ear."

189

"Okay, Nick. Okay. Tell me, did you know if the girls had any talent?"

"'Any' talent is what they had. Enough to pass an audition. But like too many rock stars and country-and-western singers today, they'd serve the public better by slinging hash. I consider you one of the smart ones, Pharoah. This is the age of mediocrity. This is a world where a nothing like Madonna can make millions by standing in a spotlight and grabbing her crotch."

He paused to light a cigarette while Pharoah wondered who was the villain who had caused Suggi to sour on the world. Who was it who'd made him sour on himself? Who had molested his soul and left a wound so deep it refused to heal? A stunning hunk of man withering on the vine called La Fontana. What a waste.

Pharoah asked Suggi, "That night at the Capri, I assume you caught the girls' act."

"Oh, yeah, it came with the dinner, along with the finger bowls. You could figure out the routine for yourself; you've seen it often enough. Entrance in stunning knee-length, blazing red dresses into which they'd had to be sewn. A couple of rock numbers, on-key, amazingly enough. Then a lightning change into Alice-blue ankle-length gowns and a medley of golden oldies. Then another fast change into top hats, tuxedo jackets, and white satin shorts that just about cover the crotch and into a sexy rendition of 'Puttin' on the Ritz,' followed by some more or less fancy footwork. Then milk the applause for three curtains and then off and good-bye. Same routine they did at the Fountain of Youth benefit."

"You were there, too?"

"There's some law against it?"

"You don't strike me as the Fountain of Youth type."

"I'm not. A friend invited me." He smiled. "I like fruit, Pharoah. But only what grows on trees and bushes."

Pharoah's fingers drummed lightly on the table. "I think you've answered one son of a bitch that's chewing away at me."

"What's that?"

"Why waste the twins? Having gangbanged and beaten them up, why send them to a watery grave? Why not just pay them off, buy their silence? It's done all the time."

"I agree with you. Marco could have convinced Rita that the girls were the victims of a—ha, ha—boyish prank. Rita'd be too smart not to cooperate." Pharoah stared past Suggi at nothing in particular, briefly deep in thought, giving Suggi an opportunity to study the detective. He wondered if he might be a closet heterosexual. Or maybe he was a switch hitter, batting both ways. He'd seen Natalya giving him the once-over the previous evening, and he knew Pharoah had been aware of the scrutiny and had played it very cool. At the same time, he caught Pharoah casting subtle glances at himself, and whereas that sort of thing usually made him uncomfortable, coming from Pharoah, he found it flattering. Now their eyes met.

Pharoah said, "A penny for them."

"Still thinking about the twins," Suggi lied.

"So was I. I think that night somebody sober pleaded with the twins to play nice and cooperate and maybe someday they'd own Cuba. And the twins were in no condition to accept any kind of terms. No, they were going to tell Rita what happened, and Rita is no lady to trifle with."

"You're probably right. Those were two tough kids, real

tough. One of those convent teachers must have been a diesel dyke who fancied them and taught them a lot of street smarts."

Pharoah laughed a soft, cynical laugh. "How many faces did the twins have? And why should I give a damn? They were murdered, and now the ripple effect is killing a lot of others. And whether they were nice guys or villains, I've got to catch a killer because that's my job." He stood up. "Thanks, Nick. By the by, who's running the Fountain of Youth these days?"

"One of Marco's Hollywood imports. You might remember him from pictures years ago when he was a teenage pinup. Roger Hart. Remember the ads?"

"Yeah. 'Roger Hart Will Steal Your Heart.'"

"Nowadays he'll steal anything else he can get his hands on. I can tell you don't know he was also at the Capri that night."

"I know now. I'm sure he wasn't in on the orgy."

"What, and give him a heart attack? He was in the meeting with us. AIDS or no AIDS, Marco's looking for a way to expand his gay circuit. He wants to open more gay bars and restaurants, the way they proliferated twenty years ago when there was Regent's Row and the East Five Five."

"And the bird circuit," added Pharoah with a tinge of nostalgia in his voice. "Ah, the Blue Parrot." He sighed. "Nick, homosexuality ain't what it used to be."

The desk sergeant buzzed Walt MacIntyre. When the chief responded, the sergeant told him, "The prodigal has returned." Pharoah heard and offered the sergeant the erect middle finger of his right hand.

MacIntyre rasped, "We got a fetid calf we can kill?"

The sergeant hadn't the vaguest idea what MacIntyre was talking about and sought consolation in his copy of *Playboy* magazine.

Pharoah sauntered past Albert West's cubicle, poked his head in, and inquired sweetly, "Care to join the ladies? Into one big lady?" He stared at the striped jacket and the slacks. "Anyone for Tennyson?" He continued on to MacIntyre's office, followed by Albert West, who before leaving his office jettisoned the gum he'd been chewing into his wastepaper basket for fear Pharoah might make bawdy jest about chewing gum locked in the deep recesses of his subconscious, waiting for the opportune moment to be sprung.

Walt MacIntyre shoved his ham and cheese on white to one side as Pharoah entered, followed by Albert West. "Where the hell have you been?"

"Please, Chief, please don't be mean to me. You know I had a miserable childhood." He sank into a chair with his legs stretched out in front of him. "And finish your sandwich. You need your vitamins. Albert, don't hover over me like a bee about to feast on a wildflower. I've had a fruitful morning, no pun intended." Albert sat down, and he and MacIntyre were soon trapped in the web of words Pharoah began to spin. They learned about Robinson and a little about Edna and a lot about what Natalya had told him and then what he had learned from Nick Suggi, who Pharoah thought was a pretty nice guy.

"You falling in love again?" growled MacIntyre.

"What do you mean by 'again'? You haven't seen me in love in months, and I can't even remember the last one's name, only his precious mother's—Hepzibah, by Christ!" He smiled sweetly at Albert. "Remember, Albert, in the affairs of the heart I'm not to be trusted. In the bad old days, as the song goes, men gathered round me like moths around a flame. I used to be known as the Great Incinerator."

MacIntyre interrupted gruffly. "What next?"

"In no particular order, I think I should introduce myself to Roger Hart at the Fountain of Youth and ask for his autograph. I'd like to meet Adelaide Benarro and then at some point connect back with Rita and risk my life by telling her the sainted twins weren't wearing their halos properly."

"You know, just because Suggi fed you a line, you don't have to swallow it. After all, his comments about the girls could be the sour grapes of a spurned suitor."

"Come to think of it, Suggi did say he liked what grew on trees and vines, but he didn't strike me as the type with a taste for sour grapes. Remember, Chief," Pharoah cautioned while wagging an index finger, "there's good and bad in all of us. I've got a feeling he's made a good call on the twins. Their not-so-still waters probably ran very deep, which led to their ending up in deep waters. What I've been wondering is, could Marco have called the shots on their final fade-out, and if he did, will this really be Italian grand opera?"

Pharoah suddenly decided to lift the veil on the information he'd been holding back. He told MacIntyre and West that the twins were Rita's bastards and that Marco was the father and ignorant of the fact that he was. And then he added, "Rita never wants Marco to know."

"And whatever Rita wants, Rita gets." MacIntyre had gone

back to his sandwich, chewing with disinterest. "Got any comments, Albert?"

"Well, I enjoy juicy gossip along with everybody else, but what's the parentage of the twins got to do with who's commiting these murders?"

"Albert?" asked Pharoah, "When you sang in the Sunday school choir, were you a high tenor?"

Albert replied stiffly, "I didn't sing in a choir. I didn't attend Sunday school. I preferred playing baseball with my gang." Pharoah waited for him to append, "So there!," but it wasn't forthcoming.

MacIntyre interrupted impatiently. "Pharoah, you think Marco's got serious financial problems?"

"When are financial problems not serious? He's got to be in some sort of trouble if he's forming networks with the Russians and Weeping Willie. Tonight he's wining and dining in Chinatown, and they're a real skuzzy bunch, those Chinese."

"I'm wondering if Marco isn't pulling a fast one on us." MacIntyre and Pharoah were eyeball to eyeball. "In the past, he's been pretty fast with the fast ones."

"You mean, is he killing off his own soldiers and sending us off on a wild-goose chase."

"It's a possibility."

"With Marco, anything's a possibility," Pharoah agreed. "But I don't see him ordering the mass murder of his shooters. And I believe Natalya when she's says he's hurting bad in the employee department. A good young gangster is real hard to find these days. The potentials are doing better in the movies and in politics. Look at all them punk actors with names ending in vowels. They're cleaning up, and I can't tell them apart without a scorecard. No, Marco's worried. I know him too well to know when he's faking. He and I haven't discussed this, but I think he's frightened that once the killer finishes mopping up the orgy boys, he'll come after the person inadvertently responsible for what happened to the twins, and that's Marco."

Pharoah was walking back and forth, hands in his trouser pockets and jingling coins to Albert's annoyance. "This killer's a dark-horse entry. He's got an ax of his own to grind, and the girls are exclusive to him. I also think Rita knows more than she's been telling me."

"I thought she was a special friend of yours."

"She is, but since when do friends have to be on the level with each other? I killed one of mine yesterday."

"So he needed to be killed. Herbie Marks was a no-good rat fink, and don't you look at me like that. If he hadn't been an old friend, would you have thought twice about icing him? Like hell you would. Herbie Marks! Marco Salino! And you! How did you escape?"

"I had a mother and a grandmother who cared. I wish you played the violin, Albert. About now, 'Hearts and Flowers' would be appropriate."

Albert said in a voice that could curdle milk, "If I played the violin, I certainly wouldn't bring it to work with me."

Pharoah sat down in defeat. He looked at his wristwatch. "Okay, Albert. Time to prove we're worth the shameful pittance we're earning. Let us requisition an unmarked car and seek sustenance at the Fountain of Youth."

"That gay bar?"

"Albert, do I hear the sound of blood draining from your face?"

Albert repeated. "A gay bar? In the afternoon?"

"Albert, have you never had a matinee? Have you been brought up with the belief that sex is only to occur in the dark, behind a locked door, and restricted preferably to Saturday nights? Gays don't keep union hours. They don't because they don't have a union. And they don't have a union because they never go on strike. They seek partners whenever the hunger strikes, which nowadays is too damned often, with too many damn fools thinking AIDS is what happens to everybody else. Oh, well. Off the soapbox, Pharoah, and follow the yellow prick road to the Fountain of Youth. Come, Albert. This is your baptism of fire."

"Pharoah!" barked MacIntyre.

"What?"

"Keep in constant touch!"

In the car, with Albert at the wheel, heading across town toward Third Avenue, Pharoah bemoaned the vicissitudes of trying to make rapid progress on a crosstown street. They were moving at a bit better than a snail's pace, and Pharoah was smoldering with impatience.

"Can't we try some other street?"

"Such as?"

"Maybe Thirty-fourth."

"How about Ocean Avenue?"

"That's in Brooklyn!"

"I know. But it doesn't get much traffic."

"Why, Albert, I had no idea you had some sass in you."

"There's a lot in me that you don't know about, Pharoah. You're too busy being eccentric to notice much of anything in anybody unless they can answer some questions pertaining to a murder."

"Okay, Albert, you've made your point. I consider my hand slapped." They crept along in silence for a while. "I'd be interested in hearing your theories, Albert. I assume you've got some."

"I've got some," he said without taking his eyes off the car ahead of him, which he thought was too close. "I agree with you. The victims aren't the targets of anyone connected with the family or the other gangs. This is strictly personal. Someone who had a passion for one or both of the twins."

"That's our strongest possibility. I'm with you on that. There's Nicholas Suggi. And Yoyo the clown. And maybe even Gino Vinelli a.k.a. Carl Turner. Most male whores are switch hitters. In fact, most whores are positively bisexual. You got to be, to be a good whore, a good, all-purpose whore." He paused and then said, "Juana Gomez, I'm sure, is clapping her hands with glee when there's another pair of murders. And I repeat, Rita has to know more than she's told me."

"What about Emmanuel Robinson?"

"Emmanuel Robinson in the role of murderer?" He smiled. "What perfectly awful casting."

"That's what they said about Ronald Reagan in the role of president of the United States."

"You're right. But still, Manny Robinson isn't the killer type. You know, it's funny." Pharoah was staring out the window at the Third Avenue shop fronts. Albert had finally made it out of crosstown traffic, and they were now heading south to East Fourteenth Street. "Something's been nagging at me about this killer. The feeling that he's right under my nose but too close for me to recognize him. Maybe Suggi. Maybe Yoyo. Now I'd like to know what he really looks like."

"Why don't we tackle him, hold him down and wash his face."

"You may be kidding, but I'm really tempted. He seems nice enough. He's no puzzle like the Grey Ghost. The Grey Ghost doesn't fit in anywhere. Those twitches, the filth that pours from his mouth. My heart goes out to him. You know, there but for the grace of God go I. And there but for the grace of God is the Fountain of Youth. Now to find a parking space."

Five minutes later, they were inside. Two middle-aged men at the bar were brawling, a waiter and the bartender trying to pull them apart.

"Good heavens," said Pharoah, "Fistfight at the All-Gay Corral."

Pharoah and Albert stood to one side as the men were ejected, presumably to continue their fracas outdoors. The waiter, a muscular man in his twenties, smoothed back his hair and said to Pharoah deadpan, "We usually book a better class of act." From somewhere in the back of the room they heard the start of a medley of show tunes played on a piano. A surprisingly pleasant tenor voice started singing "I've Got You Under My Skin."

The bartender, probably the only male in the place with a broken nose, asked pleasantly, "Gentlemen? What can I do for you?"

"I'd like a Heineken," Pharoah said. Albert signaled with

his fingers to make it two. They sat on comfortable leather stools, and Albert looked about the room. At the far end was a stage. The curtain was drawn, and there were movie-star names embroidered on it. Although the room wasn't bright with lights, Albert recognized the identities of the oversized photographs on the wall. There was Bette Davis and Joan Crawford. Mae West and Marilyn Monroe. Judy Garland and Barbra Streisand. In an attempt to appeal to more selective tastes, there were, in various forms of undress, Arnold Schwarzenegger, Tom Cruise, the late Bruce Lee, a variety of black actors, and an eclectic selection of athletes of the past and the present. Near the stage was a small space for dancing. The walls featured booths, and from the stage to the entrance there were tables covered with red checkered cloths. On each was a small, thin vase with fresh cut flowers.

"The food used to be pretty good here," Pharoah told Albert.

"Still is," the bartender told him as he returned with two bottles of beer and two glasses. "Shall I pour, or do you prefer to suck?"

"Don't be vulgar," said Pharoah good-naturedly. "Pour for my friend. He has a college degree."

Albert glared at him. "I'll drink from the bottle. It's more manly."

"Touché." Pharoah smiled at the bartender. "You look as though we might have met in another life."

"We met right here, a lot of years ago. You're the fuzz, the would-be comedian born on the wrong side of the cracks."

Pharoah explained to Albert. "I used to drink a lot before my nervous breakdown, which was brought about by a nervous breakup. I was thinking then of doing stand-up comedy."

"Actually," the bartender told Albert, "he wasn't too bad."

"Did I make you laugh?"

"A couple of times, I remember."

Albert was dwelling on Pharoah's nervous breakdown. Pharoah, the man of steel, a nervous breakdown? When was he ever that vulnerable? Brought about by a "nervous breakup"? A lover? Maybe a narcotics ring, maybe a murder like that of Herbie Marks. Pharoah tapped him lightly on the arm.

"Albert, my breakdown was purely psychological. Too much pressure on the brain from the sneers and jeers and snide remarks of my fellow officers. They didn't think black and gay was beautiful. Walt MacIntyre saved my sanity and my life. He brought me back out of the dungeon. That's one of the more important reasons why I love him."

"I didn't know you were a mind reader," Albert said, beginning to see Pharoah in a different light.

"And you didn't know I was only human. Let it rest. Someday I'll tell you about it if you think it's still important."

The singer was now into a golden oldie favored by club singers of the forties, "It's a Big Wide Wonderful World."

"Nancy Noland used to sing that one. I've got a recording, a seventy-eight. I wish I'd been born then. So many club singers I'd like to have seen in person. Noland, Jimmy Daniels, Mae Barnes. Oh, well. I also missed out on Abraham Lincoln." The room was beginning to fill up. It was getting toward the happy hour, drinks half price and free hors d'oeuvres. "Who's the tenor?" Pharoah asked the bartender.

"The boss. Remember Roger Hart in the movies?"

"Roger Hart!" Pharoah exclaimed with exaggeration. "You mean Roger Hart who'll steal my heart?" he said with a feigned archness that made Albert uncomfortable. "Those divine dimples and that adorable cleft in his chin."

"He's older now," warned the bartender.

"I refuse to be disillusioned. To me he'll always be the drop-dead, brick-shithouse dreamboat of every boy and every girl in the world."

"Stop futzing around, Pharoah," said the bartender. "He's already been told there's fuzz on the premises. You got anything special you want him to sing?"

"Why, yes, I do," said Pharoah affably. "That's exactly why we're here."

chapter

Roger Hart's fingers seemed to be floating over the eighty-eights, the fingers operating like delicately tooled precision instruments. The grand piano extended into a long bar with stools. In the center of the bar was a service area with shelves of liquors and liqueurs. Glasses of all sizes hung from a wooden rack that was suspended from the ceiling, very European in style. Pharoah and Albert found two empty stools next to the piano. This afforded Pharoah a better look at Roger Hart and what survived of his former movie-star looks.

The skin was sallow. The cheeks were sunken about as far as they could sink. The eyes were lifeless. His jacket was at least a size too large. Under the jacket he wore a T-shirt on which was stenciled "Abandon Hope All Ye Who Enter Here." On his upper lip there was a wisp of a mustache that blended into a neatly trimmed beard. Pharoah wondered about Hart's prognosis, how soon the AIDS would send him into a hospital and from there a crematorium. Hart hit a high note and held it, signifying the end of the song. He nodded at the smattering of applause while a drunken young man started singing "The Star-Spangled Banner." At this moment, Roger Hart's eyes met Pharoah's.

"They don't write them like that anymore," said Pharoah wryly. Roger Hart smiled. The second bartender, amusingly enough, was a rather pretty young woman wearing a jockey cap and a tank top that did nothing for her flat chest. She was speaking to a tall, severe-looking woman who seemed to be averse to talking. Her mouth was tight and prim. Her lips were thinner than Kenneth Branagh's. Her broad shoulders would put an outfielder to shame, and a monocle in her right eye added to the bizarre picture. Roger Hart was tackling "Getting to Know You," and Pharoah wondered if it was an invitation. Albert's bottle was empty, and Pharoah tried to catch the pretty bartender's eye. After a few futile minutes, Albert spoke sharply. "Could we have two more beers here, please?"

She turned slowly. She then leaned back against the bar, propping herself up with her elbows. The look on her face prompted Pharoah to wonder if she was thinking of challenging Albert to a hand-wrestling contest. The woman behind her wore a smartly tailored suit and man's shirt and Sulka tie. She was using the tie to polish the monocle while eyeing Albert and Pharoah. Pharoah was thinking that if she lunged at him, he'd beat her to a pulp. Roger Hart was singing directly at the bartender with anger in his eyes. She turned to look at him and with a sharp gesture of his head indicated she serve the beers or else.

Hart stopped singing but continued playing.

He said to Pharoah, "Her name is Vicki."

"Short for Victor?" asked Pharoah. Vicki glared at him. Pharoah was not about to let up. "Your buddy dislikes me intensely. If looks could kill, I'd soon be on display in a mortuary."

Vicki spoke, a rasping voice. "She's the strong, silent type."

"She better not pull any funny stuff. I could beat her up with one hand tied behind my back."

"You're not funny," rasped Vicki.

"No," said Pharoah, "us detectives rarely are."

Vicki shot a quick, unsubtle look at Roger Hart. Unruffled, he segued into "Time on My Hands" and crooned the words sweetly. A young man sat next to Vicki's girlfriend, his right wrist sporting a plaster cast. Pharoah whispered to Albert, "Must have been waving good-bye to someone." The young man ordered a brandy alexander; Pharoah was surprised bartenders still mixed them.

"Well, Mr. Detective, how can we help you?" Hart had stopped playing, and his hands were folded primly in his lap. Nothing about Hart had aged well. Not the face, not the body, not the voice. But with his head cocked to one side as he waited for Pharoah to respond, he almost succeeded in conjuring up a memory of his once-charming, delightfully boyish self.

"My name is Pharoah Love."

"Ah!" said Hart, "the legend himself. And your associate?"

"Albert West, rumored to be the bastard son of another legend, Mae West."

"Mae was a dear friend of mine. I used to go up and see her sometime."

"I'm a dear friend of Marco Salino."

"Indeed? How dear?"

"Dear enough to be trying to find who's murdering his soldiers."

"They're no great loss. There wasn't a single one who had any charisma."

"I understand you were at the Hotel Capri the night the Chic Twins were assaulted and murdered."

Hart said sadly, "Such dear girls."

"I suppose it's silly to conjecture you took part in the orgy."

Hart tittered. "Too, too silly, darling, too, too silly. I was in conference with Marco and his clones. A discussion about expanding his gay-club operation. Marco is very ambitious. Too ambitious. I reminded him that one of his possible ancestors, Julius Caesar by name, was also too ambitious and so got tickled to death by a plethora of stab wounds. All that remains to honor and remember him, of course, is the Caesar salad."

"How'd a nice young star like you get mixed up with the Mafia?"

"Just plain lucky." He played a few chords. "Oh, good heavens, what a delicious thought I'm entertaining. You don't think *I'm* the murderer, do you?"

"No, not because you aren't capable of it but because you've probably got a solid alibi with this piano."

"Absolutely right." He played a few riffs and then drifted into "Smoke Gets in Your Eyes." "Adelaide Benarro. I'm sure you've heard of her."

"All this morning at Emmanuel Robinson's."

"Oh, Gahhhhhd, that *impossible* man. Don't tell me you're a friend of *his*."

"No, I'm acquainted with some of his clients."

"He tried to lure me into his fold, but I convinced him he'd get nowhere with an old has-been. After all, there's no more Ed Sullivan TV show to take up the slack."

"Don't be so hard on yourself."

"I'm not, I'm just being realistic. There's no place for pretty boys who are no longer pretty except in a joint like this. Adelaide and her husband were old friends from the days back in the ice age when I played Vegas. When I came to New York a couple of years ago, or probably more, I was so low on money and energy, vultures were circling overhead. The Benarros to the rescue. They introduced me to Marco Salino—of course, this was long before some villain cleaned the wax out of Salvatore's ear with an ice pick. Marco used to be star struck, or something like it. The very idea of having Roger Hart playing at the Fountain of Youth was just too much for him to contemplate. When I said I'd be delighted to do it, he almost swooned at my feet. Then his manager was deep-sixed for robbing the till too much, and when Marco asked if I'd like to take over, I just swooped at the opportunity. Now he's in a rush to make the most of me before I depart for that immense gay bar in the sky. Rock Hudson promised he'd reserve a stool for me. Dear Roy—that was his real name. There are so many precious friends there awaiting my arrival, impatiently, I'm sure. By the time I get there, I'll be a fresh face. You know, hi, guys, new girl in town. What do I call you? Pharoah or Love?"

"Call me anything as long as it isn't insulting."

"Your Mr. West doesn't say much."

"He's the big, strong, silent type." Vicki the bartender flashed him a dirty look, and Pharoah responded with a wink.

Albert reached past the young man on his right who was too shy to admit that within moments he had fallen madly in love with Albert, and commandeered a bowl of peanuts.

"Excuse my reach," said Albert.

"You didn't have to reach for them," said the young man in a subdued voice. "I'd have been glad to have been of service." Albert missed the innuendo completely and contented himself with selecting a peanut with the care and intensity of a kept woman turned loose at a tray of diamonds in Tiffany's.

"I'm ever grateful to the Benarros," said Hart. "Addie is such a dear friend. Salvatore was such a dear friend. Poor dear Michael was a dear friend. He wrote such dear little ditties." He paused as he concentrated on "Remember My Forgotten Man." "If I had met Paul, I'm sure he'd also be a dear, dear friend. I'm so good with dear, dear friends. I used to be up to my ass in them until Hollywood dumped me."

"Who's Paul?" asked Pharoah.

"What was that, dear?"

"Who's Paul. You brought the name in from somewhere in left field."

"Addie's oldest. Her son. Michael's older brother."

"Where's Paul?"

"Around somewhere, I suppose. Addie rarely mentions him." Pharoah wondered if there was a space reserved for this Benarro son, Paul, in the murder case, a space waiting to be assigned by Pharoah.

Pharoah turned to Albert. "Don't feel ignored, Albert. I'm not into an easy chat with this former star. I'm wading my way through it, and I wish I was wearing hip boots. You hearing much of it?"

"I've been hearing all of it. So do you think Paul fits into this somewhere or he's just another irritating red herring."

"Don't be so quick to dismiss red herrings. Sometimes they can be very tasteful when fresh. Must you hog the peanuts?" Albert shoved the bowl to him. Pharoah selected a few and munched contentedly.

Roger Hart asked Pharoah, "Is there anything special you'd like to hear?"

"Yeah. Who's murdering Marco's soldiers?"

"Ha, ha, ha. Thank *God* I don't know. I've met very few of them. From time to time Marco sends one down here to hang around and check up on me, and of course I've met the collectors."

"What collectors? Garbage collectors?"

"Proceeds collectors, the receipts."

"How come you don't bank those?"

"Dear Pharoah. As Vivien Leigh said to Lucile Watson in dear *Waterloo Bridge* when dear Lucile asked dear Vivien, who'd been turning tricks not because she was passionate but simply because there was cash in it, 'Don't be so naive.' I'm talking about tax evasion, Pharoah Love. And if Marco hears I've said that, he'd cut my tongue in two."

"You'd have plenty left."

Roger Hart smiled. "Dear Pharoah, we should have met a long time ago. I just know we would have been dear, dear friends."

"We could still be dear, dear friends."

"Oh, no, dear Pharoah. There's very little time left. Time is running out. The sand is drifting to the bottom of the hourglass. Which is why I'm perfectly willing to chatter away with you. I'm flying on a trapeze without a safety net under me. I'm talking too much, I know, but I doubt if Marco will make me walk the plank. Why bother. I know I've overstayed my remission. Every morning when I look in the mirror I ask, 'What, my dear, you still here?' I can remember the days when I'd ask my mirror, 'Who's the fairest one of all?' but I don't dare nowadays. I'm a fucking wreck, and if there really is a God, why the hell doesn't he come around with my one-way ticket."

"I repeat, don't be so hard on yourself. You in the mood to talk about the twins?"

"I'm in the mood to talk about anything. Vicki!"

"*What?*"

"A lot of vodka on a lot of rocks and leave out the garbage." He asked Pharoah, "You recognize the diesel she's talking to?"

Pharoah glanced again at the woman with the monocle but heard no bell ring. "No bell rings."

"The alimony killer. She's the one who married a series of old men. Don't you remember? About thirty years ago."

"I was just a kid then."

"She got them to sign over their insurance to her, and then she eighty-sixed them. She got paroled about a year ago. So much for penal systems. She's in here buying Vicki, and believe me, that little monster's no bargain."

Since Pharoah wasn't interested in Vicki unless there was a chance she was the murderer he wanted, he persevered. "Let's talk about the twins."

"Two pretty nothings. They did a benefit for Addie here before they turned up in the Catskills at the Capri. Lots of flesh, not enough flash. Their voices were strictly Mickey and Minnie Mouse. They danced like ambitious amputees."

"You are not at all kind, Roger Hart."

Hart's voice steeled. "They were not nice people. We had a terrific crowd at the benefit, but those two bitches were mean and nasty about the boys. Not everybody who patronizes this place is couth. You know how raucous the boys can get when they have had too much drink and too much rejection, but they were on their best behavior that night. And I might add, they were damned generous to the twins. Nobody threw pennies!"

"Well!" said Pharoah, "What restraint that must have taken!"

Roger's fingers were caressing "Wait Till You See Her." "And yet I'm sorry they were treated so brutally. Nobody deserves to die the death they did."

"Got any bitchy ideas about who might be killing Marco's boys?"

"Well, let me tell you, if a murderer hadn't done them in, they'd have OD'd on garlic. You know, there was a bit of lavender among Marco's old lace. I've seen some of his soldiers, as you're so butch to refer to them, do some negotiating in this place. Gino Vinelli had at least two of them, on his strings. Have you met Gino?"

"Several times. Rita Genari's a . . . dear friend of mine."

"Oh, she is a dear, isn't she. She wanted me to do a guest appearance at one of her celebrity nights, but I begged off. The disease. Not fair. I hope you're using condoms, Pharoah. The lambskin ones. They're the safest." He stared past Pharoah to Albert. "What about whatsisname?"

"Albert."

"Whatever. Does he use condoms?"

"He's straight."

"His secret shall die with me. Make sure he uses condoms."
Pharoah turned to West. "Albert?"

"What?"

"Do you use condoms?"

"When?"

"When you eat pickles. What cloud you on, Albert?"

"Well, actually, Pharoah," said Albert, lowering his voice
and his head conspiratorially, "it's the conversation going on
between the two guys in leather on my right. They're talking
about doing a porn version of *Tom Sawyer*, and it's positively
appalling! I mean, to do to a classic like what they're planning
to do." Pharoah didn't want to be away from Roger Hart for
too long. There were still questions he wanted to ask. "Can
you imagine Tom and Huck as lovers and what Indian Joe
does to them in the cave when he traps them there."

"It's Injun' Joe, not Indian Joe. Eavesdrop for the rest of it.
I'm fascinated." He returned his attention to Roger Hart, who
had a forlorn expression on his face. "What hurts, Roger?"

"I thought you had abandoned me," he said coquettishly.

Pharoah smiled. He liked Roger Hart. "Roger, it *would* have
been nice if we had met a long time ago."

"Oh, yes, dear," said Roger, now playing "Where or When,"
"it might have been very nice. Except maybe now you'd also
be in remission. Now where were we?" He freed one hand to
sip some vodka.

"The twins. Addie Benarro. Rita. Marco. Soldiers. Murder.
Addie's sons."

"You should have known Salvatore."

"Why?"

"Believe it or not, he was an honest man. Addie says that's why they killed him."

"Who is 'they'?"

Hart said with irony, "His pals." The bar was getting crowded, and Pharoah marveled at how Roger Hart played the piano, conversed with Pharoah, and kept a watchful eye on Vicki the bartender. He was a damned good manager and a damned nice person, and what a pity he was damned. "You should talk to Addie."

"I plan to."

"A great gal. Contrary to what people claimed, she really loved her husband. You know, she was born into Philadelphia society."

"Is that as good as Passaic society?"

"My ancestors came over on the Oakland ferry. Addie's been through hell, but she's weathered it well. Salvatore's murder followed by Michael's death. I was at Michael's funeral."

"Was Paul?"

"I don't know. I told you I never met Paul."

"Wouldn't he have been at his bereaved mother's side?"

"Marco and Rita were at the bereaved mother's side."

"They were such good friends?"

"Marco and Salvatore had a deal going together. Rita and Adelaide go a long way back. I sometimes suspect Addie helped Rita get some of her bankroll for her house. Paradise indeed. More likely Paradise Lost."

"Why did I think Marco was her bankroll?"

"Him, too. It's possible. You're looking at your wristwatch. You're leaving. Oh, Pharoah. What will I do without you?"

Pharoah said, "I'll be back. I promise."

"Don't wait too long. There's so little time."

"You might be one of the lucky ones with more time than you realize. Maybe you've banked a little extra."

"From your mouth to God's ears." He smiled at Albert. "*Arrivederci* . . . or is it *ciao*? Oh, the hell with it. *Adieu*, er . . . um . . . "

"Albert West," said Albert.

"You must forgive me, dear. I've always had trouble with names. Even at the height of my celebrity I always referred to Clark Gable as 'Hey, you.' On my way down I was reprieved briefly as master of ceremonies at a political bash, and I had to introduce Zbigniew Brzezinski. By the time I got the name straight, I had to be taken to a sanatorium to recuperate." He sipped more vodka. He played "Lover" as he watched the detectives leave.

Pharoah turned and waved at Roger Hart.

Hart's fingers froze on the keys. That gesture. That wave of the hand. How sweet. How touching. How generous. His eyes misted. Too late, he told himself. It's much too late for love at first sight. He emptied the glass of the remaining vodka in one swig and then aborted "Lover" for "If I Loved You."

Vicki said, "I don't like that black dick."

Roger Hart snapped, "What the hell do you know about dicks, you silly twat!"

chapter

16

On the street, Pharoah stared up at the neon sign that modestly proclaimed the interior of the premises as the Fountain of Youth. "You know, Albert, years ago, when I finally got up the courage to taste the forbidden fruits of the Fountain, there used to be a line stretching from the doorway to the end of the block, and it sometimes snaked around. There were three beefy bouncers to keep the line in check. Nice guys when you got to know them. Friday and Saturday nights there was an admission charge. It used to get raided every so often before the family bought the original owners out and made some under-the-table financial peace with us."

He waved a hand with disdain. "Ah, the hell with it. It's all gone. The only thing that's the same is murder, and our plate's piled high."

"Who's next?"

"Addie Benarro." He fished in his inside jacket pocket for his wallet. "Emmanuel Robinson gave me her phone number and her address." He found the slip of paper. "I see a phone in the coffee shop next door. Let's grab some java and I'll phone her."

Adelaide Benarro and three of her personal maids were in her suite busy polishing her jewels when the butler entered to announce there was a detective Pharoah Love on the phone wishing to speak to her.

"Thank you, Fraught." Adelaide arose from the table and sauntered slowly across the room to a desk where a multibuttoned phone extension reposed. A tiny red light flickered above one of the buttons. Adelaide took a moment to tighten a loosening emerald earring and examined herself in a silver-framed mirror above the desk. She was immensely pleased with her reflection. Her hennaed hair was artfully arranged in one of Mr. Rebecca's most spectacular yet tasteful arrangements. There wasn't a line on her alabaster face thanks to her most recent face-lift. True, her surgeon had cautioned her to treat this latest lift with care, as another one might result in her ears on the top of her head. Her retroussé nose was as artificial as her eyelashes, which, when fluttered, were in danger of causing her severe cheek damage.

Her negligee was trimmed with ostrich feathers, and she decided to change into something less frivolous should Pharoah Love request an immediate audience. She'd been interviewed by detectives before and had come to realize that simplicity in appearance was an asset. Therefore, she would jettison about five of her spectacular bracelets. She would scuttle all the rings on her left hand except for her wedding band and the magnificent engagement ring that had been her late husband's first great extravagance. Yes, she would provide Pharoah with a splendid and tasteful performance the way she had dazzled club audiences when she sang as Adelaide Gibson.

She looked at her wristwatch. She mustn't overdo keeping Pharoah waiting. She picked up the phone. Her voice was pure whipped cream. "Mr. Love, do forgive me for keeping you waiting. I was seeing dear Jackie Onassis to the door." The maids exchanged glances while Adelaide sat on the desk chair.

Pharoah couldn't help but wonder how many times a week Mrs. Benarro showed Jackie O. to the door for the benefit of a telephone caller, but he was too anxious to get to his coffee and then to Mrs. Benarro. He said, "Oh, I'm sorry I missed her. We've had lunch a few times at Mortimer's."

Adelaide ignored the one-upmanship. "What is this in reference to, Detective Love?" He knew she knew, but he told her again.

"Robinson gave me your phone number. Emmanuel Robinson."

"Yes, of course. He provided many of the performers for my AIDS benefit, a memorial, in a sense, to my darling son Michael. Very energetic man, Mr. Robinson. He's such a breath of stale air." Pharoah thought he might learn to love her. "I'd certainly like to cooperate with you. I'm not sure how, but we could give it the old college try, couldn't we?"

"I like your spirit, Mrs. Benarro."

"I hope I'll like yours."

"You could give it the old college try. Muskegee."

217

She hadn't the vaguest idea what Muskegee alluded to and sought no elucidation from him for fear of exposing an area of ignorance. "You have my address? Oh, fine. How's about in half an hour or so?"

Pharoah joined Albert in a booth. "In half an hour we meet Adelaide Benarro." He forked some of the blueberry pie he asked Albert to order for him. Albert was chewing on his already. "How's the pie?"

"Tastes like shit."

Pharoah tasted it. "You're right. But what have they done with it?" He pushed the plate aside and sipped coffee. "What hath God wrought?" he groaned. "This must have been filtered through a dishrag." He leaned back. "Funny about the twins."

"Funny how?"

"From Rita and Juana's end of the pole they were deserving of beatification. From everybody else's end of the pole they were bitches on wheels."

"Rita and Juana are prejudiced."

"I don't think the twins ever let them see the side of them seen by the others. But there must have been some kind of magic that made guys fall for them."

"There's no accounting for tastes."

"Too true. When I saw Rita's pretty good portrait of them, I found myself falling under a spell."

"Gee whiz, Pharoah. Don't tell me you also go for women."

"I go for them, but not all the way." He folded his arms on the table. "Roger Hart has left me feeling very sad."

"You were very kind to him."

"Are you scolding me or complimenting me?"

"I never scold. I sometimes nag, but I never scold."

"A few light-years in the past he'd have been my type. Now he's just a stereotype. Poor bastard." Then he sighed. "What the hell. He had a pretty good run as a star. He lasted longer then most. Probably pissed away a small fortune, though back then they got paid nowhere near the kind of dough they command today."

"The money was worth more in those days. Joan Crawford didn't die broke."

"Bette Davis did. I read that somewhere. How do you know Joan Crawford didn't die broke?"

"I read that somewhere. In a book about last wills. It claimed Tallulah Bankhead left ten million dollars. Do you believe that?"

"Albert, let's stop farting around and prepare ourselves for Adelaide Benarro, who I have a feeling is one of the last of our home-grown empresses. I want to try and learn more about this mysterious older son."

"Paul."

"Yeah. Paul. Why he's been exiled to the background."

Albert thought, then suggested, "Maybe he was the black sheep of the family."

Pharoah snorted. "In Mafia families, there are *only* black sheep."

Albert said, "Maybe Paul opted for exile. Maybe he was a nice guy with more Philadelphia than Sicily in his veins and rejected the opportunity to be a soldier or a lieutenant."

"That should have been Michael," said Pharoah.

"No, Michael was Mama's baby. Soft, delicate, probably very cute, with something of a talent for composing songs." He was enjoying creating his composite of Michael Benarro from out of whole cloth. "We've both met the type before. Calls mother 'darling' and 'sweetie' and shops with her to make sure the dresses she buys are of the highest quality and in exquisite taste."

"And it's an asset if they wear the same size."

"I know you can't help yourself, Pharoah, but try not to be mean. I'm trying to paint a word picture of Michael to give us an idea of what he was like."

"Why don't we save time and ask Mama to show us some pictures of him. I'm sure she's got a rogue's gallery in his bedroom, which she's probably turned into a shrine. You know, everything in the room the way he left it on the day he died. Nothing's been moved except maybe his pile of *Playgirl* magazines. Not a bad job, Albert, not a bad job at all. What can you do with Paul?"

Albert contemplated a sign on the wall listing the daily specials. Just reading them started to give him indigestion.

"Well?" prodded Pharoah.

"Paul's not easy. Dark horses never are."

"Work on it. My money's on you." Albert leaned back and furrowed his brows. Pharoah sat up straight and folded his arms. Their waitress offered to bring them fresh cups of coffee, but Pharoah begged her not to.

Snotty *schwartze*, she thought, and waddled away.

Albert stared out the window. "Paul."

"You see him?"

"Trying to."

"Easy. Don't push it." Albert continued to stare out the window, his face a study in serious contemplation. Pharoah took the opportunity to study him. Albert West. Detective. A square in police circles. On the other hand, maybe not so much a square. Probably his homophobia was coloring Pharoah's assessment of the man. Albert wearing a jazzy sports jacket. It looks good on him, but is he comfortable in it?

His brows are furrowed. Albert's thinking hard. Trying to prove himself to impress Pharoah? But why should he give a damn what Pharoah thinks about him? Pharoah himself never gave a damn what anybody thought of him, except maybe Walt MacIntyre, his guardian angel. Self-appointed. Those years past, when Pharoah made detective, he was one of the few blacks assigned to the precinct, along with three other minority cops all Hispanics. The four suffered a lot of flak in the beginning, but it drew them together. The other three didn't like it when Pharoah named them "the *Mira* Gang," but they all proved to be so competent that they were eventually given grudging respect.

Then Pharoah decided to drop the bombshell and revealed his homosexuality. At first, when a brother detective entered the men's room and saw Pharoah, brother detective would position himself several urinals away. Pharoah only laughed. Next Pharoah acquired the famous earring and grew the ponytail. Then his clothing became more eccentric and outrageous, and he made his name solving three tough ones in a row. His picture was in the newspapers. He was becoming a living legend. Pharoah love it. There was a time when TV wooed him. He was on the *Today* show and *Good Morning, America*, *60 Minutes* did a segment, and Barbara Walters asked him, "If you could be a tree, what kind of tree would you want to be?" To which Pharoah swiftied, "The kind that could kick dogs away."

It puzzled his fellow detectives when he made it clear he wanted no promotion. He loved it in the field, and he wanted to stay there and play in it. In his infrequent spare time he began to jot down notes about his police activities, and it was Walt MacIntyre who read and liked them and encouraged him to flesh them out into short stories. Pharoah remembered the first time he had stared at the blank sheet of paper in the typewriter. After several troubling minutes, he found the courage to type the first word:

"The."

Pharoah smiled. He had typed his first word. Now he was a writer. He took a nap. That first word had drained his creative energy. It was days later before he returned to the typewriter and found the courage to work in earnest. He was a one-finger, hunt-and-peck typist, but soon invisible wisps of smoke began to rise from the overheated machine, and Pharoah was absorbed in the fantastic experience of creation. When weeks later Pharoah typed "The End" and sat back staring at the collated pages, he was plagued with the misgiving that the world wasn't ready for a black detective who was gay and fought the temptation to call his chief "Wilhelmina."

"Paul."

"Got a line on him?" Albert intruded on his autobiographical reverie.

"He's a loner."

"No girlfriend?"

"No, because he's been too often disappointed in love.

He's a romantic, and as we both know, most of them are losers."

"What's the matter, Albert, not getting much lately?"

"Not looking for it. Let's stay with Paul."

"Sure, babe. How old's Paul?"

"I'd say three or four years older then Michael, which puts him at twenty-seven or twenty-eight."

"Do you think his father liked him?"

"I think he was a big disappointment to Salvatore. He didn't want to actively participate in family matters. Paul is something of an aesthete. He prefers museums to funeral parlors."

"Who doesn't?" Pharoah asked, aching for a cup of coffee but lacking the courage to experience another one in this hash house.

"I like funeral parlors," Albert said matter-of-factly.

"You're kidding."

"No. My father was an undertaker."

For the first time in a long time Pharoah was astonished. "How come you didn't follow in Daddy's footsteps?"

"I couldn't stomach the embalming. But the parlor and the viewing room were very peaceful, and Dad had music piped into them."

"Barry Manilow, Dolly Parton?"

"I said *music*," Albert stated flatly. "I read the obituaries every morning in the *New York Times*, but in the past couple of years they've gotten very dull. I mean, they're giving space to people who in my opinion should be sent on their way with as little fanfare as possible. You know, very dull and common-place when alive, equally dreary as obituaries."

"Albert, against my better judgment you're beginning to fascinate me. Back to Paul. Why do you suppose Adelaide doesn't mention him too often, if we're to believe Roger Hart?"

"I believe Roger Hart. He's a man who's made peace with himself." Albert smiled, and Pharoah realized it was the first time he had seen him smile. It was a slightly crooked smile, which, Pharoah saw, gave it character. "I could better guess what Adelaide's attitude is toward Paul once I meet her and do a little sizing up. Mothers are supposed to favor their first-born."

"No, it's usually the baby of the family that gets all the pampering. I was the baby of my family, and I got all the pampering. The oldest, my brother Imhotep, was an epileptic."

"Imhotep? Pharoah?"

"My sister, the middle child, was Cleopatra. My mother was hipped on Egyptology. Don't ask me how come. My father thought it was because he had taken her to see a palmist when they got engaged to be married and my mom was told that in another life she'd been an Egyptian sorceress. Nice people, my folks."

Pharoah was surprised to hear Albert say, "Someday I'd like to meet them."

"That's nice, Albert. But my family's dead. I'm the sole survivor. A car crash wiped them out. It was an Easter Sunday, and they were driving in from Canarsie for dinner with me. That was five years ago. Let's get back to Paul."

"Oh, yeah. Our new buddy Paul. Well, now, I don't think Michael liked him—or understood him. Paul probably was the handball-playing type who also went in for tennis and got off on all kinds of ball games. Michael probably played jacks and cut out paper dolls for which he designed dresses inspired by what he saw movie stars wearing. He loved show tunes and went to the ballet because to him ballet was the equivalent of a football game."

"Don't be mean."

"Pharoah, believe me, I have come across some Michaels in my time. I coped with several in high school and college."

"You didn't like them. You didn't try to like them."

"They made me nervous."

Pharoah stared at him and then smiled. "Do I make you nervous?"

"You don't make me nervous as long as you don't *try* to make me."

"Albert, you're perfectly safe. I'm the laziest gal in town. Does Paul have a girlfriend?"

"Like I said, he's been disappointed too often."

Pharoah shrugged. "So if at first you don't succeed, try, try again."

"I get the feeling Paul is more interested in love and affection than he is in the physical act of sex."

"Poor Paul. Do you suppose he's still a virgin?"

"I hope not."

"Why?"

"I'm beginning to like Paul."

"Oh, for crying out loud, let's get the hell out of here. We mustn't keep the Widow Benarro waiting." Pharoah paid the check, and ten minutes later they pulled up in front of Adelaide Benarro's magnificent town house.

"Will you look at this thing? It's a palace fit for the Borgias or the de' Medicis. I wouldn't be surprised if at least one ceiling was done by Michelangelo. I'm surprised it's not surrounded by a moat."

"Maybe it once was but it stagnated and the Board of Health gave them a summons and they decided to fill it in."

"Albert, I'm beginning to enjoy you immensely. Continue to amaze me. Do you suppose the doorbell is a genuine diamond?"

Albert put a police identification on the windshield. Pharoah crossed to the magnificently carved doors while Albert locked the car. There was an ordinary doorbell with a hidden light, and Pharoah felt a pang of disappointment. He pressed the bell and from within was delighted to hear chimes playing the opening bars of *The Godfather* theme. "Well, here we are, Albert. Showtime."

The door opened, and Pharoah looked at the butler. He was positive he had seen him before in a police lineup of suspected child molesters. "Yes?" asked Fraught. Pharoah felt another pang of disappointment. The "yes" had been politely drawn out, undoubtedly from years of practice, and it was undoubtedly British in origin. Well, so what? There's a lot of child molesting in Great Britain.

"Pharoah Love and Albert West to see Mrs. Benarro."

"Yes. You're expected. Please come in."

They entered a hall that almost knocked them back on their heels, so exquisitely and expensively decorated was it, with hangings, paintings, and various forms of statuary. Pharoah looked up to the ceiling, which was five stories high above them. He wasn't disappointed. There was a mural on the ceiling depicting the Last Supper. Pharoah wondered if by chance the artist had commandeered a number of Benarro's soldiers for models. Albert's eyes left the ceiling and found Pharoah's. They were delighted by what they had seen.

Fraught said, "Madame is in the first-floor sitting room. Do you care to walk up, or would you prefer the elevator?"

"The carpeting on the stairs looks pretty plush. Will our feet sink into it?"

"Depends on how heavy your tread is."

Pharoah asked, "If we walk up, is it okay if I come sliding back down on the hand railing?"

"If you wish. We are heavily insured."

Albert said, "Come on, Pharoah. Let's get on with it." Fraught, uninterested in playing games with Pharoah, started up the stairs, and the detectives dutifully followed. Pharoah and Albert recognized several of the masterpieces hanging on the walls.

Pharoah whispered to Albert, "Phonies?"

"I'm not a connoisseur, but I doubt it."

Fraught had overheard and told them politely, "Mrs. Benarro has developed a keen eye for fine art. She can be found at the auctions at Sotheby's and Christie's very often. These are but a small fraction of her acquisitions. On the top floor is a gallery that extends the length and width of the house. It is, of course, sophisticatedly wired against theft, as are these and all the others that can be found throughout the house."

"How many rooms in the palace?" asked Pharoah.

"I've never counted." Fraught reached the landing and indicated they follow him to the left. More thick carpets, more hangings, more masterpieces; the ceilings looked as though they had recently been freshly painted. He brought them to the first-floor sitting room, which was large enough to house an off-Broadway production. There was a grand piano with an elaborate candelabra that would have brought tears of envy to the late Liberace. As an afterthought, Pharoah wondered if it might have been bought from that AIDS victim's estate. Pharoah said to Albert, "An antiques dealer could go berserk in here."

Fraught said, "Two did. May I offer you some refreshment?"

"Is there coffee?" asked Pharoah.

"There's always coffee," Fraught informed them.

"Coffee, Albert?"

"Yes. Black." Fraught crossed to a stunning Louis XV table that almost stretched the length of a wall. Amid the various vases and decorative plates and framed autographed photos was a phone extension with numerous buttons. As Pharoah and Albert studied the framed photos, Fraught spoke in precise tones to the kitchen. In addition to the coffee, he requested tea, dainty, sliced cucumber sandwiches, miniature pastries, and deviled eggs.

Albert whispered to Pharoah, "Sounds like he's ordering a proper British tea."

"What's an improper British tea?"

"One that includes coffee."

"Well, I don't care for tea."

"All right, so we're getting coffee." He returned to the framed photos. "Quite a rogue's gallery. Imelda Marcos, Margaret Thatcher."

"For crying out loud!" exclaimed Pharoah, "Benito Mussolini."

Fraught had moved behind them. "He was a close friend of Madame's father-in-law."

Pharoah said, "I don't see Jackie Onassis," positive Fraught wouldn't sense that his tongue was in his cheek.

Fraught said without missing a beat, "Mrs. Onassis is having a new portrait sitting. She didn't like the one she'd given Madame earlier so Madame had it removed."

Albert was reading off other celebrity names, including several Italian movie stars who were no longer active in films either here or in Europe but whose names would remain ever green. There were the inevitable home-grown singing stars such as Sinatra, Damone, the McGuire Sisters, and others. Albert concluded, "Last but not least, a watercolor of Jesus Christ."

"Autographed?" Albert flashed Pharoah a look.

Fraught indicated the numerous uncomfortable-looking antique chairs and several sofas and invited the detectives to sit.

"Are they safe?" asked Pharoah.

"They've been reinforced," Fraught assured him.

Albert wasn't ready to sit. He was occupied with a huge painting that was hung over the fireplace. It was a portrait of three people. A beautiful titian-haired woman sat on what could very well, in better days, have been a throne. Her left arm was around a blond teenaged boy with a very weak face— or else the artist had a very weak touch. On her right stood a young man, obviously in his early twenties, looking away from the woman and the teenager, giving an impression of disinterest. Pharoah joined Albert and stood admiring it also. The artist's signature was unfamiliar to them.

Again Fraught enlightened them. "This is Madame and her sons. The blond one on the left is Michael, tragically deceased earlier this year."

Pharoah said, "I suppose the other one is Paul."

Fraught seemed taken off guard. "You've heard of Paul?"

"Yes, as a matter of fact. My friend Roger Hart, who manages a joint called the Fountain of Youth, told us about him. Of course, you know about the Fountain of Youth."

Fraught said with a sniff of disdain, "Only by hearsay. Madame held a benefit there for AIDS unfortunates in Michael's memory. It was AIDS that killed him."

A maid entered pushing a tea trolley laden with everything requested by Fraught. Pharoah said, "The service is pretty good around here."

"Won't you sit. I'll remind Madame you're here."

Madame didn't need any reminding. Right on cue, she came sweeping in behind the maid pushing the cart. A tall, svelte woman of indeterminate age, she wore a simple black dress and a simple string of pearls. Undoubtedly worth thousands, thought Pharoah. The dress was sleeveless, and her arms were amazingly firm, no sign of flab. Her fingers were surprisingly devoid of flash except for a simple wedding band and an engagement ring that, if suspended, thought Pharoah, could light up a ballroom. She wore black pumps, and Pharoah was disappointed she wasn't wearing Nike sneakers. She had to be at least in her mid-fifties, thought Pharoah, but now he felt it appropriate to knock at least ten years off her age, as he was sure she did.

"I'm so sorry to have kept you waiting"—she spoke melodiously, as if back in front of a musical group in a midtown café, announcing her next sophisticated number—"But I was on the phone with the White House." She didn't name names, possibly because she had been sworn to secrecy or else couldn't think fast enough to conjure one up. She held her hand out to Pharoah. "Well, Pharoah Love, we meet at last. Your reputation precedes you."

"It doesn't often." He took her hand and shook it gently. She looked disappointed he didn't kiss it. Pharoah almost told her he didn't kiss hands, especially not knowing where they might have been. He introduced Albert, who also shook her hand, and she invited them to sit within easy reach of the trolley. Fraught was pouring coffee for the detectives.

"I'll take tea, Fraught, with just a few drops of milk and no sugar." She smiled genially. "But of course you know that after all your years of loyal service." It sounded to Pharoah as though Fraught might have been in the French Foreign Legion.

Pharoah decided the best tactic in dealing with the woman was to begin by turning on the charm. "Mrs. Benarro, I never dreamt I'd get to meet the famous Adelaide Gibson."

"Oh, my heavens," she gurgled, almost spilling the cup and saucer she'd taken from Fraught, "you couldn't *possibly* remember me."

"Mrs. Benarro, please, you're *highly* memorable." Pharoah took a minute to explain Mrs. Benarro's nightclub background to Albert, who looked impressed but wasn't. The only Gibson he'd ever heard of was an old-time movie star named Hoot Gibson, and that was thanks to reruns of his westerns on TV when Albert was a child.

The woman set her cup and saucer on an end table and resumed gurgling. "Roger Hart tried to get me to do a few numbers for the benefit, but much as I was tempted, I decided not to risk making a fool of myself. The pipes aren't what they used to be. Roger Hart of the movies, you might remember."

"We met Roger this afternoon. We asked questions while he played piano."

"Roger's delightfully tuneful. All those wonderful golden oldies. And your questions, Mr. Love?"

"A different kind of music. We're looking for a murderer, Mrs. Benarro. I'm sure you know that."

"Oh, yes, I do. I most certainly do. Why his victims never fled the country, I'll never understand."

"A pattern wasn't recognized until four were murdered. Besides, had they left the country, they might not have gotten back in."

"And they couldn't go to Italy," she contributed knowledgeably. "My friend Marco Salino said that with the crackdown on crime there they'd be marked men and probably killed and buried in unmarked graves. Of course you know Marco Salino."

"Me?" Pharoah then proceeded to explain about their boyhood friendship.

"How charming!" she concluded, as though Pharoah had just treated her to a violin solo. "Growing up together in Canarsie, wherever that is."

"Brooklyn."

"Wherever that is. Sandwiches? Pastries?" They declined. She took the rejections bravely. "Now how do you think I can help you?"

"I'm sure you know what triggered these killings."

"The tragic deaths of the Chic twins." She fingered her pearls. "But really, I think these killings are just *so* senseless."

"Not to the killer," corrected Pharoah.

"Wouldn't justice have taken its course? Couldn't these men have been rounded up and indicted?"

"Not easy. Their identities were privileged information."

She sipped some tea. There was a thoughtful look on her face. "Marco could have been more cooperative. It's his lieutenants who are biting the dust."

"He insists he thought they were safely hidden, that is, the remainder who went into hiding after the first four killings began to suggest the pattern. That's when Marco came to me for some special help."

"And I'm sure you are special." She remembered Albert. "I'm sure you're both special." Her eyes widened, and now there was a smile on her face. "Oh, look who's here. What a pleasant surprise!"

Nick Suggi came into the room, but Pharoah wasn't in the least bit surprised.

chapter

17

"I was in the neighborhood, so I thought I'd drop by and bum a cup of coffee. I suppose I should have phoned." He leaned over and kissed Adelaide's cheek.

"Not at all, darling. You're always welcome! These gentlemen are detectives."

"Nick and I are old buddies," said Pharoah. He introduced Nick to Albert. Albert was tempted to ask Nick the name of his tailor but discarded the thought as inappropriate.

"Something tells me I'm intruding on a private conversation," said Nick as Fraught brought him his coffee.

"Investigation," corrected Pharoah. "Stop squirming, you're making the chair squeak. In fact, you might be of some help." It was obvious to Pharoah that there was something going on between Adelaide and Nicholas. In fact, he thought she might be courting indigestion the way she was devouring Suggi with her eyes, although he didn't blame her one bit. Suggi was a morsel of a mortal. He told Nick, "We're discussing at the moment the Chic Twins."

"Your favorite topic," said Suggi. He told Adelaide, "I've played this scene before."

"You were a big help," said Pharoah, "and I'll bet you can be even more of a help." He now favored Adelaide. "Your husband's murderer is still at large."

"Yes," she said, fingering the pearls again.

"I suppose you think we haven't given his case its best shot."

"That isn't what I think. I know the police haven't closed the books on it. I'm in touch from time to time with your Mr. MacIntyre."

"He's our chief."

"Oh, how nice. Such a lovely man," said Adelaide.

Pharoah said, "He's adorable," and Albert's cheeks flushed. "I suppose you held your benefit at the Fountain of Youth because it's all in the family."

"Not my family," said Adelaide, "Marco's family."

"A very dysfunctional family," said Pharoah. "But still, I assume that, despite your husband's death, you still maintain his connections."

"But of course, darling. May I call you Pharoah? I'm not very comfortable with calling anybody Mr. Love."

"You call me Pharoah, you call my partner here Albert, and we'll call you Adelaide—and I'd like to hear more about your connections."

She was smiling, and Pharoah suspected that if she left the

room, the smile would stay behind, like the Cheshire cat's. "I'm very involved with the wives of my husband's associates. The husbands appreciate my keeping them busy with committees and socials. It gives the boys more free time to play on their own. I keep a hand in because I inherited all of Salvatore's financial interests. It takes a lot of money to live in the style to which I've become accustomed. Whatever has this got to do with the murders?"

"I never know when one thing can lead to another. Like I didn't know at first that Nick here was up at the Capri the night of the unpleasantness."

"How quaintly put, Pharoah." She was still smiling, but suddenly Pharoah found himself wondering to what degree she could be deadly. He also wondered if by any chance she knew who'd ordered the ice pick stuck in Salvatore's ear.

"I didn't mean to be quaint," said Pharoah. "When I'm feeling quaint, I think about wearing a tutu." He went for broke. "Any ideas of your own as to who ordered your husband's death? Maybe it's the same son of a bitch I'm after."

She said grandiosely, "Murder can wear so many faces, can't it, Pharoah? Who ordered my beloved Salvatore killed? I can't put a face or an identity to him, but quite obviously it was a contract. Capos don't do their own dirty work. They line up a soldier for that. For all I know, this person has already gotten his just desserts from the one you're looking for."

"That's an interesting thought. Don't you think so, Albert?" Albert shrugged. "Who ordered Mr. Benarro's murder isn't half as important as why they wanted him snuffed."

"There were a lot of people out to get Salvatore. He had this one serious shortcoming. He was an honest man. He didn't pull his punches or hedge his bets. He called a spade a spade, and there were certain deals in which he refused to become involved. He wouldn't touch narcotics. He wasn't interested in prostitution."

"Marco is."

"Pharoah, I'm sure you're aware Rita and I are somewhat friendly. We're not constantly on the phone with each other, but we're friends. She helped unselfishly with the benefit. She bought a lot of tickets. She contributed generously."

"There's a rumor you're in on her action."

"Nonsense. I lent her money. It was a loan, not an investment. Rita had inherited money, but it turned out not to be enough. Marco invested, too. You probably know that. Rita's is Marco's home away from home. He detests his wife almost as much as she detests him. But he keeps her well provided for, which is all she cares about. She can eat to her stomach's content, and she feeds her soul with her church and constant confessions. She's a peasant with a peasant mentality. If the TV networks ever cancel their soap operas, she'll suffer a fatal stroke."

"So will I," said Pharoah. "I tape three a day."

"It's nice to know you have a secret vice," she said, smiling at Suggi.

"It's not a secret, and it's not a vice. Your husband and Marco didn't like each other."

Her voice coarsened. "Who told you that?"

"I think I heard it someplace." Suggi was lighting a cigarette. "We all know the capos are all jealous of each other, even though they often do business with each other. I suspect your husband and Marco had something going despite the fact I'm sure they loathed each other's guts. I know they both had pieces of action in Las Vegas and Atlantic City."

"Oh, my dear, dear Pharoah, there is so much apocrypha about the Mafia, so much mythology."

"A myth is as good as a mile. Forgive me, I couldn't resist."

Fraught passed among them, refilling cups, and Pharoah thought that perhaps Fraught was his least likely suspect. The butler could have done it, as was suspected in so many of the thrillers he had read in his teens, but the butler rarely did. "Marco's involved, for instance, with Weeping Willie."

"Marco is involved in a great many things, I've been told."

"Have you also been told Marco is also hurting financially?"

"Yes."

"And his manpower's being severely depleted."

"Obviously."

"You don't like Marco."

"Is that a question or a statement?"

"It falls somewhere in between."

"What does how I feel about Marco have to do with your investigation?"

"You might be withholding information, valuable information, because you're glad Marco is hurting. And please don't give me any crap about the recession. I'm as bored with the recession as I am with the civil wars in central Europe. Do you think Marco ordered Salvatore's death?"

"His is one of the names that have been hip-hopping in my brain from time to time."

"If you're looking forward to being in on Marco's fade-out, may I suggest viewer discretion is advised."

"Your loyalty is admirable in view of your childhood association with Marco, but I think at present, in your position as a detective conducting an investigation, your loyalty is a bit misplaced."

Pharoah switched tracks. "That's a lovely portrait of you and your sons."

"Thank you. It's one of my treasures."

"I'm sorry about Michael."

"It was God's will," she said with unbecoming piety.

"Where's Paul these days?"

She stiffened visibly. "Paul?"

"Your older son. Your firstborn. Paul."

"How'd you know his name?"

"From Roger Hart."

"Oh, of course. You saw Roger today."

"Is Paul supposed to be a secret?" Pharoah wondered what was bugging her. She was uncomfortable now. Her eyes darted from Pharoah to Suggi and then to Albert and back to Pharoah.

"Of course he's no secret. It's just that Paul is off in a world of his own."

"Which hemisphere?"

"Paul's a maverick. He listens to a different drummer."

"I can see you don't like talking about him."

"I don't mind talking about him. It's just that there's not much to talk about."

"Don't you like Paul?"

"I'm his mother. Of course I like him."

"Except he's never around very much." Pharoah continued tenaciously. He felt he was on to something. He wasn't sure what, but a second sense told him to pursue the subject of

Paul Benarro. He didn't realize he had Albert mesmerized. "Where does Paul live?"

"I'm never really sure."

"Don't you care?"

She was visibly ruffled. "He's an adult. He can look after himself."

"Did he know the twins?"

"I don't know."

"You knew Annie and Millie. If they had met Paul, wouldn't they have told you they knew him? At the benefit. Wouldn't they have told you at the benefit?"

"Neither one of them mentioned it."

"You're sure?"

"Very sure."

Pharoah aimed his mouth at Nick Suggi. "Did you ever meet Paul?"

"Me?"

"Who else?"

"I didn't know either one of Addie's sons."

"Yet you attended the benefit in Michael's honor."

"Out of respect. To Addie. Addie invited me."

"Are you two lovers?" Albert's shoulders sagged.

Adelaide bristled. "Now really, Pharoah. That's none of your business."

"Sometimes I think it is. I don't trust lovers. They lie for each other when they think it's necessary. They withhold information. And that makes my job tougher. You know, Adelaide, I think you're pussyfooting around about Paul because he's somehow involved in this investigation."

"That is absolute and utter nonsense. Paul never knew any of the victims."

"How can you be sure?" Pharoah was on his feet and crossing to the painting. "How long ago was this thing painted? Five years ago? More? Look at Paul's eyes. Like blue steel. Fierce." They reminded Pharoah of someone, but he couldn't put a finger on it. "How can you be sure Paul didn't know some of those lieutenants."

She machine-gunned him with words. "Because Paul hated everything his father represented. He hated the families. He hated the Mafia. He was a very sensitive child, and it was a constant bone of contention between him and his father that he fought against becoming one of the Mob."

"So he despised his father."

"No, damn you! He didn't despise him!"

"He wasn't soft and pliant like Michael."

"Michael was a saint!" she shouted.

"It didn't bother Salvatore that Michael wasn't macho like him? Weren't both his sons two big disappointments to Salvatore? One an eccentric creep and the other a flaming faggot."

"Pharoah Love, you have gone too far." She didn't try disguising the menace in her voice.

"Addie, I haven't gotten as far as I intend to get."

Suggi spoke up. "You're getting too rough, Pharoah." Pharoah dismissed him and his statement with a disdainful wave of a hand.

"Does Paul have a profession, Addie? Did he maybe want to be an actor, a performer. Didn't he know you used to be a well-known singer?"

"Yes, of course he knew. He was very proud of that. He and Michael were both proud of my professional past."

"Did either one of them inherit any of your talent?"

"Michael had a pleasant voice."

"What about Paul?"

"I didn't hear him sing much."

"Not even "I'm Only a Bird in a Gilded Cage'?"

"Paul was a very unhappy child," said Adelaide softly. "And yes, Salvatore was terribly disappointed with his children. But he was a devoted father. For crying out loud, he was Italian. They're always devoted fathers. The sons are everything. As much as he was capable of loving, he loved the boys. Salvatore was a very generous man." She waved a hand to encompass the interior of the room. "He gave me all this and more. And believe it or not, much of his income came from legitimate investments. He was trying to wean himself away from the Mob. He wanted respect. He hungered for respect. He wanted to produce movies and own record companies—"

"Oh, come off it, Adelaide. He was into movie companies and recording companies and porn movies and massage parlors—"

Adelaide interrupted peevishly, "And on the seventh day he rested."

"Where's Paul?"

"Why is that so important? Oh, my God. Do you think Paul might be your killer? Oh, that is to laugh."

"Adelaide, is there a photo of Paul within easy reach by any chance?"

"No. He was camera-shy."

"Camera-shy. But he stood still long enough to be captured on canvas."

Adelaide arose and regally crossed to an armoire. She opened a drawer and rifled among papers and photographs it contained. She found a snapshot of her son Paul. "I just remembered. There's this one taken five years ago at Michael's birthday party." Pharoah crossed to her and took the photo. He studied it and asked, "Do you mind if I hold on to this?"

"It's the only one I've got!" she protested.

"I promise I'll guard it with Albert's life."

Suggi smiled at Albert, who looked displeased. He wasn't sure what Pharoah was after, though it had been easy to see that Pharoah had been dropping clues. What was the enigmatic Paul all about? *"Look at Paul's eyes. Blue steel. Fierce. . . . Did he maybe want to be an actor, a performer?"* Albert now recognized in Pharoah a man who neither wasted words nor theories. Albert knew now he was nursing a hunch, a suspicion, and hunches and suspicions were a lot of what criminal investigation was about. Albert could almost see Paul as Pharoah composed a portrait of Paul that was a revision of the interesting young man in the painting. He realized that Pharoah was standing, looking down at him. He gave Albert the snapshot. "Albert West, meet Paul Benarro."

Albert took the photo and studied it. It was a candid shot: Paul looking uncomfortable in a party hat. It was a colored photograph, and what dominated the young man were his eyes. It was the picture of an unhappy young man who undoubtedly wished he was anywhere but at this party. A girl was standing next to him, but she was looking elsewhere. She, too, was obviously unaware that she was being photographed. She was laughing. She was holding a drink. Five years ago. Five years ago. If this girl was who he thought she might be, five years ago she should have been in a convent. He couldn't be sure, but the girl in the snapshot might be either Annie or Millie Cicci.

He handed the snapshot back to Pharoah with one word: "Interesting."

Pharoah put the snapshot in an inside jacket pocket, the one next to his artfully hidden holster. He heard Adelaide saying something to him.

"You're being absolutely ridiculous if you think my Paul has anything to do with these murders."

"Adelaide, let me displease you a bit more. Paul wasn't also gay, was he?"

"Hell, no!"

"Am I too far off the mark guessing he had other problems? Like did he at some time in his youth undergo psychiatric treatment?"

"You bastard. You absolute bastard."

"Did he?"

She looked at Suggi, but he could offer her no help. He knew Pharoah's reputation. He had experienced his interrogations. His look told her, "I can't help, honey. With Pharoah, you're on your own."

"Paul had problems." Peevish again. Fingering the pearls again. Pharoah could see they gave her some sort of comfort. Should all else fail, there'll always be wealth. Jewelry. A magnificent town house. Superb art on the walls and some probably stashed away in the attic and in closets.

"Had? Not has?"

She was once again poised and cool. "Didn't everybody

have problems when they were young? Some overcome them as they mature, don't you agree?"

"Thank you, Joyce Brothers." Pharoah said in an aside to Albert, so softly that the others couldn't hear him, "I think we should be wearing garlic. Let's get the hell out of here."

Albert was grateful. He needed air. The atmosphere in the room had become close with foreboding. Pharoah was positively on to something, and though Albert was looking forward to the conclusion of the investigation, the knot in his stomach told him he dreaded it as well.

Now he and Pharoah were standing. Albert saw Adelaide out of the corner of his eye, and the relief she felt was evident. The look on Pharoah's face, however, told Albert that he was about to spring some fresh afterthoughts. Pharoah was studying the snapshot again.

Pharoah said, "Gino Vinelli."

"Pleasant young man," replied Adelaide smoothly. "Nice voice but nothing special."

Pharoah indicated the snapshot. "I don't suppose he looks like Paul."

"I most certainly don't suppose," said Adelaide. "He's at least five years younger, several inches shorter, and much too pretty. He's also a whore. That word could never describe Paul." The snapshot was back in the jacket pocket.

Pharoah zeroed in on Nick Suggi. "You didn't just *happen* to be in the neighborhood, Nick, did you? Adelaide phoned you for moral support."

Nick didn't flinch. "I *was* in the neighborhood. My dentist is around the corner."

"How convenient. Okay, Albert, let's go. It's time to break this case."

Adelaide and Nick were on their feet. Adelaide said, "I'll ring for Fraught to show you the way out."

"Don't bother, Adelaide," said Pharoah. "We can show ourselves out." He turned to Nick. "Marco's favorite table at La Fontana."

"Number five. What about it?"

"It's bugged, isn't it?"

He feigned surprise. "It is? Do you think so?" Nick was patently uncomfortable. "I'll tell Marco."

"For the role of Little Boy Blue, Nick, you need a toy horn for a prop. If it's bugged, you know it's bugged. The way Marco's office is probably bugged, and his house. They're closing in on him, Nick. It's on the grapevine. I'm sure Rita knows, and I'm sure"—his eyes moved to Adelaide—"Adelaide knows. And who knows, Adelaide, maybe there's bugs placed in a lot of corners of your sanctum sanctorum."

Adelaide paled. "Why would the feds be after me?"

Feds. Not "Why would there be hidden listening devices in my gorgeous mansion?" Pharoah told her, "You know a lot, Adelaide. You're one smart lady. Salvatore trusted you, confided in you, even though you fell short in the offspring department. Adelaide, why do I keep thinking you know who ordered the curtains lowered on your husband but are too frightened to talk? Why is this rat of suspicion gnawing away at my insides that it's Paul who's killing Marco's lieutenants?"

"Go to hell." She spat each word.

Albert hurried after Pharoah, feeling he was on the verge of hyperventilating. They met Fraught in the hallway, coming up the stairs, and Pharoah saluted him smartly. Fraught nodded his head with dignity.

Back in the house, Adelaide was looking behind some of the paintings. Nick said hotly, "For crying out loud, you don't believe Pharoah, do you?"

"I could be bugged. Why couldn't I be bugged?

Fraught entered and asked, "Shall I remove the trolley?"

"Fraught!" She shouted his name.

"Is something wrong, madame?"

"There may be electrical devices planted in the house. Eavesdropping devices!"

Fraught thought of questioning her sanity. "I don't think the cleaners have come across any."

"The cleaners! Yes, of course! They have access to the house. They could have planted them!"

Fraught threw Nick a questioning look. Nick shrugged. He had something more important on his mind that concerned him. If Marco was being targeted by the feds, could he be in danger of being implicated as a confederate? La Fontana was one of Marco's many "laundromats"; a lot of hot money came into the restaurant to be cleaned up.

Fraught attempted to reassure his frantic mistress. "Madame, the cleaning people are bonded. They are supplied by a highly respectable company. Why, I believe your husband is a partner!"

"*Was* a partner." She turned to Nick. "He's frightened me. That son of a bitch has frightened me. Pour me a brandy."

Nick crossed to the bar, which was set up near the entrance to the room. Adelaide stood with her hands on her hips.

Fraught was looking unhappy. He watched Nick pour the brandy. He, the butler, should be pouring the brandy. These people have no class. Thank God Mrs. Benarro overpaid him or he would have made tracks long ago. Could this place, after all, have been wired by the authorities? There *had* been a lot of activity, with plumbers and electricians, and one would have needed a dozen pairs of eyes to keep watch on them. Wired? Wired, indeed. Wired and be damned.

Adelaide swallowed the brandy, then wrinkled her face with disgust. "I forgot I hate brandy!" She slammed the glass down on a table. "Fraught, I want every inch of this house examined carefully for strange devices. Do you understand?"

"Yes, madame."

Nick intervened. "Now, Adelaide, let a cooler head prevail. They couldn't bug this entire castle! It's impossible!"

"That's what *you* say! Didn't we have to scrap an embassy in Moscow because the Russkies had bugged every square inch of it?"

"Calm down, Adelaide. Why don't you move down to your place in Palm Beach for a couple of weeks. While you're gone, I'll supervise the search."

"It's a good idea, but I can't leave town."

"Why not?"

She sat on a couch, her hands limp on her lap, watching Fraught wheeling the trolley out of the room, his lips moving as though talking to himself. Adelaide said, "I can't leave Paul."

chapter 18

Albert was steering the car back to the West Side. To Rita Genari's house. "You were real rough on Adelaide, Pharoah. At one point there I thought she was going to wind up and throw something at you."

"What she was throwing a lot of was that stuff that hits the fan."

"You kept going on about her son. Do you think Paul is the killer?"

"He has to be."

"Why are you so positive?"

"Because Marco had to have ordered Salvatore Benarro's murder. Don't give me that look. Sure, sure, they were mixed up in deals together. But you heard Adelaide. Salvatore wanted out of the mob. He was trying to wean himself away so he could go straight. Straight! I'm beginning to hate that word."

He cast a sly look at Albert. "Present company excluded. To start a fresh, clean record you have to make peace with the government, and that means cooperation. Salvatore, I suspect, was readying a deal with the feds to delight them with some rarefied arias, and he'd be singing high C above G."

"I don't know anything about singing. I like to listen to it, but I don't really know it."

"Albert, why am I beginning to think you might be an endangered species?"

"Come off it, Pharoah."

"I mean it in a nice way, Albert. No offense intended. You are very sweetly naive about certain things, and I find it refreshing. Salvatore had the families frightened. And when the Mob runs scared, they hit first and then ask questions afterward. They question each other. They ask why didn't they ice the bastard ages ago. Salvatore wasn't popular. He wasn't about to win any awards."

"You knew him?"

"Not to break bread with, but our paths have crossed. At Rita's. Back in the days when, if you didn't feel like getting laid, you could always sit in on a game of poker to pass the time. Salvatore was a very abrasive man. God, how he must have suffered about those sons, probably cursing the fact he'd never be a grandfather unless he had some anonymous bastards roaming around out there in the great nowhere."

"What about Paul? Paul isn't gay."

"You didn't listen clearly, Albert. Paul's the other misfit. There's something wrong with Paul. I suspect I know what Paul is all about." He thought for a moment. "It's all so meshuga, meaning 'crazy' in case you don't know any Yiddish."

"I don't."

"I know some, thanks to Herbie." He went silent. Herbie. Now Marco. All that will be left is Pharoah. The Three Musketeers will soon be a memory.

Albert said, "What a terrible sigh. What's wrong?"

"Better you shouldn't know," Pharoah said, sounding like Herbie's mother.

"Is Adelaide in danger?"

"Only from herself," Pharoah said flatly. "The Mob rarely kills women. The women know enough to keep silent, especially if they've inherited all the goodies."

"Don't you think Adelaide worries about being squeezed out of Salvatore's shares?"

"Why, shame on you, Albert. Members of the Mafia are gentlemen; they honor a gentleman's code. Adelaide worries about old age. She worries about how much longer she can hold on to Nick Suggi or his unreasonable facsimile, with age approaching and encroaching. I mean, from the look of her, one more face-lift and her lips will cover her nose." He paused. Another sigh. "Adelaide's wealth is safe. She's probably got a shrewd lawyer or a staff of them protecting her interests for interesting fees. Whether they can protect some of those interests from Suggi is something else."

"He's not a murder suspect?"

"He is if he committed them by remote control. When you manage a restaurant, you have to be on the premises a lot of long hours. His alibis are sound."

"Gino the whore? Could he be Paul despite what Adelaide said?"

"If Gino was in a room and a mouse appeared, he'd be the

first to hop on a chair and scream for the marines to come to his rescue. I'm narrowed down to two possibilities, and that's why I need to talk to Rita." He stared out the window in silence for a few minutes. They were almost at Rita's place. "My friend Rita. Oh, why the hell didn't I listen to my mother and learn to play the saxophone!"

"Why didn't you?"

"Because I was too busy with another kind of blowing."

Albert felt courageous. "Didn't sex ever get you into trouble?"

"No, Albert, I took the advice of a United States president who advised, 'Speak softly and carry a big dick.'"

In Rita Genari's private living room, Rita sat behind her desk, entertaining Marco and Natalya Orloff, Natalya—a strange vision in a Bob Mackie nightmare. She was unaware there was tension between Marco and Rita. Adelaide had phoned Rita to advise her of Pharoah's unpleasant visit, to suggest that perhaps she, too, might be privileged enough to be bugged. Rita had reached Marco on his car phone, and as he was in her neighborhood en route to La Fontana with Natalya, he had his chauffeur detour to Rita's place. It was a first meeting for the women, and they sized each other up warily, like boxers squaring off in the ring for the first time. Natalya came out punching, telling Rita that a whorehouse was a new experience for her.

"Ve have many in Russia, of course, and once I had an opportunity, but I vas not interested. That time I had ambitions to be great musician; I vas studying at conservatory. I vas determined to be great concert penis."

"Cool it, Natalya," Marco cautioned. Natalya cooled it at once. She had been trained well by Sergei Paskudnyak. She crossed a leg and stared at Marco. Sergei has warned her that Marco was in trouble—big trouble—financially, with the government determined to see as many of the families wiped out as were being wiped out in Italy. Natalya didn't understand why she was feeling a twinge of sympathy for Marco until she reminded herself she was a Russian and therefore subject to strong, sympathetic emotions. She listened quietly and carefully while Rita repeated Adelaide's information for Marco's benefit and comment.

Rita said softly, "She thinks Pharoah is getting too dangerous. She wants him iced."

"No way!" snapped Marco.

"He'll nail your hide to a wall."

"You listen to this, Rita. I'd rather take a stiff sentence and go inside for the rest of my life than be stalked like a wounded animal for whatever days I've got left. Herbie and me, we always did think alike except in one respect. I don't mind being poured into the jug. I'll arrange for someplace decent like where they're holding Gotti. And like him I'll read books. Maybe I'll learn to play chess. I've always wanted to know that stuff about Kings jumping queens, or whatever the hell they do in that game. Nobody touches Pharoah," he warned her. "You should be ashamed of yourself. Pharoah's been damned good to you; he looks after you. Shame on you."

"Don't you go accusing me of anything against him, Marco. I said Adelaide wants him put down. She sounded dangerous. That's not cottage cheese between her ears. That's one shrewd bitch, which is why I go out of my way to keep on her good side. There's a hair trigger in her brain, and one of these days it's going to snap."

"I'll have a talk with her."

"That'll do no good. She was screaming about Pharoah telling her that her place was probably bugged."

"Ah, she's bug nutty."

Natalya broke her silence, prompted by her insatiable curiosity. "Vot is bugs? Is like sleeping with person and getting crobs?"

"Crabs," corrected Marco. "I'll explain later."

From what she'd been hearing, Natalya suspected that Marco didn't have much "later" left. She wondered, If Sergei was privy to Marco's whirlpools of misfortune, why hadn't he warned her? Perhaps, she wondered, Sergei is bored with me. Perhaps—she brightened at the thought—it is time to encourage Nicholas Suggi. *Da.*

Rita asked Marco, "Do you think I'm on the verge of some serious trouble?"

"You'll be questioned. You've been questioned before. You handled the heat real good when they had you in when Salvatore bought it."

"I don't want to be in trouble, Marco."

He was about to speak when the door opened and Pharoah entered, followed by Albert. "Forgive me for not knocking," said Pharoah, "but I've got no time for amenities. I used my passkey on the front door. Albert, close the door. Hello, Marco. I'm glad you're here. It saves time. How's the girl, Natalya?" He crossed to Rita, uninterested in any response from

Natalya. "You ain't been on the square with me, Rita." He then looked at Marco. "And likewise you, old buddy."

Rita was lighting a cigarette and frowning.

"What's the beef?" asked Marco.

"Okay, Marco. You first. Where's Paul Benarro?"

"How should I know? I got no interest in him."

"You should. I think he's murdering your lieutenants." Pharoah saw the look Marco gave Rita and marveled that Rita hadn't died instantly. "Rita, where's Paul Benarro?"

"You mean right this minute?"

"I'll rephrase. *Who* is Paul Benarro?"

"Adelaide's oldest."

As Pharoah reached into his jacket for the snapshot he'd gotten from Adelaide, he said, "You want to play games? Pharoah will play games. Pharoah is fed up to his teeth with lies and subterfuge and double-talk and 'remember the good old days,' which weren't all that good."

He placed the snapshot on the desk. "Take a good luck, sweetheart. I got it from Adelaide, who I'm sure told you I had it when she phoned to repeat the scene I just played with her. Her and Nick Suggi. "He asked Marco. "Is Nick banging her?"

"He'll bang anything." He didn't hear Natalya's heart sink. Rita said softly, "Adelaide told me this is her son Paul."

"Did she also remind you of the identity of the chick standing behind Paul?" He waited. She said nothing. "Which one of the twins is it? Annie? Millie? You having a stroke, Rita?"

"Oh, go to hell!"

"For a few seconds there you looked like a somnambulist."

"Vot is that?" Sequins reflected and glittered in Natalya's eyes.

"Better you shouldn't know," said Pharoah, and Albert smiled. He wished he had known Herbie Marks's mother.

"When that picture was taken," resumed Pharoah, "the twins were supposed to be away in a convent school."

Rita said angrily, "They weren't there three hundred and sixty-five days of the year. They came home for holidays. This snap, the party, it was over the Easter holidays."

"Which one is it? You can tell them apart."

"What difference does it make?"

"I want to know. Tell me. Bless me with some honest information for a change."

"It's Millie."

"Paul was in love with her?"

"She was only fifteen then!"

"So what? My mother was pregnant when she was fifteen." Natalya's eyes rolled up as she lit another cigarette. "I've had enough of this horsing around, Rita. You painted a very pretty picture of the girls for me. Saints, virgins, placed on unreachable pedestals. Well, since then I've heard different. They were a pair of good-time Gerties, no better than what you got in the bedrooms upstairs."

"You shut up!"

"It's okay. It's no skin off me. They were murdered, and that triggered more murders. Paul is out there dispensing justice, a very sick justice—but what the hell. From my point of view his justice is better than no justice at all. But it's my job to bring him in. Come on, Marco, how many are left?" Marco stared at the floor. With a roar of anger, Pharoah rushed at Marco, grabbed his lapels, and pulled him out of his chair.

"Please!" Natalya shrieked, "no violence!"

"Where are they, you son of a bitch. How does Paul know where to find them? Who tells Paul where they're hiding? Oh, shit!" He let go of the lapels, and Marco fell back into the chair. "Rita, you bitch! Rita of the infallible grapevine. You've been feeding him the information!"

"Yes!" she shouted, now on her feet, leaning across the desk with a ferocious look on her face. "What you heard about my girls was slander! Stinking, rotten slander! They were good girls! I loved them! I miss them!" She broke into sobs. "They were all I had. They were going to be stars!"

Natalya whispered to Albert, "No vay," and took a deep drag of her cigarette.

Rita pointed an accusing finger at Marco. "Your garbage killed Annie and Millie. Violated them. Raped them." She turned to Pharoah. "Sure, Paul was in love with Millie. Everybody was in love with the girls. Paul worshiped her. She was all he ever wanted in his life. But Paul's sick, very, very sick. And I don't mind telling you, with me coaxing on the sidelines, I drilled it into him to avenge the death of Millie and her sweet, sweet sister. But it's too late for you, Pharoah. Paul is probably there by now. I gave him my Lamborghini. It's worth hundreds of thousands. Right, Marco?"

"You're crazy, Rita, you're crazy." Marco seemed to have shriveled. Pharoah, looking back on this scene, would recall how his old pal suddenly grew smaller and older in front of his eyes.

"Not so crazy, Marco. You told me too much, Marco. I told

you very little. I don't give a damn anymore. Pharoah, there's two left to kill. One's named Leo Scarpi. The other is Danny DiLuca." Rita looked crazed.

Marco stared at her with disbelief. "Weeping Willie's boy?"

"A mole, Marco. A mole I helped put into your army. Danny's been feeding the authorities everything he could find out. It was a deal Willie made to protect himself. You're going belly up, Marco!" Marco made a move that triggered Pharoah's reflexes. He leaped at his old friend, and Albert moved in to assist. He knew Marco was reaching for the gun in his underarm holster. Together they wrestled him to the floor.

Natalya shouted, "*Borgiamoy!*" appealing to God for help. She watched Albert remove Marco's gun and cram it into his own jacket pocket.

"When'd you lose your marbles, Marco?" asked Pharoah as he loosened his grip. "When'd you get so dumb? Offing Rita isn't going to make things any easier for you."

There was a bridge of hatred between Marco's and Rita's eyes. Natalya looked from one to the other and back again, wondering if she herself was capable of such venomous feelings. It was sad. It was tragic. It was grand opera without the music. Suddenly, with a ferocious display of strength, Marco sent Pharoah and Albert crashing backward. As they fell to the floor in a tangle, Marco ran from the room, out of the house, and into his waiting limousine. He barked an order to his lieutenant behind the wheel, and with a screeching of wheels, the car disappeared in the direction of Eighth Avenue.

"That stupid son of a bitch!" cried Pharoah.

Natalya stood with outstretched hands, a little match girl in a state of bewilderment, and pleaded, "Vot is going on?"

Pharoah shouted at Rita, "Where's he going?"

"The Capri," she said quietly, "and I hope he gets one between the eyes."

"Rita," said Pharoah, "I'm rarely given to understatement, but you're one hell of a big disappointment to me. Come on, Albert. Let's make tracks."

Natalya watched Pharoah and Albert's hasty exit.

Rita, trembling, sat behind her desk. Her shoulders shook with a life of their own, and she sobbed pathetically. Natalya went to her, knelt at her side, and put a comforting arm around her shoulders. But there was no comforting Rita.

Juana Gomez entered the room with Lily Davis in tow, Lily dressed for an outcall. Juana cried, "What's going on here? What's wrong?"

Natalya stood up and said darkly, "Very Dostoyevski." She tried her best to describe the previous scene with some degree of accuracy, building up to Marco's attempt to kill Rita. When she finished, as Juana was attempting to console Rita, Lily Davis put her hands on her hips, eyed Natalya from head to toe, and then asked in a voice filled with awe and a soupçon of envy, "Honey baby, wherever in hell did you pick up that far-out outfit?"

chapter

19

"How many cannons you got stashed in this heap?" Eddie Parma, the chauffeur, wondered if Marco knew he sounded like some old-time Warner Brothers gangster, like Stanley Fields or even George Bancroft.

"I got four. Two in the glove compartment. Two on the floor next to me. What happened to yours?"

Marco leaned back and said, "Somebody stole candy from a baby. What have you got?" He might have been inquiring about an assortment of petits fours.

"Two forty-five automatics, two three fifty-seven Magnums."

"Give me a Magnum."

The chauffeur was beginning to feel uneasy. "We going to war or something?"

Marco told him what lay ahead at the Capri Hotel.

The chauffeur suggested, "Maybe when we get there, I should park on the road, and maybe we creep up on them, sort of quiet-like, you know?"

Marco knew he was speaking, but he wasn't hearing the words. He was dwelling on Pharoah and Rita and the meaning of friendship, the necessity of friendship, the treachery of friendship. As clear as though it had happened that afternoon, Marco could see himself with Herbie Marks and Pharoah jumping off the Canarsie pier into the polluted waters of Jamaica Bay. Pollution, Marco reminded himself, all my life there's been pollution. From Canarsie to the Olympian heights of the Mafia, all pollution.

Rita. The true love of his life. He was glad he had never admitted it to the bitch. Rita, he mused while staring out the window at the view from the West Side Highway. Past the Hudson River, New Jersey and its half-empty high-rise apartment houses. Seventy-ninth Street and the houseboats rocking back and forth, nauseating the rats who sought food on them. Ahead, through the windshield, loomed Grant's Tomb, scrawled with graffiti. Marco stroked the weapon that rested on his lap. He wished it was a Cobray M-11, which could fire a thousand rounds a minute. A Street Sweeper would also do. It could hold twelve shotgun shells and fire as rapidly as a machine gun. He wished he knew people as well as he knew guns.

There were times Rita could fire a dozen rounds when she opened her mouth to yell. Rita, years ago, soft and warm and pliant; she was the best. He had had nothing better. He should have married her when she told him she was pregnant.

He shouldn't have shut the door on her. He should have kept her from running off to Mexico. Mexico. Juana Gomez.

Mexico and Juana Gomez. The twins?

"Oh, my God!" he howled. "Oh, my God!"

"What's wrong, Marco? What is it?"

"Oh, Christ! Oh, Christ! Oh, Christ!"

"You want me to turn off someplace? You want a coffee?"

"No! No! Oh, God forgive me! Dear Jesus, forgive me! They were my babies! The twins were my babies! Why didn't she tell me? Why didn't the bitch tell me? I'd have looked after them. I'd have taken good care of them! They'd be alive today! Oh, my God. Oh, my God. Oh, my God!"

What Eddie Parma was seeing in his rearview mirror was the picture of a man losing his sanity. A man slipping away into a fearsome new dimension.

The tears ran down Marco's face into his mouth. His eyes were lowered, and his jaw was slack. It was as if the chauffeur were at a tennis match. His eyes darted back and forth between the rearview mirror and the road ahead of him. There was little traffic, and he was grateful. In the mirror he could see Marco wiping his eyes with the sleeve of his jacket. Then Marco reminded himself he had a handkerchief and blew his nose. He sat limply, staring at the weapon, looking forward to Armageddon.

Albert leaned over the wheel of the unmarked patrol car, staring ahead intently, passing cars and trucks while doing close to ninety, the reincarnation of the late speed demon Barney Oldfield. Pharoah had radioed Walt MacIntyre to tell him

265

they were headed for what would undoubtedly be a very bloody climax at the Hotel Capri.

"I'll inform Sullivan County," said Walt. The Capri was in South Fallsburg, and that was Sullivan County.

"Not yet," Pharoah urged. "They'll storm the place now and screw up everything."

"I'm in trouble if I don't tell them."

"Walt, please," Pharoah pleaded, "develop temporary amnesia. Give me a couple of hours. Paul Benarro belongs to me. He's mine. I want to bring him in."

"There's just the two of you, for crying out loud! You're outnumbered."

"No, we're not. Paul's on our side. And baby makes three."

"You nuts or something? There's DiLuca and Scarpi. The other soldier. By the time you get there, Marco will be there with his chauffeur. You'll be outgunned."

"Walt, my money's on Paul. He's lowered the odds. The DiLuca son and Scarpi are goners by now. How I wished I owned a florist's in Little Italy."

"You could order a wreath for yourself!" MacIntyre shouted.

"Two hours, Walt, two hours," Pharoah pleaded.

"If you don't think of yourself, then think of Albert!"

Albert barely missed sideswiping a pickup truck as it swung onto the highway from out of the darkness of an entrance ramp.

Pharoah said, "Tell Albert he should be thinking of me."

"Sorry, Pharoah," said Albert as sweat formed on his upper lip. "The son of a bitch sneaked up on me."

MacIntyre finally acquiesced. He and the chief in Sullivan County were on good terms. MacIntyre had helped him crack another case in which a nanny was accused of murdering her charge, one of an epidemic of similar cases that had broken out in Sullivan County and its environs. Mary Poppins must have been spinning in her grave.

It was now more than an hour since Pharoah had been in touch with MacIntyre. He kept touching the gun in his holster for reassurance. He checked the glove compartment for additional ammunition. It was there; he had put the box of bullets in it himself. He looked at Albert, hunched over the wheel, reminding himself of how he and Herbie and Marco must have looked when competing against each other in Soap Box Derbies. Soap Box Derbies! Whatever became of Soap Box Derbies! Whatever became of Roller Derbies? Whatever became of derbies?

He put a damper on his thoughts. He was getting giddy. He envisioned the impending shoot-out. He and Albert against Paul. Against Marco and probably Marco's chauffeur. He knew Eddie Parma and liked him. He had met him years ago at the Fountain of Youth when Eddie was trying to decide if he was straight or gay or bi and finally had settled for straight as being less complicated. A homosexual emeritus.

"What's so funny?" asked Albert.

"People," replied Pharoah. "People are so funny. I sometimes wish there was a way to rewrite or redefine the past."

"Don't go sentimental on me, Pharoah, and spoil everything."

"And spoil *what* everything?"

"I'm coming around to appreciating you, Pharoah. I'm

finding a few things to admire. Your insensitivity. The way you don't hesitate spitting in somebody's eye. The way you've invented yourself. It's not my way, but I appreciate how it works for you, and I think I'm little envious. If I find out you cried when Lassie came home, I just might have to kill myself."

"Albert" Pharoah spoke the name solemnly—"please don't see me as a role model. The world, as I have created it, can only deal with one Pharoah Love." He stared out the windshield at the Hotel Capri, which materialized ahead of them, bathed in the light of the moon. Pharoah was impressed. It was quite a construction. He said lightly as he drew his weapon, "'Last night I dreamt I saw Manderley again.'"

A huge billboard with an arrow directed them toward a narrow road leading up to the hotel's front entrance. There another sign proclaimed that this was indeed the Hotel Capri, its most recent incarnation since the hotel was constructed in the early thirties, when the Catskill Mountains grew and prospered despite the Wall Street crash of 1929 and its ensuing, crippling depression. The lavish-looking Capri look-alikes promised three meals a day, fishing, swimming, boating, and entertainment nightly except Mondays. At the other end of the scale were the bungalow colonies where families did their own cooking and provided their own entertainment, known to the almost exclusive Jewish renters as '*Kuchalanes*' (translation: Do your own cooking). Herbie Marks's family rented one one summer, and Pharoah and Marco had been invited up for a week, Pharoah's presence proving unsettling and provoking a heady panorama of racial slurs that Mrs. Marks fielded with a barrage of slurs of her own, many of them highly creative and shockingly meaningful. How Pharoah had adored that woman. Thinking of Mrs. Marks brought him back to Herbie, which led to a hopscotch to Marco Salino, which led to the stark reality of the drama involving Pharoah that was now unfolding.

Albert had taken the winding roadway slowly and cautiously. The roadway was bordered with untrimmed shrubbery that provided excellent cover for any would-be sniper. He steered with his left hand, a revolver occupying his right. Pharoah, his weapon at the ready, was amazingly relaxed. He was always that way when faced with the inevitable.

"There are an awful lot of lights on in there," said Albert.

"I guess somebody's afraid of the dark," said Pharoah.

"It's awful quiet," said Albert.

Pharoah replied, "If we've missed the fun, I'll spit." They heard an exchange of gunfire. "The curtain is up. The comedy is under way. There's French windows over there. I've always wanted to make an entrance through French windows. Loretta Young used to enter through French windows. I wonder if she was ever told they were French. Follow me, Albert, on little cat feet."

Slowly and cautiously they made their way. The detectives saw a massive dining room. "This dining room," commented Pharoah, "must have been an occasion for teardrop earrings." Albert hadn't the vaguest idea what he was talking about.

The windows were locked. Pharoah chose the line of least resistance. He broke a pane with his gun and reached in and released the latch. He pushed open the window and entered slowly, his partner right behind him. Albert gasped. He grabbed Pharoah's arm by way of caution.

"What? What?" Pharoah asked, momentarily confused.

"Over there. There's a guy sitting at the table over there, his back to us."

"Must be deaf if he didn't hear the window break." Albert released Pharoah's arm. Slowly, they crossed to the man.

"Freeze!" said Pharoah. But the figure was already frozen. His throat had been cut. Albert felt ill. "This is one of Marco's shooters."

"How can you tell?"

"Tan loafers with yellow tassels. It's a trademark." He had found the man's wallet. "Leo Scarpi." He pocketed the wallet. They heard gunfire. "I haven't been in a decent shoot-out since yesterday, and that one was mostly indecent. Let's go."

They crossed the dining room to a heavily draped entrance, the drapes sorely in need of vacuuming. Pharoah said to Albert, "I've always wanted to make an entrance through drapes."

"That's an awful lot of entrances you've wanted to make."

"It's due to my crying need for acceptance." He parted the dusty drapes with caution. Beyond lay the hotel lobby. "Oh, good. A familiar face."

On the floor lay Weeping Willie's teddy bear. Pharoah told Albert quickly about Weeping Willie and his teddy bear. "Danny DiLuca must have SOS'd Daddy for backup. Now where do you suppose the unhappy twosome have themselves barricaded? Where the hell's Marco?"

"Where the hell's Paul Benarro?"

"Also a good question."

Pharoah was able to identify the location of the last round of gunfire. "Downstairs. The club. There's the stairs leading down. Goodness, the carpeting. It's to die from. Ultraviolet liberally sprinkled with artfully stippled drops of blood. What won't these outré designers think of next? Let us follow this well-laid trail."

At the end of the trail, at the bottom of the stairs, lay Eddie Parma, Marco's chauffeur. "Poor bastard," said Pharoah, "I was hoping he'd save the last dance for me." The club was big and gaudy, with a bandstand behind that sparkled five silver-and-gold letters that spelled CAPRI. Placed around the room were artificial palm trees from some of which hung puppet monkeys. There were three liquor bars. Marco Salino stood at one. He was holding tightly to the bar and managed a smile for Pharoah. The front of his shirt was bloodstained. His Magnum lay at his feet, a useless ally. "Hi, Pha'." Pha', the nickname Pharoah now rarely heard. Marco started to slip to the floor. Pharoah caught him and eased him down gently.

"Where are the others?" asked Pharoah.

"Don't worry. You'll hear from them. Willie and his boy are behind the bandstand. Willie's hopping mad. He plugged me. He knows I ordered Salvatore killed. So he says he's mad at me, the hypocrite. Pha'."

"What?"

"Were the twins my kids?"

Pharoah didn't answer.

"That tells me. Oh, Pha', I humped my own kids!"

Albert blushed.

Pharoah said weakly, "They're always humping them in the Ozarks."

"But never in Italy, Pha', never Italians."

"Baloney. They do it all the time in Sicily. I think I read that in *Vanity Fair*."

"Go easy on Rita."

"I got nothing on Rita."

"Oh, my fat, ugly wife," groaned Marco.

"What'll I tell her?"

"Tell her to go fuck herself."

"Don't make me promise."

"To think she'll have all that money."

"I thought you were broke."

Marco managed a smile. "Ain't you heard of offshore investing? My lawyers will handle it." He was fading. "Careful. Paul Benarro's here. He's true meshuga. That disease of his. Those rotten parents. Pha'. . . ." Pharoah had to move his ear closer to Marco's mouth. "'My mother thanks you, my father thanks you, my sister thanks you,' and . . . Oh, Mother of God! Is this the end of Marco?"

Pharoah released the body. "Good old Marco. Corny up to the very end."

Albert sensed Pharoah was fighting back tears.

Pharoah took a deep breath. "Okay. Behind the bandstand. Let's go get 'em."

With caution, they proceeded to look for a way to get to the back of the bandstand. They found it easily enough. There was another trail of blood. Propped up against a wall next to an antique player piano were Weeping Willie and a younger man they assumed was his son. Their throats had been slashed. Both faces were tearstained. "Like father, like son." Pharoah added wickedly, in Natalya's voice, "Poor Veeping Villie. He has vept his last." Albert felt a bugle playing taps might be appropriate and told Pharoah, who agreed. "Come on, let's go find Paul Benarro."

A QUEER KIND OF LOVE

They heard a clash of cymbals followed by a drum roll. In the shadows at the far end of the dimly lit space they saw the outline of a man crouched over a set of trap drums.

Pharoah squinted and asked, "Is that you, Ghost?"

chapter

20

Obscenities.

More obscenities.

Then twitching. Violent twitching.

Paul Benarro, the Grey Ghost, fell from the stool he'd been sitting on. Pharoah and Albert saw the wound in his chest, which was bleeding profusely. Pharoah knelt at his side, staring into the steely blue eyes. The Ghost had cleaned himself up for the grand finale. He was clean-shaven. His fingernails were manicured. His hair was neatly combed, if now somewhat disheveled. His jacket and trousers were tailored to perfection. And the obscenities continued to spew forth; the twitching grew more violent. He was trying to talk. Finally, with an effort, he formed words. Pharoah and Albert strained to hear them.

"Tell Mama . . . I got them all."

Pharoah winked and said with a somewhat British accent, "Good show, Ghost." He grabbed hold of a twitching hand. "And nice to meet you at last, Paul Benarro."

"Freeze!" shouted a voice behind them. Pharoah stood up, and he and Albert faced what they assumed to be members of the Sullivan County police force.

"Good evening, gentlemen," said Pharoah Love amiably. He identified himself and Albert. "Gentlemen, this is supposed to be a private party. May we see your invitations?"

The newspapers had a field day. The tabloid headlines were ingeniously sordid. A grieving Adelaide Benarro ceased grieving long enough to instruct her attorneys to instigate lawsuits against the tabloid press for printing such unflattering candid photographs of her taken when she was found entering or leaving the funeral parlor where her son Paul was at rest, no longer twitching or spouting obscenities.

When Pharoah had phoned her from the hotel to tell her Paul was dead, she had burst into tears. Pharoah had hoped her grief was genuine. She asked him to come see her as soon as he returned to the city. She would wait up for him and Albert.

A few hours later, they were with her in the upstairs living room. Fraught mixed and served drinks. Pharoah was telling Adelaide, "You understand you'll probably be charged as an accessory. You, Rita, Juana."

"We'll get off," she said coldly. "And I have no regrets." She smiled, a thin, unpleasant smile. "He got them all. Thank you for telling me. Once I found out Marco had ordered Salvatore's murder, I was determined to destroy him. The incident at the Capri was a stroke of luck. For me, not for the twins, of course. Rita and Juana wanted revenge, I wanted revenge, and Paul, in wanting his revenge, became a useful instrument." She said it so coldly, in such businesslike tones: a useful instrument, her son a useful instrument. The Philadelphia lady of breeding had truly metamorphosed into a Mafia wife. "Murdering them in pairs was really mere coincidence. The twosomes were always twosomes. They always palled around in pairs. But it was a nice touch, I thought." She stared at the portrait on the wall of herself and her sons. "Poor Paul, from birth he was so unfortunate."

"You let him live on the streets."

"Don't be ridiculous!" She was genuinely angry. "He lived in this house, in an apartment we built for him in the basement. Fraught can show it to you if you like."

"But he was always showing up at Rita's for handouts."

"For information, Pharoah Love, for information. Rita knew where the lieutenants were hiding out. She knew when it was safe to get to them. And destroy them." She thought for a moment. "So of course this incriminates Rita and the Gomez woman."

"Rita's also got smart lawyers as well as friends in high places who like to come to her for a high. So tell me, Adelaide, you going to run a memorial for Paul at the Fountain of Youth?"

She drew herself up regally. "No, I'm not. I'm planning a gala performance at Radio City Music Hall. Tomorrow I shall instruct Emmanuel Robinson to book it at any price, and my lawyers will meet the fees of Liza Minnelli and Tommy Tune and Mick Jagger and . . ." She wrapped her arms around herself. "Fraught, I'm chilly. Come put your arms around me."

The butler crossed to her and took her in his arms somewhat stiffly. Pharoah thought, So the butler *did* do it, but then where did Nick Suggi fit in this jigsaw puzzle? He told himself, in the words of a very great lady, "Fiddle dee dee, I'll think about it tomorrow."

Adelaide said, "Paul was unstable—did you recognize that? Did you?"

"To me, Adelaide, he'll always be the Grey Ghost. I really liked that dude. Come on, Albert. Walt's waiting, and I'm near dead on my feet."

In the car heading toward the precinct, Albert wondered if the women would be indicted and brought to trial. Pharoah forecast with remarkable accuracy the battle of the two-hour TV movies among the three major networks. "Let's see," said Pharoah. "They get Kate Jackson to play Rita, probably Loni Anderson for Adelaide and—"

"Oh, come off it!" said Albert. "Let's hope Walt's got us squared away with Sullivan County."

Walt MacIntyre, however, turned out to have no problem with Sullivan County. They had reminded Walt that they owed him one, which he already knew. While MacIntyre chewed some antacid tablets, Pharoah, between yawns, explained, "For a while there I thought it might be Yoyo the clown who was Paul Benarro. But when the murders were taking place, he was mostly on the street performing in full view of a lot of witnesses. It was the snapshot." He paused for a moment. "Those eyes. The whole sad look of Paul Benarro. I could think of nobody but the Ghost. You know, I didn't want it to be him."

"You sorry he was shot?" asked MacIntyre.

"No. He didn't have much time left. Tourette's syndrome takes no prisoners. The hell with it." He stood up. "Me for bed. Come on, Albert. Drive me home."

As they left his office, MacIntyre yelled, "I want full type-written reports on my desk by no later then two P.M."

Pharoah turned in the doorway and with a hand on a hip said, "Beast!"

Several hours later, in bed, Pharoah heard the merciless cacophony of garbage cans being tossed around by the Department of Sanitation. "Mothereffers," he murmured, "mothereffers." He sat up and said, "Albert, let's get dressed and get breakfast."

Albert groaned and hid his head under the pillow.

Pharoah patted him on the back. Albert groaned again. Pharoah's grin stretched from ear to ear. "Albert, I've got the feeling this is the beginning of a beautiful friendship."